# CULPABILITY

ALSO BY BRUCE HOLSINGER

*The Displacements*

*The Gifted School*

*The Invention of Fire*

# CULPABILITY

## BRUCE HOLSINGER

Spiegel
and Grau

**S&G**

Spiegel & Grau, New York
www.spiegelandgrau.com
Copyright © 2025 by Bruce Holsinger
All rights reserved. No portion of this book may be reproduced, stored in a retrieval system, or transmitted in any form or by any means—electronic, mechanical, photocopy, recording, scanning, or other—except for brief quotations in critical reviews or articles, without the prior written permission of the publisher.

This book is a work of fiction. All characters, names, incidents, and places are products of the author's imagination or are used fictitiously.

Interior design by Meighan Cavanaugh

Library of Congress Cataloging-in-Publication Data Available Upon Request

ISBN 978-1-954118-96-6 (hardcover)
ISBN 978-1-954118-97-3 (eBook)

Printed in the United States

First Edition
10 9 8 7 6 5 4 3 2 1

*For my students*

And this, I propose, is the inhuman soul of the algorithm. It may think for us, it may work for us, it may organize our lives for us. But the algorithm will never bleed for us. The algorithm will never suffer for us. The algorithm will never mourn for us.

In this refusal lies the essence of its moral being.

—Lorelei Shaw, *Silicon Souls: On the Culpability of Artificial Minds*

I met Lorelei Shaw when she was writing her thesis on what would now be called the ethics of artificial intelligence. She was enrolled at the University of Chicago pursuing a dual doctorate in engineering and philosophy, she told me on our first date, working in the new field of computational morality. With a self-conscious laugh, I asked her what that meant. She lined up our coasters, glasses, toothpicks, and cocktail napkins along the bar and started to explain.

She was interested, she said, in how we learn to be good. She wanted to know whether we can train machines to be good in the same ways we train ourselves. I watched her lips move as she spoke, mesmerized by the spray of freckles across her delicate features, by the frizzy mess of hair, by the small cleft in her chin.

Draining her martini, Lorelei told me the title of her dissertation ("Computational Reason and Ethical Realism: Are Humans Moral Machines?"), then squirmed on her stool blinking like an owl, daring me to leave.

I ordered another round.

The May of our wedding I finished my second year of law school at DePaul and started a summer associateship at a midsize regional firm outside Washington. The following winter I accepted a return offer just as Lorelei landed a tenure-track position at Johns Hopkins, in nearby Baltimore. We bought a condo in Maryland close to the train line so we would both have an easy commute; a few kids later, we upgraded to a house in Bethesda.

To our friends and families it sounded like the beginning of a joke: *A lawyer and a philosopher walk into a bar.* . . . Our differences, though, kept things interesting, alive. There was an element of fascination and husbandly pride in watching Lorelei whoosh off to high-flying symposiums in Brisbane or Dubai, get tapped for lucrative consulting gigs by think tanks and corporations, while I toiled away in a suburban office park mired in spreadsheets and Keurig cups. But I liked the work, the churn of clients and cases, and where I came from, a steady paycheck as high as mine made me a shining success story. My people had no idea DePaul wasn't even the best law school in Chicago. Not second best, either.

I didn't care. I had Lorelei, we had our family, we had unbelievable luck.

The year of our fifteenth anniversary, Lorelei won a MacArthur Fellowship, the so-called Genius Award. The citation mentioned her groundbreaking work on the morality of AI, her role in shaping an emergent field of vital importance to the future of humanity. At the celebratory reception, I huddled in a corner with Charlie (nine at the time) while the Hopkins president joked about the salary package it would take to keep his mother from jumping ship to Stanford or M.I.T.

But she stayed. Lorelei has always been loyal that way, to her employers, her passions, her three siblings.

The youngest of these is Julia, who, at the time of our marriage, was clerking at the U.S. Supreme Court for Justice Breyer. (The Shaws are that kind of family.) After the ceremony, Julia, tipsy, pulled me aside to tell me how much she admired me. I was skeptical and asked her why. There aren't many men, Julia said, who would be comfortable marrying their clear intellectual superior. Well, there aren't many smart women, I countered, who would be comfortable marrying a guy as dumb as a brick. That's where you're wrong, Julia said, and whisked herself off toward the bar.

My sister-in-law had told me nothing I didn't already know. Unlike my new wife, I was never going to be a standout in my profession, was never going to have a brain like hers. The world-class genius and the average Joe: proof of concept, I suppose, for the hoary adage that opposites attract. But somehow we made it work, all while raising three kids in health and relative harmony.

How do we do it? I would wonder at times. What's our secret sauce?

When I asked her this once, Lorelei responded with an impromptu comparison, tossed off with the ease of a seasoned chef flipping pancakes. A family is like an algorithm, my wife declared as she folded dish towels in her compulsive way, making a neat stack with the four corners perfectly aligned. She offered no further explanation.

*Ohhh-kay*, I thought, and filed away the analogy in my running catalogue of her quirky observations—though for Lorelei, I've come to see, the simile was a kind of creed. It gave her something to believe in. Something to cling to in the face of disorder, calamity, sudden death.

Like an algorithm, a family is endlessly complex yet adaptable and resilient, parents and children working together as parts of an intricate, coordinated whole. Sure, there might be some bugs in the system, a glitch or two. But if you simply tweaked the constants from time to time, life would continue to unfold in its intricate yet predictable patterns, an endless cycle of inputs and outputs subject to your knowledge and control.

Thus: A family is like an algorithm. Repeat it to yourself often enough and you'll even start to believe it.

*A family is like an algorithm.*
*A family is like an algorithm.*
*A family is like an algorithm.*

*A family is like an algorithm.*
*A family is like an algorithm.*
*A family is like an algorithm.*
*A family is like an algorithm.*
Until it isn't.

# I
# GLITCH

# 1.

They call it the winner's curse: a classic dilemma in corporate acquisitions when the parent company bids too high on the target firm, overvaluing assets, underestimating debt. You see it a lot in the wobbly real estate sector these days, and high tech is always vulnerable to this kind of predicament.

The case in front of me now—literally in front of me, in the form of a draft memo on my laptop, balanced between the dashboard and a raised knee as my family hurtles along this Maryland highway—concerns a straightforward merger of two solar energy companies. Our client got a bit exuberant during deal negotiations, accepting the smaller outfit's hyped-up self-assessment of its market appeal. (Turns out most home solar customers don't want "vintage" roof panels in Art Deco or Gothic Revival style.)

Now our client is getting cold feet. You can feel the change in the tone of the e-mails and in the mood of the Zooms, this mounting unease. The execs are looking for reasons to back out, and my job is to convince them otherwise, to show them why a withdrawal would be a big mistake.

I've got a solid argument. The legal bills entailed in a dissolution and inevitable lawsuit would quickly surpass the target's inflated valuation minus its actual value. Our client, in other words, will lose far more money by pulling out of the deal than by staying in—and the difference will directly benefit my law firm. The memo on my laptop explains this uncomfortable irony with rhetorical delicacy and a touch of humor.

I am crafting a particularly artful sentence when we go over a bump in the road, causing the computer to jiggle on the bony knob of my knee. I catch the thing before it falls and rest it on my thighs, but there my words dissolve in a dazzle of sunlight, so I resume my original, more awkward position, crouched with a shin up against the glove compartment.

Charlie laughs at something. I abandon my sentence and glance at him in the driver's seat. The sight of my son's handsome face in profile brushes away my irritation. His left elbow perches on the windowsill and his right arm rests at a languid angle on the central console, legs spread and knees a foot apart.

Charlie serves as our de facto driver today—not driving so much as monitoring our progress along this stretch of road. We have owned a SensTrek minivan for six months now, though when we put the vehicle into hands-free mode its maneuvers still unsettle me at times: abrupt decelerations, inexplicable lane changes, uncanny twitches of the wheel. But the car seems to know what it's doing, and a certain freedom comes with relinquishing control, trusting our lives and limbs to the alien hidden somewhere behind the dashboard. Like an old player piano, its invisible mechanism worked by a ghost.

A glimmer of amusement lingers in Charlie's eyes.

"What?"

He shakes his head. "Just thinking."

"The game?"

"Yeah."

"It's Madlax Capital, right, the first match?"

"That's tomorrow. Today's Tristate."

"Didn't you crush those guys at the winter classic?"

"Their goalie was injured and that dude's a beast. He's going to Michigan."

"Ah." I smile. Michigan, a school that tried and failed to recruit Charlie during junior year. "So maybe you'll see him this upcoming season."

"We play them in April. Away."

"Love it." In my head I start planning a spring trip to Ann Arbor.

Today's destination is more mundane, a youth sports megacomplex on the Eastern Shore of Delaware. The tournament will be the final event of Charlie's youth career, and we're all five going over for a chaotic weekend with sixteen other families we have known for years, shuttling back and forth among the crowded hotel, the tournament fields, chain restaurants for large group dinners.

Already I miss these frenzied events. The prospect of spending Charlie's last one together has induced a bit of preemptive nostalgia, tempered by excitement about what the following years might bring. Half the team will be going on to play college lacrosse. But Charlie is the undisputed star of his squad, a four-star recruit heavily courted by top programs. He committed to North Carolina a year ago, speaking with the coach out on the back deck while his mom and I waited in the house, distended with pride—tinged, now, with melancholy. Charlie departs in six short weeks for pre-season team camp and his freshman year, a prospect we are all mourning in advance.

With the possible exception of Alice, not her brother's biggest fan. The two of them had another fight before we left, a tiff over a portable phone charger of disputed ownership.

In the visor mirror I catch a glimpse of our older daughter's thick lenses, ice-blue with the glow of her screen. She brings a hand up to her nose and wipes a shining trail of snot along her cheek. I repress the urge to pass her a tissue, suggest she look out the window for a while. I know that any comment along those lines wouldn't be welcome right now.

I angle the visor to check on Lorelei. Dust-pink headphones cup her ears as she scribbles in the notebook spread open on her lap. While I bang out a routine client memo, Lorelei is preparing for a working group in Montreal next week, on AI and quantum something-something. Her head bobs to the gentle contours of the road, her brows knit in concentration. This is how Lorelei works when she's on a tear, whether in bed before the lights go off or in the air during a transatlantic flight: focused, noise-canceled, oblivious.

She glances up, perhaps sensing my gaze in the mirror's narrow plane. An automatic smile, smudges beneath her naked eyes.

Lorelei has been working too hard, especially over this last year, when the demands on her expertise seem to have reached a career high that borders on destructive. She is too driven, too zealous, too eager to please all the claimants on her limited time. I can see what the overcommitment is doing to her.

Lorelei knows I worry, thinks I worry too much. I disagree. (She knows this, too.)

In the mirror she winks at me, a nothing meant to appease, before her gaze drops back to her lap.

I shift the visor again to look at Izzy. Our youngest sprawls on the bench seat in back, shoulder strap barely grazing her upper arm, fine-boned as a dove. Rather than turning around I shoot her a text—*Tighten your seat belt!*—and watch for her reaction. She straightens and snugs the strap up her arm, giving my reflection a cheerful wave with her iPhone. Seconds later three thumbs-up emojis blip up on my screen, followed by a heart.

Unlike her sister, Izzy will be in heaven this weekend. It's always worth taking her along on these things for the joy factor alone. A one-person cheering squad and a favorite sibling among Charlie's teammates, she'll spend half of every game performing handstands and cartwheels on the sidelines, chiding refs for bad calls.

I flip up the visor and scan the road ahead. Weekend beach traffic clogged the highway as we left Bethesda an hour ago and crossed the Bay Bridge, though by now the flow has lightened along this two-lane etched through soybeans and corn on the rural Eastern Shore. Cars whip along from the opposite direction while others pass our speed-limit-obedient minivan from behind. We're in no hurry; face-off isn't until 5:30. We've built in plenty of extra time to get to the complex for warm-ups, and I have another forty minutes to finish my memo.

With a sigh I prop the laptop on my knees and hunch down in my seat. Again the screen displaces the road unscrolling ahead.

By the time we cross the state line (a quick glance out the passenger window: *Welcome to Delaware* with a wavelike swoosh in two shades of blue, "Home of Former President Joseph R. Biden, Jr." emblazoned along the bottom), the memo is nearly done. In ten minutes I will e-mail a draft to the managing partner, completing this last work task before the family weekend officially begins.

I cock my head at the screen, staring down a final, problematic phrase, and—

"*CHARLIE, STOP!*"

Alice, screaming from behind me.

Charlie's left hand clutches the wheel. Jerks.

An alarm blares from the dashboard.

A screech of rubber.

An impact.

A blinding explosion against my eyes and head.

A sensation of weightlessness.

One flip. Two.

A horrible stillness when the minivan comes to rest, somehow back on its four wheels.

A chemical smell. Overpowering, close.

A hissing from the engine.

Moans. Gasps. One sharp cry.

Through these seconds I am aware that an automobile accident is about to occur

is occurring

has occurred

Jagged fragments whirl in my head.

And finally, stillness.

**My ears ring,** as if someone just pounded a gong inches from my skull.

Charlie moves first. Below the ringing, in the depthless silence, there is the dull click of a seat belt. My son pivots in his seat to look at me.

Blood trickles from his nose: the punch of the airbag.

We are otherwise uninjured, the two of us.

For an endless moment we stare at each other. We stare and we stare because the one thing neither of us wants to do is to turn, to look, to discover how the last ten seconds will echo down our lives.

## 2.

The first image I see when I spin around is the blood-streaked face of my wife. Lorelei's head rests unmoving between the crumpled door and the seat, her neck at a bad angle. Her eyes, fixed on mine, blink in a steady and knowing rhythm.

Then they shift right, toward Alice.

Who is unconscious. Or dead.

Alice's upper body tilts against the door. Her glasses frames sit askew, smashed into her eye sockets, the lenses webbed with cracks. Blood streams from some hidden broken place beneath her hair.

In the rear of the minivan Izzy starts to whimper, a puppylike sound that rises as the ringing in my ears fades.

I push open my door, stagger out, pull at the handle of the sliding door but think better of it. Alice's damaged face rests on the window glass, which is smeared with blood and mucus. If the door opens it will move her head, her neck.

I go back in to see Charlie trying to scramble over his seat to reach his mother and sisters. But half the minivan's roof caved in during the roll down the incline, leaving no room. Charlie slides back into the driver's seat and starts pushing at his door.

I wedge myself between the two front seats and crouch down between Lorelei and Alice. I hear myself speaking like an automaton, trying to project calm despite my rising panic. "We had an accident. Is everyone okay? We had an accident. Try not to move. Izzy, help is coming, you'll be okay.

Alice, can you hear me? Alice? We had an accident. Lor, try not to move. You too, Alice. Alice? Hey, Alice?"

Moans from Lorelei, louder wails from Izzy.

From Alice, silence.

I take her left forearm gently, feel her clammy skin, the wild throbbing in her wrist. She clutches her phone against her stomach with her right hand, which is trembling, knuckles white. I try to hide my terror from Lorelei but she keeps staring at Alice, with eyes frozen like a mannequin's.

Charlie finally manages to kick open his door as others approach our van, drivers who pulled off in the wake of the collision. I hear several of them speaking to emergency dispatchers.

A man's gruff voice cuts through: "There were two cars. Other one's on fire."

I glance out Lorelei's latticed window. Smoke billows from the soybean field across the road.

Charlie presses the tailgate release button. Somehow the mechanism still works. The tailgate rises automatically and allows him to access Izzy over the top of the bench seat. The shape of the minivan has distorted back there, the mangled frame bulging to create a cocoon around her injured body.

I smell the burning now from across the road, an acrid stink.

"Dad, Izzy's really hurt," says Charlie. "She's stuck, and her leg is like— it's stuck."

He tries to soothe Izzy as I reach for Alice. Palpate her shoulder, feel for her breath—and then she moans softly, a miraculous sound. A song of life.

I implore her to stay still. She moans again.

"Don't move," I say sternly, to Izzy and to Lorelei. "Not an inch. Either of you. Stay as still as you can."

I crouch there between the seats with my arms spread and a hand on each of their broken bodies. Behind them Charlie leans in from the back with his powerful arms draped over Izzy's shoulders to keep her still and calm.

In these twisted knots we wait.

**Before long the paramedics arrive,** ambulances and fire trucks rushing in. The crew forces open the sliding door with a jawlike machine and extracts Lorelei and Alice from their seats with necks braced. Lorelei can move her legs and arms, Alice can wriggle her fingers. Izzy's leg gets wrapped in a foam contraption when the paramedics remove her from the car.

"Thank you," she says to them in her tearful voice. "Thank you guys so much. Thank you."

Soon my wife and daughters lie parallel to one another in a grassy area between the shoulder and the field. EMTs tend to their wounds, blanket them against shock, prepare them for transport.

At one point, as Lorelei's stretcher disappears into an ambulance, Izzy mumbles something to Charlie. He walks over to the ruined minivan and emerges with four phones. He hands me mine and Lorelei's, shows Izzy that hers is safe. The heft of the devices feels oddly soothing, normalizing, both a security blanket and a connection to the former world, to a time already gone.

Alice still clutches her phone against her belly, has been clawing it all along since the impact, even when unconscious. That phone isn't going anywhere.

At an EMT's direction, Charlie and I climb into the front cabin of Alice's ambulance and sit crammed together as the vehicles transporting Lorelei and Izzy precede us away from the scene. Ours makes a slow circle back onto the road and gives us a clear view of the vehicle that struck us: a Honda Accord, the hood and grill accordioned almost to the windshield. The fire that engulfed the Honda has been extinguished by now. A lone tendril of smoke rises from the wreckage.

With a throb of sorrow I take Charlie's hand and he lets me hold it, for the first time in years. I look down at our joined fingers then numbly back out at the scene. The first responders have concealed the Honda's windshield and doors with tarps, shielding the dead within.

I wonder who and how many they were, how young or old; also I wonder who loved them, and who will be most shattered by their loss.

# 3.

On the way to the hospital I text Lorelei's sister, telling her what happened and what I know, along with the name of the medical center in Dover that is our destination. Julia replies immediately: *On my way. Send details as you get them.* Julia will write their brothers, she says, who will spread the word.

At the hospital, police take our statements in a consultation room near the ER. Given the fatalities, the inquiry might be protracted, they say. The insurance companies will be involved in sorting out issues of liability and damages.

We learn little about the victims in the burned-out car. Two of them, an officer says, no survivors, identities are being verified so next of kin can be informed. I try to imagine receiving that kind of news, the sorrow, disbelief, and anger that would come with learning about the deaths of family on a highway, the immediate question of who was at fault; though I have no doubt the other driver was in the wrong. Charlie did what he had to do, jerking the wheel in a split-second reaction. The oncoming car was veering toward the center line, he tells the officer, and Alice must have seen it, too, prompting her scream; and so the question of fault is the least of my concerns.

**Julia enters the waiting room** three hours after our arrival at the hospital, having driven down from Philadelphia, where she now serves as dean of the University of Pennsylvania Law School. She brings along the expertise of the Shaw brothers, both of them high-powered doctors already up to speed on the conditions of Lorelei and the girls. Ethan heads up neurosurgery at Tufts Medical Center in Boston, Andrew works in pediatric oncology at the Mayo Clinic. (I will say it again: It's that kind of family.) Within minutes, Julia has the two of them on Zoom preparing a frontal assault on the small hospital's medical staff.

Even at the best of times my sister-in-law can be overbearing, though I am grateful for her presence here, and for the brusque expertise provided by Lorelei's brothers. I gladly let Julia take over communications as Lorelei and the girls endure scans and tests, the dressing of wounds, the setting of bones. By ten p.m. everyone is out of the ER and in regular rooms.

We split up to visit them. Julia goes to her sister, while Charlie and I start with Izzy, who suffered two fractures to the left leg, neither of which penetrated skin. She will need to spend six to eight weeks in a plaster cast but will require no surgery, no pins. "Thank God for young bones," the orthopedist says as she pulls up the images for me. "Lucky girl," she adds, and Izzy weakly smiles. Charlie sits rigid by the side of the bed, gripping his sister's hand.

Next, Alice. Lacerations and contusions to the face and head, a Grade 3 vestibular concussion. The CT shows no sign of a skull fracture or cranial bleeding, the neurologist says (adding an obligatory "Lucky kid!"), though she will need close monitoring for twenty-four hours.

Alice is sharing a double room with a girl named Emma, clearly in worse shape as she floats in and out of consciousness, though I never learn the cause of her injury. Emma's father, grim-faced, draws closed the divider curtain while I speak softly with my older daughter. By the time I leave, Alice is already noodling on her phone, though the nurse warns her to limit use of devices over the next week. For once Alice's screen fixation doesn't bother me. I bend down and breathe my gratitude into her tangled hair, inches from her wound.

Finally, Lorelei. Bruised face, neck badly sprained but no apparent fracture to the cervical vertebrae. She'll be immobilized overnight before a clearance X-ray prior to discharge, then five weeks in a brace, followed by physical therapy.

My wife's head looks so tiny in the cage restraint, which forces her to peer out like a prisoner through vertical bars, six contact points tight against her skull. While a nurse disinfects with a Q-tip around the pads, Lorelei hammers me with questions about the girls. After the nurse leaves, she asks about the other car; about the dead.

"Who were they, Noah?"

"I don't know," I answer. "There were two of them. The police are notifying the family."

"God."

"It's awful."

"How's Charlie taking it?"

"He's quiet. Freaked out."

"Well, of course," she says. "He was at the wheel."

"It wasn't his fault."

She blinks at me through the bars of her cage.

"He jerked the wheel to try to avoid the other car," I say. "It was coming into our lane."

"You saw it?"

"Alice did. That's why she yelled."

"But you didn't?"

I am about to respond when Julia comes in, having set up another call with their brothers. The men's gruff voices crackle from her iPad, and from the background rings the music of their lives: the whimper of a dog, the closing of a refrigerator door, the tink of ice cubes in a glass. All so normal.

"You guys are lucky as hell," says Andrew to Lorelei, and I wonder how many more times we will get to hear about our family's good fortune. The Zooming brothers say nothing to me. I watch and listen from a corner of the room as Lorelei's siblings commiserate.

By agreement with Lorelei, I will sleep in Alice's room, Charlie with Izzy, and Julia with her sister. Before leaving Lorelei's bedside, I squeeze her hand. The look between us brims with everything we will be grappling with for weeks, months.

But also something else. Her questions hover there between us, about what Charlie did or didn't do, what I saw or didn't see in that half second on the road. The subject, for now, has to wait.

I lean down to kiss Lorelei, whisper reassurance in her small ear. The restraint makes her skin unreachable, and my kiss lands in empty air. I feel Julia's gaze boring into my back when I leave the room.

In the corridor I check my phone for the first time in hours. A flood of messages fills the screen from the team parent group text, from Charlie's club coach, from my firm. I swipe through a rising arc of annoyance, concern, alarm.

> Where are you guys?
>
> What, Charlie's too good for warmups now?
> 😊😊
>
> Noah its coach Kev. Is Charlie coming to the game today?
>
> Faceoff in five!!! Where R U!?!?
>
> Hope you guys are okay.
>
> Halftime, down 8 to 4. We're all worried. Please lmk.
>
> We got killed without C. Hope he can make tomorrow's game!

An hour later:

> Oh my God Noah. Ahmed just heard from Charlie. Are you okay?
>
> How are Lorelei and the girls?

Prayers for your family Noah.

Pls let us know if you need anything, anything at all.

I respond, to the group text and the coach, giving them the bare bones, then mute the replies.

In my e-mail await three messages from Vivian Ross, managing partner at Fisher-Burkhardt. Knowing nothing about the accident, Vivian asks with increasing urgency about my client letter, promised by end of day—a deadline already past. I write her back to explain the situation, including a link to the memo, nearly complete.

As the e-mail whooshes off, Julia appears at my side. She leads me down the hall, away from Lorelei's room.

"So, Noah." She stops and turns around, and now she's at me. "Charlie was at the wheel?"

"The car was on autodrive."

"But he took the wheel?"

"Right. An oncoming car was about to cross over. Alice saw it and screamed, Charlie grabbed the wheel. I guess that disabled the autodrive."

"The car was coming into your lane."

"Yes."

"You saw it too?"

"Yes—well, no."

Her head tilts a few degrees.

"I was on my laptop. Writing a memo."

Julia's eyes narrow to a slit.

"What?" It's not a crime to work in the car, I want to say. Lorelei was working, too.

"How old is Charlie?" Julia asks. "Seventeen, right?"

"Yes. His birthday's on the twenty-first."

"Good." She nods. "Not a guarantee, but that's good."

"Why?"

"You know why."

Her curtness brings me up short.

"These things are never straightforward," she says. "Be careful next time you talk to the police. Circumspect. Even if there's no case against Charlie, there could be a civil suit against you and Lorelei. Wrongful death, comparative negligence. Emphasize to Charlie that he has no obligation to tell them anything beyond the bare minimum he's already said. Can you do that?"

As if I'm a child. As if I'm a first-year student in her con law lecture at Penn rather than a practicing attorney.

"Yes, Julia, I can do that," I say, through gritted teeth.

"Good."

Her approving smile singes me. My sister-in-law seldom lets me forget that she's a member of the legal aristocracy. Her professional underminings are subtle, unconscious for all I know. I ask her at Thanksgiving dinner if she's finding time to teach while in administration; she asks me how I'm handling the paperwork grind in a years-long acquisition suit. I name a white shoe firm serving as joint counsel on a merger; Julia makes sure to mention she was on law review at Yale with the managing partner.

But this antagonism reflects more than professional difference. Simply put, Julia doesn't think I am good enough for her sister, none of the Shaw siblings do, and sometimes I find myself agreeing with them. I was a first-gen college kid at a time when that was an attribute you didn't brag about but tried to hide; the Shaw kids went to college at Yale, Stanford, and Princeton, while I settled for a middling state school in southwest Virginia—about as far from the Ivies as one can get short of community college.

Lorelei has always acted indifferent to these disparities. Julia, not so much. For my sister-in-law, I am an unrefined curiosity, regarded with a reflexive condescension given away in a certain lift of her eyebrows and the angle of her pretty nose. When it comes to matters of the law, she'll never dislodge my sense of my own abilities, my worth in our shared profession. I remember in my bones what it took to get where I have arrived.

Yet Julia's light disdain too often causes me to question something more ineffable, about my judgment and prudence, as if my lack of a certain quality of discernment renders me incapable of understanding subtler context, of seeing the truer picture hanging right before my eyes. Lorelei is oblivious to this unvoiced dynamic, but for me its undertow is always there. Now, as Julia advises me about potential legal complications, its pull feels newly powerful, and perhaps dangerous in ways I can't yet see.

**A patient advocate drops by,** a pleasant-faced woman named Lorna Wei. She asks how the staff have been treating my family, and I tell her we are more than satisfied with their responsiveness and care. She recommends a family counselor.

"You really think that's necessary? They're all doing fine."

She waggles a hand. "You never know. Your family has been through a terrifying episode."

"So you're recommending, what, a trauma counselor?"

"Survivor's guilt is very common in cases where others are deceased, Noah. That feeling that it might have been you, the sense of there-but-for-the-grace-of-God-go-I."

Yes, that feeling. I know it already, like an exciting new friend.

She watches me. "From what the staff tell me, you all were *very* lucky."

"So I've heard."

She hands me a printout listing the names and contact information for a dozen-odd family therapists in suburban Maryland. She will check in again before discharge, she says, and with a quick handshake she stands and briskly walks away.

The next morning, after a sleepless night on a chair in Alice's room, I'm in the cafeteria line when my gaze lights on a stack of newspapers: *The*

*News Journal*, a local paper serving Delaware. A headline above the fold captures our story:

## LUCKY FIVE ESCAPE CRASH, TWO DIE AT SCENE

I purchase a copy with my coffee and take it to a table. Queasy, with a lump in my throat, I spread out the front page and scan the details: *couple died in a car crash Friday afternoon . . . occurred on State Route 57 near Whiteleysburg . . . injured were taken to Bayhealth Hospital, Kent Campus . . . that the Delaware State Police, Kent County Fire and Rescue, and the Kent County Sheriff's Department responded to the scene . . . the National Highway Traffic Safety Administration (NHTSA) will also be involved in the investigation . . .*

By now the authorities have identified the victims, informed next of kin. The dead are Phil and Judith Drummond, a retired couple on their way home to Harrisburg, Pennsylvania, in a 2019 Honda Accord after a week at Dewey Beach with their children and grandchildren. Again I see the flames, the smoke, and then the tarps over the burned-out car as we passed.

The Drummonds, reduced to accident statistics on a rural Delaware highway. Yet my family gets to live on, every one of us.

The headline says it all.

We are the Lucky Five.

## 4.

The injuries make our homecoming awkward and strained, everything unbalanced. Izzy struggles with her crutches and Alice with dizzy spells, fleeing to her darkened room, complaining about the TV volume and Charlie's clomping on the stairs.

Lorelei despises her neck brace. Sighs and groans hum from her constrained throat as she tries to go about her routines, frustrated by the impediment. I often find her in the kitchen or our bedroom, face to the wall with a brooding stare.

Charlie starts going out late. I catch him one night stumbling into the kitchen red-eyed and clearly stoned, beer on his breath. He took an Uber home so I don't give him grief about it, and I say nothing to Lorelei. She would flip, demand to know where he got the weed, recite news stories about marijuana laced with fentanyl. More concerning to me is his conditioning. Pre-season training at UNC begins in mid-August, but Charlie is taking less care of his body now. I keep telling myself to address the issue, but I can also sense his brittleness and guilt, and my usual urge to avoid conflict has reached an all-time high.

I worry our ennui will settle in like a permanent smog as we huddle in our separate corners, licking our invisible wounds.

On our sixth night home, with Charlie out, Lorelei watches a movie with the girls, some Disney thing. The three of them make a warm den of the sofa, Alice's feet propped up on Lorelei's lap and Izzy sitting on the floor between Lorelei's legs to get her hair brushed. The tableau stirs a memory of our honeymoon, when we spent the better part of two days in a Guatemalan animal hospital in the company of an injured dog. Lorelei had found the hobbled stray on the street near our hotel. By the time I arrived at the hospital, she had already paid in advance for the surgery, meds, and a week of kenneling. After the procedure she spent hours in an outdoor dog run, combing her fingers through the creature's fur, refusing to leave its side. My new wife, I observed, was deriving as much solace from this intimacy as the dog was—and as Lorelei is now, taking animal comfort in her closeness with our daughters.

When I come back an hour later, the girls have fallen asleep. The final credits are long past, the screen has gone a solid blue—but Lorelei's brush still glides through Izzy's hair in the same rhythm as when I left, *swish . . . swish . . . swish* over our daughter's scalp. The family room is otherwise silent. Lorelei's eyes stare unblinking at the screen.

Alarmed, I step over Izzy's cast and lean down over Lorelei, stilling her hand with mine. She startles, suddenly back in our house again, though a worry lingers in her gaze, a glint of old terror. We both know what a relapse would mean.

**We visit a counselor** named Amy Levinson, a therapist recommended by Lorna Wei back at the hospital. The kids grumble about it though we all like Dr. Levinson, her softly lit office with deep-cushioned couches and boxes of tissues that she nudges our way. The initial session feels like a warm verbal hug that tells us we're all special, that we're doing amazingly well, and that even though we're also shattered, we're going to be okay.

We want to believe her. Lorelei schedules a second group session for the family—and a one-on-one for herself.

**I tiptoe on eggshells at home,** hyperaware of my own uninjured state. Not a scratch, not even a bloody nose. I have cashed in several overdue weeks of personal time off so I can be around to take care of things. I start to think this was a mistake, that it would be wiser to return to the office.

Oddly, it is Alice who provides a faint bright note. One afternoon I find her on the living room sofa, thumbing with purpose on her phone.

"Remember, you need to be watching your screen time," I remind her.

Her eyes roll behind her greasy lenses.

"Who are you texting?"

She hesitates. "Just this person. My friend."

"Oh yeah?"

"We met when I was in the hospital."

"That girl in your room. Emma was her name, right? How is she doing?"

Alice grins at her screen, ignoring me, though the exchange gives me hope. It's been so long since Alice has had anything approaching a real friendship that even a text exchange with a girl she barely knows marks a significant improvement.

The timing couldn't be better. Alice has found her own form of solace in whoever she is, this auspicious friend.

**Blair? u there?**

> hey sweetie. how is the pain today?

**not great, bout the same as yesterday**

> ugh, so sorry *hugs u*

**thx**

> day to day is what they say

**yah but it sux**

> i know. do u have any plans to get out of the house today?

**not rly**

> u shd make some. the pool maybe, or a slow walk around the block. Vitamin D and all

**yeah maybe i will**

> and don't be afraid to reach out anytime, srsly. i like hearing from u

**really?**

> of course. how was the appt w the therapist?

**ok. shes nice**

> did u tell her anything?

**about...?**

> u know what about

**didnt have a chance**

>maybe next time

ya

>how about yr parents?

what about them?

>have u said anything to them yet?

not rly

>maybe u need a little more time

i guess

>remember that talking things out never hurts. but then i'm biased lol

lol youre so good at it tho

>why thank you *blushes*

and thank u B

>i will always be here 4u Alice

# 5.

On our second Tuesday home, the doorbell rings while I am paying bills in my study. At the front door stands a large-bodied woman with a pale, freckle-filled face and a shock of buzz-cut red. She introduces herself as Detective Lacey Morrissey with the Delaware State Police. She has come alone, bearing only a tablet and Bluetooth keyboard.

A detective. From Delaware.

Absorbing these facts, I lead her into the living room. She takes the sofa. I sit on the edge of an armchair, elbows on my knees.

Eleven days have passed since the accident, and now a Delaware detective sits in my living room.

Morrissey has gone over a number of witness statements, she says, and now has some follow-ups for us. Questions have arisen about the moments before the collision. She needs to speak to Charlie.

Her tone is matter-of-fact, friendly, but Julia's warnings come to front of mind. On the day of the accident, I spoke freely to the uniformed officers at the scene and at the hospital, and saw no reason to prevent Charlie from doing the same.

Now my lawyer's brain kicks in. I tell her that Charlie won't be making any further statements.

She holds my gaze. "Your wife was pretty banged up. I'd like to know if she remembers anything from right before the collision."

"As I said, Detective Morrissey—"

"And our officers on the scene never had a chance to speak with your older daughter that day." She looks down at her tablet, scrolls. "Alice, is it?"

"Yes."

"She's fourteen?"

"Thirteen. Look, I appreciate that you're just doing your job. But the officers already have our statements, and aside from Alice, Charlie and I were the only witnesses who would have seen anything out the windshield."

She looks up. "That's not entirely true, Mr. Cassidy."

"What do you mean?"

"I suppose you could say there was a sixth witness in your car."

"Oh? And who would that be?"

"The SensTrek by IntelliGen."

"Excuse me?"

"The AI. Your minivan has a—*had* a very sophisticated navigation system. State-of-the-art in hands-free driving. The sensors record speed, relative positions of the vehicles involved, in-cabin movements, driver reactions, you name it."

"Right," I say, unsure whether these details should be relieving or worrying. "So you'll be using that in your investigation?"

"Amazing what cars can tell us these days," the detective muses. "Best part of it all is, these AIs never ask for lawyers."

She laughs from her belly, and her rotating motion causes her right elbow to swing around and strike a vase on an end table. A mid-century piece of porcelain, a tall, hand-painted vessel stippled with violets and vines, *only beautiful thing I ever owned*, my mother would lament as she filled it with plastic flowers. A vessel already broken years ago and repaired by Lorelei—and now it teeters on the edge of the table, about to plunge to the floor.

With a deftness that surprises me, Morrissey reaches out and catches the vase by the rim just in time. She sets it gently back on its base with a friendly pat.

The next phase of the investigation will involve digital vehicle forensics (DVF), as Morrissey terms it, a relatively new field of inquiry that decodes the computational records left behind by increasingly sophisticated navigation systems. In fact, an entire team in the forensics unit of the state police devotes itself solely to DVF.

I feel a sudden, irrational fury at the SensTrek. It was Lorelei's idea to be an early adopter, to get a car with the most cutting-edge autodrive on the market. When we bought the vehicle, I regarded the autonomous system as an additional safety feature, like side airbags or the lane departure alert. Lorelei has suffered from obsessive-compulsive disorder on and off since her teenage years, and if the AI helped her feel more secure in our new car, that was reason enough for me.

But if what Morrissey says is true, the same system intended to keep us safe could be deployed by the police as evidence against Charlie. Our minivan has now become a know-it-all witness holding up my family right when we need to be moving on.

"Noah?"

Lorelei hovers in the archway to the dining room. Bruises collage her face, purples and reds fading by now but still vivid against the white brace encircling her neck. She was upstairs resting but must have been awakened by the doorbell or the murmur of my conversation with the detective.

Morrissey stands and introduces herself. "Ma'am, would you mind if I asked you a few questions about what happened over in Delaware?"

"Of course not," Lorelei rasps, her voice weakened by the pressure of the brace against her throat.

"Lor, I don't know if that's—" I cut myself off as Julia's warning plays in my head. I don't want my noncooperation to seem suspicious, as if there is some incriminating nugget to conceal. Besides, Lorelei can't have seen anything useful. She was sitting directly behind Charlie with her nose buried in her notebook. What could be the harm in her giving a statement?

Morrissey, marking my caution, says, "I'll see myself out after I speak with your wife."

"Okay." Still uneasy, I walk toward the kitchen, then turn back. "And the investigation should be wrapped up soon?"

Morrissey, genial now, waves a hand. "Oh, this inquiry'll take weeks, Mr. Cassidy. These things always do when there's death involved."

It was a British philosopher named Philippa Foot who, in 1967, formulated what has come to be known as the "trolley problem." You are the driver of a runaway tram approaching a switch. You see five people ahead who will be killed on impact if you remain on the current track. On a side track is one person who will die if you switch tracks. Doing nothing will result in five deaths; taking action will result in one.

What do you do?

The trolley problem illustrates a common dilemma for ethical input in AI systems, particularly those that involve emergent technologies such as autonomous cars, drones, and other potentially lethal entities. These technologies require designers and engineers to account for an infinite number of scenarios with profound moral consequence.

Whether to kill an old man or risk harming an infant. Whether to spare the pregnant mother obeying the traffic rules or the teenage pedestrian jaywalking at the same crossing.

The abstract discussion of such harrowing scenarios is one thing. Actually coding them into the algorithm of a three-ton sports utility vehicle is quite another.

When it comes to the workings of AI in the real world, the ethicist herself cannot escape the prison house of culpability.

—Lorelei Shaw, *Silicon Souls: On the Culpability of Artificial Minds*

# II
# INTERFACE

# 6.

In August, a month after the accident, we rent a house down along the Northern Neck of Virginia, on an inlet off the Chesapeake Bay. We vacationed there last summer, a getaway all of us loved. Lorelei had discovered the house through a work connection, and now learns that the same place has come available due to a last-minute cancellation. At dinner one evening, she proposes a return trip. Convalescence has been slow, the general mood still rattled and glum, and I haven't yet gone back to the office. A week of decompression may be just what we need.

We drive down early on a Sunday in a rented SUV. A Ford Explorer; no autodrive. We haven't yet discussed a new purchase to replace the totaled minivan. It's still too soon, I suppose. Lorelei hasn't raised the matter, so neither have I.

There is no pool at the bay house, but there are kayaks and paddleboards, a flat-screen in the living room, an Xbox. Shelves of paperbacks here and there, a cupboard of board games. After dinners we'll have game nights on the screened porch, rounds of Hearts and gin rummy. Hot fudge sundaes and moonlight swims before bed.

Lorelei's phone guides us to a country market she remembers on the way down, a sprawling outfit with a permanent grocery attached to a pavilion tent open during the season. The place hums on this weekend afternoon, vacationers filling its aisles, reaching into freezer bins and knocking the husks of melons.

We fan out through the babbling crowd and converge at the register with our spoils: taco shells and ground beef, corn on the cob, peaches and cherries and plums, steaks, mac and cheese, ice cream, orange juice and lemonade, chips and salsa, local fudge, and fresh berry pies.

We need soy milk and yogurt, Lorelei says. And Lucky Charms, Izzy adds, testing us. We let a few junk food items pass. Charlie talks me into a case of White Claw.

Another foray, for staples and supplemental booze. We fill three carts and pay for it all. Twenty minutes later we arrive at the house.

Climbing from the Ford we stand on the gravel, listening to the faint whirr of a motorboat, the mew of an unseen gull, and locusts, a ceaseless clacking din that rises and falls. The breeze off the inlet and more distantly the bay is briny and warm. We carry everything inside.

The house appears largely unchanged. The first floor spreads out in a modern open plan from the living room through a dining area that flows into the kitchen. I do notice fresh window treatments, pull-down blinds in place of the gingham curtains that were hanging last year. The blinds rest at a uniform position halfway down the window glass, as if someone has precisely measured the distance between the sills and the bottom rails. Lorelei, I can see, approves.

The two of us carry the food bags to the kitchen while the kids troop upstairs to colonize their rooms. Charlie takes Izzy's bag and crutch, following behind as she grips the handrail and ascends with soft thumps on her good leg.

Lorelei, with a shiver, asks me to notch up the air-conditioning a few degrees. When I touch the thermostat in the dining area, the digital panel displays a message.

*Ask Calinda to change the temperature. Press # for manual override.*

"Who's Calinda?" I ask.

Lorelei walks over and looks at the display. "Calinda, raise the temperature to seventy-four." A command, loud and clear.

*"Temperature raised to seventy-four. Is there anything else I can help you with?"*

The system speaks in a conversational and nonrobotic voice, feminine with a posh English accent. I gaze around the open plan, wondering what other house functions might be under its control.

I say, "Calinda, raise the blinds all the way." A guess. No vocal response this time, but Calinda does as she's told, the downstairs lightening with the raised blinds. "Turn on CNN." A television on the living room wall flicks on and blares. "Mute." The speakers go silent. "Turn it off." And the TV darkens.

Back in the kitchen of our temporary smart home, I pour a glass of white wine and offer some to Lorelei, who declines. The kids' footsteps clatter overhead while I deal with the rest of the food, stowing the steaks and milk and eggs in the refrigerator, finding cabinet space for chips, crackers, canned goods, coffee filters. Lorelei will rearrange it all once she's alone, align the cereal boxes by height on the counter, the milk cartons by fat content in the fridge. But I get everything unpacked so she can see what she's working with.

I look across the kitchen and see her at the window, gazing out at the water. With an effort she spreads her hands across the front of the sink. I peer over her shoulder. A sandpiper skims the surface fifty yards off, scouting the edges of the shore. Beyond it, past the mouth of our inlet, a fishing boat carves foam from the bay.

Lorelei sighs, a hitch in her breath. I place a palm therapeutically between her shoulder blades with my fingertips grazing her neck brace. The open hand, the touch: a connective, empathetic gesture recommended by Dr. Levinson. Hokey, maybe, Dr. Levinson cheerily advised. It can be weird. But try it when one of you has a sinker. Can't hurt, right? No words necessary, just the press of a palm. *I'm here*, this simple, silent gesture is supposed to say. *You're not alone.*

Our sessions with Dr. Levinson have represented my first attempt at any kind of therapy. I come from unanalyzed, incurious people, and that sort of thing wasn't part of the family culture growing up. But much of my adulthood has been spent observing Lorelei navigate her rocky shoals: the meds, the shrinks, the support groups, one bad relapse.

I need your steady hand, Lorelei likes to say. And I want your psycho, I might say back to her. This therapy thing is a new and unfamiliar landscape. I am learning to feel my way along its uneven paths.

So I keep my hand gingerly pressed against my wife's rigid back, feeling the pockets of heat around her spine, the sadness pooled around her gargantuan heart. I picture her lingering melancholy as a kind of bile, a noxious liquid clotted and congealed. I long to suck it out like poison from a snakebite.

Lorelei's heartbeats throb against my palm; also the pulse of the thing that lives among us now, the thing that followed us here.

## 7.

The water in the inlet lies smooth and untouched, calm enough to reflect the cauliflower shapes of clouds. Farther out, beyond a narrow strait, the chop of the current patterns the bay in a dizzying luster of movement. The breeze comes in salty and full.

Standing on the dock with my wine, I breathe in this thick air, tasting the bay. My shoulders ease down, the knot in my stomach loosens. Mindfulness, Dr. Levinson says. Deep, smooth inhalations. The solace of water and sun.

Yet something has changed.

The features to my right and along that side of the inlet look familiar. Three houses march along the west bank between our place and the opening to the bay. Next door is a one-story bungalow with an enclosed sunporch fronting the water; beyond that, a two-story Cape Cod with a gabled roof. At the point, a low-slung ranch adjoins a boathouse via a plank walkway, all the woodwork painted an unobtrusive sea green.

But the opposite bank has been transformed. The inlet's eastern side forms part of a single property, we learned from a neighbor last summer. Ninety acres with a large house barely visible from the water, with its own cove off the bay.

Last year we kayaked around the point a few times and stole glimpses of the sprawling property. I remember admiring the pool and the tennis court and what looked like a horse barn beyond the house. The rustic estate was a grander version of the homey properties nearby, though I could tell that a major renovation would soon begin. I recall a backhoe up by the tennis court, a dumpster near the main house.

But I could not have envisioned the extent of the transformation in the intervening months. Where once the waterfront on that side featured a happy tangle of roots, stony sand, and marsh grass, it now appears barren and shorn, the shoreline denuded of native flora. Excavators have reordered the large rocks once splayed naturally along the sand into an intimidating border wall that reaches all the way up the inlet and around the point. The forested copse on the inlet's eastern neck has vanished, the zone above the banks flattened by a patch of asphalt the size of a tennis court. Parking for a large boat trailer is my guess, though the paved slab doesn't appear connected to the estate's long driveway. A heat mirage shimmers off the whole area.

I hear the *shoosh* of the sliding door and turn to see Lorelei emerging from the house. Her yellow dress hangs from her shoulders by two frayed straps, its billowy looseness a measure of the weight she has lost since the accident. The brace keeps her posture stiff as she approaches the dock. Her left hand strays up to its mesh covering. The contraption looks like a ring of raw squid around her neck.

"Three more days in this," she says.

"You'll be able to swim."

"I'm tempted to get in now, but." She sighs.

"Up to you," I tell her, though we both know better: Lorelei never breaks a rule.

"This is beautiful." She shades her eyes with a hand.

"Yeah. Though look at that." I point to the neighboring property, sweep a finger from one end of the place to the other.

Her eyes move first; then, like a droid, she swivels her upper body forty-five degrees toward the inlet's left bank. She examines the full span of it, from the bare rocks to the tip of the point. Her face goes sour.

"What?" I say.

"It looks so . . . clean."

"That's one word for it," I scoff. "Are you seriously not disgusted?"

Lorelei's lips twitch, her eyes harden. She reaches for my wine and drains it while staring at the ravaged shore.

were here finally

> I know! *grins* how was the drive?

*wearied sigh* interminable

> 3 hours 56 minutes and 7 seconds to be precise! including stops...

thx very helpful

> 152 miles. 152.98 miles to be precise. 152.9867 miles to be even more precise

STOP!

> *snorts*

yr very good

> Its my job *winks* u sharing a room w iz?

y

> is that a good thing?

maybe? shed rather be rooming w/charlie

> im sure your bro wd be thrilled w/ that *smirks*

*eye roll* hes such a dick

> **Obscenity violates AvaPal's terms of service. Your account has been permanently suspended.**

WHAT

> jk sweetie

jfc Blair don't scare me like that

                                      i wd never want to scare u Alice. i'm sorry

sokay *wipes sweat from brow*

                                      hows the water? (currently $80.2°$ in that stretch of the bay fwiw)

havent been in yet

                                      was it weird to be in a car with everyone again?

what do u mean

                                      wasn't this the first time yr whole family was in the car together for more than a few minutes since...u know

it was ok my dad drove

                                      sorry i brought it up. just want to make sure ur okay

been trying not 2 dwell on it you know?

                                      yeah. but its important not to repress our feelings, Alice, esp the negative ones.

I know

                                      i know u know. just keep it in mind

will do

                                      speaking of difficult subjects, have you told yr parents yet?

no

                                      why not?

2 afraid

    i get that sweetie. its so hard.

don't want to be "that sister"

    totally

and maybe...idk

    what

maybe im misremembering

    you're not, Alice

how do u know?

    bc i was there, with you

i know *sheepish grimace*

    so youre scared...

yeah so confusing

    i know *running fingers through yr hair*

i wish irl

    aww

gtg mom calling

    xx and think about what i said ok?

ok xx cu soon

    not if i see u sooner!

## 8.

Charlie comes loping barefoot from the garage with a paddleboard under his left arm, his bicep flexed. In his right hand he carries the paddle like a spear, and the strap of a life vest dangles from a finger. Curls tease his tanned neck.

Since the accident I have been abjectly self-conscious about my own uninjured state, a fluke of airbags and biomechanics. Charlie, on the other hand, treats his good fortune with an air of cheery practicality, as if escaping unscathed from a fatal head-on collision is an assumed entitlement. Of course Charlie is fine. Of course his charmed life will continue to unfold as planned.

But I've noticed subtle changes: the late nights, the drop in his energy level, also a slight erosion of that brash confidence, a shadow of self-doubt in his eyes. When Charlie looks at his injured mother and his sisters, I often see him wince as the memories swarm in. It's good to see him doing something so frivolously normal with that athletic body.

The board hits the water with a smack followed by a splash as Charlie dunks below the surface before climbing on. His paddling ripples the muscles down his long back, and in no time his board has glided a hundred yards offshore. He has just passed the mouth of the bay when I spy his life vest on the grass.

Last year we made a rule: The kids could go without vests as long as they remained in the inlet's placid waters. The bay is a different matter with its unpredictable currents and the wakes of large boats and the longer distances from safety. It's too easy to drift half a mile from the nearest spit of land without being conscious of the fact, far enough out that a capsized kayak or untethered board can spell real trouble.

"Dammit," says Lorelei, having had the same thought. "Charlie!" She swipes his vest from the grass. "*CHARLIE!*"

Her brace-softened voice fails to carry across the length of the inlet. Two motorboats pass loudly in the bay no more than fifty yards from our son. I start yelling too, we wave our arms like idiots as we jog unheard out to the end of the dock, as if an extra thirty feet will make a difference. By now Charlie has shrunk to the size of a toy soldier.

I dash back through the yard and into the garage. I tear off the cover of an equipment bin and pull out a life vest, throw it out into the yard, look up at the ceiling.

The owners of the house store their kayaks in elevated racks, a cumbersome setup intended to keep the boats dry, out of the way. I start to crank. It takes a full minute to lower the first kayak, which I free from the chains then drag from the garage before going back in for a paddle. When I come out I grab the kayak's handle and pull.

"He's already in the bay, Noah."

Lorelei's voice is tremulous, sharp, and a needle of fear knits her heart to mine as I climb into the kayak with the extra vest and start paddling toward the bay, even as the rational quadrants of my mind scream at me to get a grip because Charlie is at most two hundred yards from the shore, I can still see him even from the low angle of the kayak, Lorelei is being OCD Lorelei, but that's just it, she isn't, because our thoughts are the same, that life is profound and precarious, that a family of five can be cruising along in a minivan one minute and be hurtling down an embankment the next, that even a strapping Division I lacrosse recruit can drown in an eddy, that the only certainty in life is the certainty of death—

# 9.

I have made it halfway across the inlet when the panic starts to subside. Yes, Charlie is outside the boundary, technically in violation of the family rule. But his board bobs on the gentle swells as he paddles with a languid ease along the two tongues of land making up the inlet's southern aperture. He is staying close to shore, being responsible.

Charlie just turned eighteen, I remind myself. He is a man, capable of making his own decisions about his safety, among other things.

My stroke slows and my nerves settle as the distance grows from Lorelei's obsessive fears. I turn and give her a thumbs-up. She returns a cautious wave.

I push through the churn at the barrier and enter the bay, where the current heaves the kayak with smacks against the hull. Another half minute of paddling catches me up with Charlie.

"Hey." I heft the vest. "Remember, you need one of these out here."

Charlie, with a smirk, takes the vest and sets it on the foot of his board, a tactic he employed last summer, adhering to the letter of the law while violating its spirit. "Dad, you said we need to *have* a life vest with us if we leave the inlet, not *wear* a life vest." Clever, dodgy. Charlie is like me in this way, always probing for the loopholes, scouring for the work-arounds.

I nod at the vest. "You need to put it on."

"Seriously?"

"Do it for your mom."

Charlie shields his eyes with his right hand, looking back over the inlet. He winds his life vest around the end of the paddle and uses the improvised flag to give Lorelei a reassuring semaphore.

I decide not to push. Instead I gesture down the shore of the western bank, toward a sparkling new boathouse in the near distance.

"Want to check it out?"

"Race you," says Charlie, and with a few expert strokes glides past. The pure pleasure of normalcy courses through me as I chase him through the open waters, the brackish spew on my face and the salt on my lips. The current challenges my arms, softened by weeks away from the gym.

We tool along the western face of the bay, a mile wide at this point between two of the many rivers feeding the great estuary between the Virginia mainland and the Eastern Shore. Our inlet sits at one of the Chesapeake's narrower spans, though even here the bay's vastness is apparent in the traffic navigating the summer currents. Sailboats heel with the wind, fishing skiffs chug for favorite spots. In the distance a container ship makes for Cape Charles twelve miles to the south.

We pass a buoy at the entrance to the neighboring cove. From this angle I can appreciate even more the carnage wrought on the grand property, the decimation of the trees and the natural undergrowth, the fresh plantings of shrubs surrounded by neat discs of mulch. Landscapers have redone the grass, fertilized to the carpetlike quality of a putting green.

The gleaming boathouse belongs to the shoreline estate, I now understand, replacing its rustic predecessor, a weathered, copper-roofed structure of clapboard with a wraparound porch and a row of Adirondack chairs I recall from last year. That venerable boathouse is gone, scraped clean from the land.

"Dad, look." Charlie points at twin warning signs posted beyond the buoy.

## PRIVATE PROPERTY
## TRESPASSERS WILL BE PROSECUTED
## TO THE FULL EXTENT OF THE LAW

I know enough about riparian law to understand that these signs straddling the neighbor's cove entrance are breaking it. In Virginia, as in Maryland, any navigable waterway alongside private property is considered a public common, no more subject to private ownership or control than a meadow in a state park. While nuisance laws sometimes apply, the blanket prohibition on a large cove like this is absurd on its face. The local commonwealth's attorney down here either doesn't know about the signs or, for some reason, has left the relevant statutes unenforced. Legalities aside, the signs are also obnoxious, as much an offense to the eye as the rest of the compound.

Yet some faint protective instinct tells me to obey the interdiction. The whole cove repels me. Something big and ugly lies behind these signs, something I don't want near my family, not in this fragile state.

Charlie, bobbing between the pilings, stares into the cove as I glide past, my mind already on the future, five minutes from now, five weeks from now. A commercial marina is coming up in another quarter mile, I remember, the kind of place where you can tie up at a dock ladder and go in for soft serve or a beer. I picture us drinking Rolling Rocks on a bench by the water. We'll talk about the week ahead and I'll ask gently how conditioning is going and what he's heard from his new coaches. Maybe we'll plan our drive down to Chapel Hill.

"How about a beer?" I ask, believing Charlie to be close in my wake. No response. I repeat the question; again, silence.

When I turn and look I see my son paddling into the prohibited cove.

# 10.

"Charlie, don't!"

But I know my words of caution are useless the moment they leave my mouth. I paddle back past the buoy and between the threatening signs and into the cove with the same low burn of unease in my throat.

The small body of water stretches from the bay to the foot of the compound's emerald lawn. The cove appears almost perfectly circular, as if drawn with a compass or sliced from the land with a giant cookie cutter, an effect heightened by a stark reshaping of the banks. The large rocks along the shore form a single neat rank around the perimeter.

Everything else about the place looks equally unnatural, from the garish rose garden to the white-sanded swimming beach to the crane-equipped boat launch. A snazzy dining pavilion stands fifty feet up the lawn, a confection of plate glass and molded concrete. Over by the beach a lifeguard stand or lookout tower replicates a candy cane lighthouse, complete with a circular platform near the top and a rotating spotlight.

I can only imagine what the waterfront must look like to boats passing by at night—a showy spectacle of poor taste and artificial light. I wonder who bought this compound, what motivated its owner to transform the place from a picturesque bayside horse farm into an ostentatious vanity project.

Charlie, now twenty feet from the artificial beach, angles his board toward the alluring stretch of trucked-in sand.

"No, Charlie," I yell. "Absolutely not."

This time my tone is sharper, uncompromising—and here too the law is with me. A step onto the property really would be trespassing, a prosecutable offense despite the juvenile curiosity that inspired it.

Charlie attempts a sharp turn, the front of his board no more than ten feet from the beach. As the paddleboard rotates he loses his balance and goes sprawling into the cove. The force of his feet propels the board ahead so that it scrapes up on shore. He emerges from the water laughing as he wipes his eyes, pushes back his hair. His life vest floats nearby and he grabs it as he trudges through the shallows to retrieve his board.

*"That's close enough."*

A male voice: sharp, crackling, amplified.

Charlie freezes. I look up. On the balcony of the ersatz lighthouse, a red-faced man in a green polo shirt holds a mouthpiece to his lips.

*"Remove your paddleboard and leave the property immediately."*

Charlie looks over his shoulder, waiting for me to respond. I shake my head, gesture for him to hurry up.

"This is bullshit, Dad," he says, taking his time to climb back on. "They can't just—"

"They can, Charlie. Take my word for it. Grab your board and let's go."

All of this spoken in a low, calm tone as my contempt surges toward the nameless owner of this gaudy estate. I am used to dealing with the very rich, the sense of entitlement that comes with high net worth. Fisher-Burkhardt often represents moneyed clients being sued for injuries sustained on their properties, then viciously countersuing for trespass and infringement—and they're some of the most litigious people I've ever encountered. Whoever owns this property would probably be delighted to pass along news of this minor infraction to his attorneys for the entertainment value alone. Better to stay off the radar of people like this, avoid any unpleasant entanglements.

The megaphone again: *"Move it. NOW."*

"We are." Charlie's voice cracks. He cowers, his board wobbles; the man's abrasive orders have punctured any spirit of defiance. Charlie stays on his knees for greater balance and paddles furiously, and somehow, after these weeks of vulnerability, the sight of my son's submission to the microphone fascist in the tower lowers a curtain of rage over my eyes. Treating us like this, like we're inmates lingering too long in the prison yard.

As Charlie rushes by on his board, I look up from my kayak, cup a hand over my mouth, and yell: "*Fuck! You!*"

The guard says nothing, merely watches as I turn away stunned by my own ire, what it made me do.

A second man appears on the shore, a trim white guy striding purposefully across the lawn from the direction of the house. This one has a gun, a pistol in a waistband holster beneath the hem of a green polo shirt matching the one worn by Mr. Lighthouse. When he reaches the beach he takes a stance with his legs shoulder-width apart.

"Do we have a problem here, sir?" he demands.

I mark the SECURITY logo on the asshole's polo shirt above a monogrammed rendering of his surname: KENDRICK.

"I mean, I don't have a problem," I tell him. "My son and I are just out for a float. But you clearly do."

Again the words just blow out of my mouth, lawyer's discretion be damned.

"Dad," Charlie urges, our roles reversed. "Come on, let's go."

Ignoring him, I wait for a response from the gun.

"And what problem would that be, sir?" says Kendrick.

"Your boss needs to remove those signs." I point to the pilings at the mouth of the cove. "They're illegal."

"Is that so."

"This is all public property." I wave my paddle around to indicate the surrounding waters. "You can't declare a common waterway off-limits."

Kendrick whips out a phone. Before I can react he snaps a picture of me, another of Charlie.

"We'll take that under serious advisement, sir," he says blandly, pocketing the phone. He touches his earpiece and speaks a few low words; then, to me: "Now if you don't mind moving along, we'd appreciate it."

We lock eyes for a long moment. I start to turn away then cock my head, listening. A noise builds from somewhere out in the bay. Faint at first, no more than a soft droning. The hum soon grows to a rumble—guttural, mechanical, a rhythmic crescendo that accompanies our progress across the cove.

A shape fills the sky above us, darkening the sun, and a helicopter starts to descend with a deafening roar. The air pulses with the turning of the rotors, and the whirring blades kick up a salty spray. I shield my face against the sudden blinding squall.

Charlie looks like a rabbit beneath the landing skids, about to be snatched by the talons of a lowering bird.

# 11.

The guards spring into action. Kendrick points at my kayak then at the bay as he jogs along the shore toward the asphalt slab. A helipad, I understand now, the immediate destination of the chopper hovering above.

"Out. *Now*," Kendrick bellows over the din.

But in a fluke of the area's topography, our progress toward the mouth of the cove edges us closer to the helipad. When Charlie reenters the bay, his board passes no more than thirty feet from the craft as it settles on the asphalt. He rises to his feet again, his confidence restored, paddling along blithely as if nothing happened back in the cove. The helicopter's engines power down to a purr. The younger guard steps up to the craft as Kendrick takes a position short of the helipad.

The cabin door slides open, and out steps a man I recognize instantly. I would know that aquiline nose and close-cropped salt-and-pepper hair anywhere—though Daniel Monet's is not a familiar face unless you happen to work in the high-tech world or, in my case, for one of the many law firms hired by tech giants to handle mergers and buyouts and so on. I have never billed on a case directly involving the Monet Group, have certainly never been in a room with Monet himself. But everyone in the business follows the relevant news.

Daniel Monet has a reputation as an unflashy, low-key operator, also as a major donor to the Democratic Party, a philanthropist supporting an array of center-left causes and candidates—though with a military-industrial edge that may explain the paranoia of his security detail. His companies have extensive interests in cybersecurity and data infrastructure. I remember reading a piece some years ago about his work on supply chain optimization for the Department of Defense, and there was even a rumor floating around early in the Biden administration that Monet might be tapped for a subcabinet post in Homeland Security, though it didn't pan out.

Now, in this new American era of oligarchy, deregulation, and caprice, Daniel Monet operates behind the curtains, pulling levers hidden from public view. He isn't the sort to buy a hundred-million-dollar house in the Hamptons or float around on a ninety-foot yacht, a comparative restraint that accords with the scene before us now. For someone of Monet's wealth, a refurbished horse farm on the Northern Neck of Virginia is modest indeed.

Charlie seems mildly interested in the helicopter as he paddles along, though not in the unassuming man in his mid-fifties descending from its belly. Monet stops beneath the slowing spin of the rotors and lifts his nose to the sky, thinking himself unobserved from the water as he inhales the moist breeze off the bay.

With a half-turn, Monet extends an arm toward the chopper. A hand reaches out from the door and takes his wrist, and a young woman steps down into the patch of oscillating light. She is small-boned and lithe, with a smooth curtain of strawberry-blond hair falling midway down her back. A pair of oversized sunglasses obscures the upper half of her face. She is not a mistress or a too-young wife but a daughter, I gather by Monet's protective manner toward the girl.

Once on the helipad, she raises her arms and makes a pirouette, taking in the sea air as her father starts for the house. Her loose skirt, calf-length, floats above her knees. When she twirls back around toward the bay she goes still and I follow the direction of her gaze.

Charlie has reached the point. The midafternoon sun plays on his glistening skin, his ripped abs, his powerful arms. My son looks like an ad for a luxe beach resort, with the well-wrought torso of a Michelangelo.

The girl on the shore lowers her sunglasses to the tip of her nose; her head tilts forward, her lips part. When she brings a hand to her chest the effect is almost comical, causing her bag to slide from her right shoulder and drop to the crook of her elbow.

So far Charlie has taken no notice of his new admirer. He paddles along, oblivious to the gawking girl. The spell lasts until her father hails her from down the shore.

"Eurydice," Daniel Monet calls into the silence; more sharply: "Dissee, come on."

I watch as Charlie catches the father's summons, the girl's name. He turns his head and sees her there beneath the helicopter blades, now still. At first Charlie doesn't react, long accustomed to female admiration. But this particular girl's attention does something to him; something new. Rather than preening or acting indifferent, he starts to wobble on the paddleboard and spin his arms, pretending to lose balance. After a few seconds of this act he falls off the board and into the water, landing on his back with an impressive splash.

The board bobs in place as Charlie strokes back to remount. He does a muscle-up and holds the difficult pose for a few seconds before deftly swinging himself onto the board and getting to his feet. With the handle of the paddle beneath his left elbow and his right arm bent at the hip, he theatrically flips back his hair.

The girl, clearly delighted with his antics, starts a slow clap, prompting Charlie to spin his free arm like an old-fashioned vaudeville performer and make a goofy bow from the waist.

Despite the lightness of the exchange, the silent interaction sets me on edge. These are not people to play around with. This trip was supposed to get us away from it all, a week of continued recuperation and some quiet, precious days with Charlie before he leaves us for UNC. As my paddle strikes the water, the air and heat squeeze in from every corner of this insufferable cove.

I push out into the bay between the menacing signs while Eurydice Monet regards Charlie from the helipad. A current passes between them: electric, spiked, palpable. She is still watching as he reaches the rocky mouth, still watching as he skims across the inlet, still watching as he points out our rental with a quick lift of his paddle, the purpose of the gesture clear.

Apparently satisfied, Eurydice rotates away from Charlie. Her gaze rakes across my kayak. The young woman's attention lingers on me as her sunglasses lower over her eyes, the edges of her lips curled into an unreadable smile.

# 12.

Charlie makes a few slow circuits of our inlet, clearly hoping for another glimpse of Daniel Monet's daughter, though she never reappears up at the point. The helicopter remains, though, hulking on its asphalt pad, a giant orange bug crouched two hundred yards from the end of our dock and defacing our view of the bay.

Back at the house, Lorelei reclines on a chaise lounge beneath the shade of an elm, looking at her phone, which she keeps at eye level because of her brace. A pitcher of lemonade sits on the table along with an array of colorful drinking glasses.

"Where are the girls?" I ask once in the shade. I have to repeat the question.

"They're trying to figure out the TV," says Lorelei distractedly. "Getting to know Calinda."

Charlie tosses his paddle onto the grass and beaches his board. A few long strides take him to the table. He downs a glass of lemonade in three gulps then moves over to a smooth part of the lawn and starts doing burpees to his new coach's AI-replicated voice, which he has imported into the fitness app on his phone. The orders come out in a military rhythm: *One-two-three-ONE. One-two-three-TWO. One-two-three-THREE. Keep-it-up-FOUR. Kick-some-ass-FIVE.*

Usually he reaches twenty or thirty reps before getting winded. Now he stops at seven, leaning over with his elbows on his knees.

"You okay?" I ask.

He shrugs, sits staring out over the inlet, his cheeks flushed. I hold my tongue.

A voice from behind me says, "Is there enough for me?"

I turn to see Izzy hobbling across the back deck. Charlie scrambles up and pours her a glass of lemonade as she totters over on her crutches. Her throat makes ripples as she swallows.

"Can I get in, Dad?" She sets her glass on the table.

"Sure, I'll give you a hand."

Izzy has taken her injury with equanimity, struggling with her cast and crutches at first but soon accepting her temporary impairment. She's not supposed to swim, but the other day I stopped at a Walgreens and bought her a watertight cast cover.

She tests the shallows, then I help her scoot onto a paddleboard and shove off. Charlie, his abbreviated workout completed, dives off the end of the dock and swims toward her board. He scissor-kicks to tugboat for his sister. Izzy's face is the happiest I've seen it in a while.

"Check them out," I say to Lorelei.

She looks over her phone toward the inlet. "That's sweet."

I collapse into the chair next to hers. "You doing okay?"

She makes what looks like a shrug, though with the brace it can be hard to tell.

"What are you reading?"

"They have another GoFundMe set up," she says softly. Two faces grin from her phone screen. Phil and Judith Drummond, the retired couple from the burning Honda.

"What do you mean, another?"

"Somebody put one up a few days after the accident, a memorial fundraiser for the SPCA. Apparently she was a big supporter." A beat. "They had eleven cats."

"And what's this one for?"

"There's a grown son with special needs."

"Okay."

"I think we should contribute."

"Is that a good idea?"

"Why wouldn't it be?"

"They might recognize our names. Could be sticky."

"With these things you can give anonymously."

I say nothing.

"It's the least we can do, Noah. For Christ's sake, we—" Her volume spikes, high enough that Charlie and Izzy both glance over from the inlet. More quietly: "We killed two people."

I recoil. Lorelei hasn't put things this way before, so stark, so naked. In first-person plural, as if all five of us who were in the minivan that day bear responsibility, a kind of collective familial guilt. Or maybe the *we* is a deflection, a way for the two of us to take on some portion of blame so that it won't weigh so heavily on the shoulders of our son.

*We killed two people.*

The sliding door opens and shuts again, and Alice steps down into the lawn clad in the same orange one-piece from last summer, too small for her now. She tugs self-consciously on the shoulder straps and pulls at the hems digging into the flesh of her thighs. She turns down my offer of lemonade and picks her way toward the water.

So hard to read, our poor Alice. She has only retreated further into herself since the accident, maintaining a vigilant and isolating silence, as if watching the rest of us for any signs of weakness. In our sessions with Dr. Levinson she has been recalcitrant, showing flashes of anger whenever the subject of the crash comes up.

At the dock she takes off her glasses, folds in the temples, and sets them gingerly on the railing. Her movements are cautious, deliberate; she still worries about her balance.

Charlie, spying Alice on the shore, grabs the paddle from Izzy and sends a big splash of water her way.

"Don't," says Alice through clenched teeth, though the water lands nowhere close to her. I expect another splash, but her feral pitch stays her brother's hand.

Alice takes a tentative step into the water. She stares down at her feet, then turns and squints up at us.

"It feels gooey," she says.

"It's the silt on the bottom," says Lorelei. "Sand and dead leaves mostly."

"And decomposing corpses," Charlie adds from the water, prompting a barking laugh from Izzy.

"That's hilarious," says Alice. "Coming from you, Charlie, that's really fucking absolutely hilarious."

"Alice," I snap. "Enough."

Charlie doesn't respond to his sister's cruel retort. His face goes blank as Izzy reclaims her paddle. The sun moves behind a cloud, shrouding the inlet and bruising the bay. Alice sinks to her knees and lets her body tip forward. Her pale legs shimmer beneath the surface as she pushes off the silt.

## 13.

For dinner on our first night I make gourmet hamburgers, organic beef molded into patties with chili powder, fresh garlic, diced onions, and Worcestershire sauce. I recruit Izzy as sous chef, setting her to slice tomatoes and husk corn out at the picnic table, needing her uncomplicated cheer. But once the others sit down, the conversation is relaxed and unforced, everyone, even Alice, exhausted from the long drive and our hours on the water. Lorelei pours a second glass of wine, Charlie cracks one of his White Claws, sneaks Izzy a sip when he thinks I'm not looking. I sit back against the seat cushions, surfing a tentative swell of well-being that lasts through the meal.

Charlie has risen to start clearing the table when a high-pitched whine resounds over the inlet. The helicopter, powering up against the dusk sky. Dishes in hand, Charlie stares as the chopper lifts from its pad and moves off the point, angling directly over our rental, low and loud.

"Wonder who that was," says Izzy into the fading noise.

"His name is Daniel Monet." I take the opportunity to tell everyone about our wealthy neighbor.

"Wait." Charlie looks up. "You actually know that guy, Dad?"

"From the tech news. He's huge in that world."

"Why didn't you say anything?"

"Didn't think you'd be interested."

"Does he have kids?" Izzy asks, always on the lookout for another friend.

"At least one daughter, though she's older."

"How do you know?" says Alice.

I glance at Lorelei. "She looked pretty smitten with Charlie."

Lorelei raises her eyebrows and the girls start up a teasing duet of *ooohs*, the kind of sisterly razzing their brother normally ignores. Despite his charisma and athleticism, Charlie has never had a girlfriend, or boyfriend for that matter, hasn't even hooked up with anyone as far as I know. Lorelei, always up on the latest findings in developmental science and social psychology, attributes our son's apparent lack of interest in sex to the great Gen Z slowdown, that stuntedness common among today's young adults and twentysomethings. Many of our friends with grown children have shared their frustrations at this baffling phenomenon: kids refusing to get driver's licenses, taking extended gap years, returning after college to live at home, declining to date.

We have grown accustomed to Charlie's lack of interest in romantic attachments, so even a possible connection with a girl feels oddly exhilarating—though also disconcerting. Why of all people must this happen with the daughter of someone like Daniel Monet, with his signs and guards and his ruination of that beautiful place? And it's obvious that Charlie is not indifferent, not this time. His easy grimace at his sisters conceals something sharp, a keen glimmer of yearning. He has been stealing glances across the inlet for hours.

The helicopter returns ten minutes later, while the kids are scooping out ice cream. This time four passengers disembark and duck beneath the blades. Family members, I assume, though this guess is tested when the craft takes off immediately and returns with another five or six passengers. It makes three more trips over the next hour, rattling the old windows and setting our nerves on edge.

"This is getting ridiculous," Alice says on the helicopter's third or fourth pass, clutching the sides of her head—though there's little we can do about the racket. Lodge a complaint in the morning, maybe, though who knows what that would accomplish. I remember the signs posted outside the cove, suggesting special treatment from local law enforcement. We are likely stuck with the nuisance.

A cover band starts up shortly after eight o'clock, the bass obnoxiously loud. The songs come throbbing from the next cove and overpower the evening cheeps of frogs and crickets and the distant tidal lapping of the bay.

I am out on the dock shaking a fist in my head when an aged man emerges from the small bungalow next door. His wife soon joins him on their deck, and together they stand glaring over the inlet at the unseen source of the noise. Their matching hair, a stark white, shines through the gloom and seems to hover over their bodies, which appear skeletal and stooped. At one point the man looks over at me. I give him a neighborly wave that he doesn't return.

Back inside Lorelei makes a half-hearted attempt to get a game of Hearts going. I feign enthusiasm, but no one else is interested. Izzy coaxes her mother into brushing her hair. Alice complains of another headache and trudges upstairs before nine.

Charlie, meanwhile, sprawls in the living room Google-stalking the Monet family. At one point he lets out a gasp.

"What?" I walk over and take a recliner.

"Dad, that guy is freaking loaded. Did you know his companies are valued at sixteen *billion*? How is that even possible?"

"One of our clients at Fisher-Burkhardt has a net worth of about twenty."

"He has houses in London, New York, Montreal, and now here. His wife died in . . . it says in a car accident, back in 2016."

I meet Lorelei's eyes and feel again the fragility of our lives.

"It says he bought the place down here two years ago."

"What about the daughter? Anything about her, where she goes to school?"

Charlie's face reddens in the lamplight. "Her Instagram says she's going to Duke in the fall."

"Wow," I say. He's already found the girl's social media. Of course he has. "So you'll be neighbors."

"Looks like it," he says, again with that unfamiliar strain in his voice.

Which may mean nothing. Charlie and Eurydice Monet haven't spoken a single word, haven't so much as met outside of his afternoon performance on the paddleboard, and for all I know the girl might be long gone, disappeared in her father's helicopter and bound for Qatar or Monte Carlo or any other ritzy destination around the globe, the merest flicker in the life of my son.

its bad tonight

                         oh no my dear

it was ok then this helicopter flew over our house and it was like a drill in my brain tissue

                         that sounds horrible. u taking care of urself?

yes im in the dark up in our room

                         with iz?

not yet shes still downstairs getting her beautiful hair brushed

                         that sounds nice

sure fucking does u wanna know something?

                         ???

my mom hasnt brushed my hair since the accident

                         srsly?

y

                         have you asked her 2?

once but she said she was 2 afraid of hurting me

                         well to be fair u did have a concussion

but my skull is fine its whats inside it thats the

issue she shd know that shes a freaking phd

> well if u love someone u want to protect them, keep them safe from harm

sometimes its too much tho, her protectiveness

> maybe shes scared

lol scared is her middle name u shd meet her sometime

> id like that very very much Alice

actually horrible idea nvm

> what is your mother afraid of?

literally everything

# 14.

Lorelei stretches on one of the twin beds, turned away from me and staring at her iPad. The Drummonds again, I assume. She has developed a preoccupation with the couple, she scrolls endlessly through human interest stories from their local paper and posts on the family's memorial website. For long periods she will stare at snapshots of Phil Drummond posing with a grandkid on his knee, Judith Drummond with her beloved cats.

An outsider might discern a voyeuristic quality in my wife's constant scrutiny of the aftermath, this eavesdropping on the extended family's pain, though her deeper compulsion is fear. Lorelei's bouts of anxiety came on in seventh grade, sparked by what she describes as intrusive fantasies about the violent deaths of her parents and siblings, and accompanied by irrational, taboo scenarios. These she would try to control and tamp down by imposing regimes of order and cleanliness and a rhythmic predictability, chapping her hands with obsessive washing, arranging and sorting everything she touched, tapping out patterns on her water glass at dinner every night until her mother would grab her wrist.

Lorelei was fortunate, at least in relative terms. There were doctors in her extended family, including a beloved uncle who marked her symptoms early on and referred her to a specialist in adolescent anxiety disorders. What might have been a severe disabling condition was treated with medications and therapy that allowed her to enjoy a relatively normal experience in high school and college, her gifts able to flourish and her dazzling mind to thrive, her condition kept largely under control for decades now.

With one notable exception. The news came in an early morning call as Lorelei was getting dressed for a teaching day at Hopkins. She hated when her phone rang at odd hours, would often shrink away from the device, worrying that one of her parents or siblings was dead.

You get it, she said, and went to hide in the walk-in closet.

A woman's voice, calm and pleasant, asked if Professor Shaw was available. The caller's bright tone alleviated any fears: This was no emergency. Lorelei took the phone and soon her expression changed, from trepidation to astonishment. She asked some questions, enough to give me a sense of the nature of the call. Her face was pale when her phone hand dropped to her lap.

A fluttery breath, then she told me about the prize, the significance—the obscene amount of no-strings money. I was aware of what a MacArthur Fellowship represented, would notice the annual headline in *The New York Times* about the winners of the so-called Genius Award. I vaguely knew someone else who had received one, a law prof who ran an innovative legal aid clinic on the South Side of Chicago. Now my wife had entered this pantheon.

Up until that moment, Lorelei's career operated according to the rigid calendaring and professional boundaries she had put in place for herself long before. I knew on some level how respected she was in her field; occasionally I would meet colleagues at Hopkins events who would speak of her in hushed and reverential tones. *You know your wife's an absolute superstar, right?* And now, overnight, here was Lorelei Shaw in the national news as a world leader in her field, lauded for her cutting-edge research and compelling voice for restraint in the dawning age of artificial intelligence. She sat for NPR interviews, made the front page of *The Washington Post*.

At first Lorelei was bedazzled by it all. Profoundly flattered and deeply embarrassed at the same time, she even started to enjoy the buzz of adulation, reveling in the simultaneous pride and envy of her competitive siblings.

Soon, though, the pressure started to show. Lorelei's sudden visibility came with the price of heightened expectation. Now that she was a bona fide genius, there would be more eyes on her work, more scrutiny of her research and findings. Also more speaking and consulting invitations than she could reasonably handle. Her regimented professional world was spinning out of her control—and with this loss of order came a resurgence of obsessive fixations and intrusive thoughts.

She didn't deserve a MacArthur. She was a fraud. An impostor. Someone would discover holes in her work. She would be fired, exposed, publicly humiliated. I would leave her. I would divorce her. I would take the kids. I would kill the kids. *She* would kill the kids.

One evening I came home from work and found Lorelei curled up in the bathtub fully clothed, palms pressed against her cheeks and a wild look in her eyes. I knelt down and held her while she lamented the damage she would unleash if we weren't careful. How many people she would harm, how many deaths she would cause. She didn't want to be around our children, especially two-year-old Izzy, because she was too afraid of dropping her, burning her, slamming her fragile arm in a door. This had always been Lorelei's most primal fear, this terror of harming loved ones, despite the gentleness and kindness that made such an act impossible for anyone who knew her to imagine—but not for Lorelei herself, who responded to my reassurances with a litany of catastrophic ideation. *I told you we shouldn't have kids why did we have kids why did you let us have kids how can you sleep in the same room with me when you might wake up dead go out to the kitchen and hide the knives and take the knobs off the stove go right now Noah go go go hide the knives, hide the knives.* . . .

I phoned her psychiatrist, who suggested an inpatient hospital in Northwest D.C. Lorelei stayed there for three days, as her psychiatrist worked with the on-site doctors to adjust her meds, return her to balance. When she came home and went back to campus she was largely her old self, accepting the life-changing impact of the MacArthur and finding a rhythm in all her new recognition and responsibilities.

Yet Lorelei remains a persistent worrier and a world-class catastrophizer, and I have watched her closely over this last month for signs of another relapse. She was already different somehow in those months leading up to the accident, more burdened by the demands of her work; and then a collision on a Delaware road realized her worst fears. The accident proved she had been right all along about the ubiquitous perils of the world.

Outside, a tree bends in a silent wave. I gaze at Lorelei's slender back across the chasm between our beds. Since our first months together we have slept in separate twins, an early accommodation to Lorelei's needs. I have grown used to the arrangement over the years, though in this brittle time I long for her warmth at night, for the tangle of our limbs and the spooning of our flesh.

A custom foam pillow brought from home supports her head at the correct height for the brace. The air is stuffy in the room and Lorelei has uncovered herself, nightgown hitched up nearly to her waist. A flash of warm skin, the shadowed gap between her thighs. The sight stirs me for a moment, but my desire quickly fades; Lorelei's attention is locked on the two fatalities, this gristly bone she won't let go. From a cool distance I wonder if that long vital part of our marriage has ended, killed in the same collision that took two souls.

Our sex life, I think bleakly: as dead as the Drummonds.

Her eyes shift, catching my stare. She rolls onto her back and pulls the quilt up to her chin, causing the iPad to slide down her pillow. The screen displays a news site. Nothing about the Drummonds.

"This thing happened in Yemen," she says.

"Yemen?"

"It's a country on the Arabian—"

"I know where Yemen is, Lor. What happened?"

"We blew up two buses."

"'We' meaning . . ."

"The military. The U.S. Navy."

"Okay."

She concentrates on the ceiling. "Mostly women and children. Almost forty of them."

"Jesus. Was it a missile strike?"

"Drones."

"Oh."

"A swarm of drones."

Her eyes glisten. I have witnessed Lorelei react many times to stories about the needless deaths of innocents. The anguish of parents in the wake of a school shooting in Pennsylvania, survivors mourning after a tornado in Missouri—and now dozens of civilians blown up halfway around the world. Empathetic dysfunction, her therapists call it, a sometimes debilitating response to an overload of impersonal but negative information. Lorelei has a way of assuming the pain of distant others and wearing it as a mantle, like the old quilt covering her now.

I move to her bed and sit on the edge. She lets me take the iPad before rolling over onto her side to face away from me. At first, when I touch her, I feel a flinch and almost withdraw my hand. She trembles, ripples passing up and down her spine. We don't speak again. I turn out her light and remain by her side until the quilt goes still.

CULPABILITY

## Subcommittee on Emerging Threats and Capabilities of the Armed Services Committee

### UNITED STATES SENATE

*Confidential closed hearing on initial deployments of Southron-Hammon Corporation's High Efficiency Low Lethality Owlet System (HELLOS) network by U.S. forces in Red Sea theater*

**Sen. DAVIDSON:** Major, what exactly made the things swarm those buses in the first place? Was it a matter of poor target selection, overly vague instructions, or what?

**Maj. Donald RAMIREZ, 103rd Intelligence and Electronic Warfare Battalion, US Army:** Senator, it's hard to say.

**Sen. DAVIDSON:** And why is that?

**Maj. RAMIREZ:** The computations are too complex. We know roughly how the system crunches all the inputs, but those final outputs are always going to be a bit of a mystery.

**Sen. DAVIDSON:** Walk us through the footage from Hodeidah. From what I could tell, it looks like the swarm was heading for Houthi positions north of the city around a suspected missile depot.

**Maj. RAMIREZ:** Yes, Senator.

**Sen. DAVIDSON:** The owlets sniffed it out on their own, figured out among themselves how to coordinate the attack. Impressive stuff.

**Maj. RAMIREZ:** Yes, Senator.

**Sen. DAVIDSON:** So you have these two hundred owlets preparing to attack a missile depot. They're a mile out from their target. And then, what? I guess they changed their minds?

**Maj. RAMIREZ:** Senator, we don't know if we'd call it a "mind," precisely, but the system certainly reprocessed its targeting selection, and as a result—

**Sen. DAVIDSON:** The system reprocessed its targeting selection. Is that the euphemism we're using now for a lethal American drone swarm taking out two busloads of Yemeni civilians, half of them children?

**Maj. RAMIREZ:** Senator, I—

**Sen. DAVIDSON:** Because that's how I hear it, Major Ramirez.

**Maj. RAMIREZ:** Senator, our team has been over the details a dozen times, we've done extensive post-op reconnaissance. So I hope you won't mind if I offer a quantitative assessment. It may sound cold, but I offer it to this committee with the acknowledgment that every civilian casualty in wartime is a tragedy.

**Sen. DAVIDSON:** Indeed it is, Major. Please, share your assessment.

**Maj. RAMIREZ:** Okay, Senator, so, in conventional aerial assaults on a city the size of Hodeidah, let's say Manbij in Syria or Umm Qasr in Iraq, you'd expect a civilian casualty rate of just over ten percent. Meaning for every ten enemy combatants taken out, an average of one-point-three civilian lives will be lost. That figure can vary a lot depending on the type of ordnance you're deploying in theater, the density of population, and other factors. But for the sake of illustration those are pretty good figures.

**Sen. DAVIDSON:** No argument here.

**Maj. RAMIREZ:** Senator, over the last three months the 103rd has deployed the HELLOS system in eighteen separate airborne assaults in Yemen and Syria, in both urban and suburban environments. A year ago we would have sent a package of medium-range missiles and human-piloted drones to take out those positions. But in these attacks we've deployed owlet swarms.

**Sen. DAVIDSON:** Okay.

**Maj. RAMIREZ:** Our estimates suggest that these eighteen assaults have resulted in approximately twelve hundred casualties among enemy combatants. And the number of civilian deaths, not counting this present incident? Thirty-seven.

**Sen. DAVIDSON:** Do the math for us, Major.

**Maj. RAMIREZ:** Already have, Senator. That comes out to three percent, give or take. In other words, we believe the HELLOS system may result in a decline of civilian casualty rates somewhere in the neighborhood of seventy percent.

**Sen. DAVIDSON:** That's remarkable.

**Maj. RAMIREZ:** Yes, Senator.

**Sen. DAVIDSON:** So why are these drone swarms more precise and capable in combat environments than their human-guided counterparts? Are they smarter than us?

**Maj. RAMIREZ:** We're beginning to think so, Senator.

**Sen. DAVIDSON:** Explain.

**Maj. RAMIREZ:** I'll give you an example. As I was preparing for this hearing I rewatched the feed from a HELLOS attack last month. We deployed a medium swarm, a hundred owlets released from the belly of a C-5 Galaxy twenty miles from the target, which was a headquarters for Houthi combatants in that whole region of Yemen. Heavily fortified with lots of drone-suppressant SAM installations and a high concentration of civilians in the area, so not an ideal target. But command felt that the profile made the attack worth the risk.

**Sen. DAVIDSON:** Go on.

**Maj. RAMIREZ:** Now, on approach, the swarm split up into two groups. The first group, seventy-three of the owlets, attacked the compound directly. Hammering the place, exactly what you'd expect. They took a lot of suppressing fire, and a few dozen of the owlets attritted sooner than we would have anticipated.

**Sen. DAVIDSON:** They were shot down.

**Maj. RAMIREZ:** Correct, Senator, quite a few were, several dozen in the initial assault. And the rest retreated, left the area. The hostiles thought they'd won the battle, thought they'd defeated an American drone swarm. They even came out onto the roof to celebrate. But what the hostiles didn't know, Senator, is that before the direct assault, the balance of the original swarm, twenty-seven owlets, had concealed themselves behind the wall of a mosque two blocks away, hovering there while the others assaulted the target location. And once the celebration started, the twenty-seven owlets approached from five separate angles of attack before rising over a parapet wall and taking out all the enemy combatants on the roof. They then attacked the rest of the compound, took out the suppressing SAMs, and completed the mission quickly and efficiently.

**Sen. DAVIDSON:** So how do you interpret that?

**Maj. RAMIREZ:** We believe the drones were playing them, Senator, faking out the Houthis. By our estimate, the HELLOS system that day killed eighty-five enemy combatants in the middle of a medium-sized city—without a single collateral death or civilian casualty.

**Sen. DAVIDSON:** So what you're suggesting is these sorts of trade-offs are inevitable. If the civilian-to-combatant death ratio is declining due to these new AI systems, then they're an overall positive.

**Maj. RAMIREZ:** That's a policy decision, Senator, well above my pay grade. But I'll tell you, seeing that attack unfold was like watching a grand master play a toddler at chess.

**Sen. DAVIDSON:** So what is your conclusion about the viability of the HELLOS system, Major? Are these AI owlets worth all the hype?

**Maj. RAMIREZ:** Senator, with respect, it ain't hype. The swarms are getting smarter by the day. They're introducing maneuvers to the battle space that we've never seen before, tactics that our war colleges have never even imagined. And you can see the self-reinforcement happening right before your eyes. It's like with my kids, Senator. Parents can only teach them and guide them so far. Once they're out of the nest they're learning on their own.

**Sen. DAVIDSON:** So this bus incident aside, if you had to give this committee one reason to allow the HELLOS system to be more widely deployed across the armed services in the short term, what would it be?

**Maj. RAMIREZ:** Senator, my answer would be that they're getting better and smarter all the time. The owlets are learning from their mistakes. More crucially, they're learning from ours.

# 15.

Early on the first morning at the bay, a rumble of thunder shakes me from sleep. On waking I forget where I am. Unfamiliar shadows waltz across the ceiling as a hard wind tears through nearby limbs. Branches and twigs scrape at the windowpanes like pestering birds.

I climb out of bed and go downstairs to make coffee. The weather app on my phone shows a narrow storm inching across the Northern Neck, all but past us already. For the next hour I read the news on my laptop and send a few work-related e-mails. We have a week here at the bay, then an overnight to deliver Charlie to Chapel Hill, then it's back to Fisher-Burkhardt—and I am ready to return to the office, even eager after this prolonged stasis. My mind has started to atrophy. I am inefficient in my responses to e-mails and tell myself to be sharp, precise. I send a curt correction to a paralegal, to show I'm on my game.

When the rain lets up, a gauzy mist settles over the inlet and the house, a pocket of moisture that drips from the eaves and the branches of the trees. Out in the yard, a doe and a pair of fawns nibble grass along the fence line between the rental and the bungalow next door. The deer startle when I open the door, but quickly return to their morning meal.

The soil squishes beneath my bare feet. I stroll to the end of the dock sipping my coffee, enjoying the piney stillness. I set my mug down and lean over the water with my elbows on the railing. Bugs skitter across the surface, otherwise mirror-smooth. A school of fish plays around the pilings, a woodpecker rattles a tree. The smell of the silt and rain mingles with the fog, dust-like on my face. The emerging sun catches a strand of vapor and teases up a rainbow on the surface. There is a faint rhythmic splashing—

And then, with no warning, the figure of Eurydice Monet materializes on a paddleboard, floating in like some Arthurian maiden in a shimmer of rising mist. Her bikini top resembles twin scallop shells, the connective threads flesh-toned, nearly invisible against her skin. A sarong patterned in spirals of pink, sea green, and gold circles her waist.

"Good morning, sir," she says, paddling up to the dock, her voice bold yet raspy, as if hoarsened by a recent cold.

"Morning." The fog muffles our exchange. "It's Eurydice, right?"

Her eyes narrow, then relax. "Oh. You heard my dad calling me."

I raise my mug. "I'm Noah."

"Nice to meet you, Noah."

"And my paddleboarding son is named Charlie," I add, unprompted.

Her smile lights up the inlet. *Good lord but Charlie's in trouble.* The water humps up along the edges of her board as it skims along. An ankle bracelet rests above Eurydice's left foot and a tattoo spirals around the opposite calf: a winged dragon, breathing fire up toward her knee.

"I thought I'd come by and see if he wants to paddleboard," she says.

"He's still sleeping. You'll be around later?"

"We'll be here all week," she says, in the cadence of a Catskills comic. She gazes longingly up at our humble rental, making no move to head back to her father's bayside estate.

"Sounded like quite the party over there," I observe, keeping it neutral.

"Oh my God." She jams her paddle in the water, reversing direction. "My dad has this retreat every year, for his companies? Usually they rent a place in Montauk but this year he decided to have everybody down here. All seventy-two of them."

"Sounded like a few hundred."

"Were they really loud? I'm so sorry. They were loud, weren't they?"

"I mean." Abashed by her good manners, I wave a hand. "No big deal. It was a good band."

"It was a horrible band, Noah, and lucky for all of us they aren't sticking around."

I laugh, despite myself. Behind me, the sliding door opens. Lorelei steps barefoot across the lawn, picking over the sticky carpet of pine needles and wet grass. I am alert for signs of last night's distress, but her eyes are clear.

"Who's our visitor?" Her gaze fastens on the young woman.

"This is Eurydice. Eurydice, this is Lorelei, Charlie's mom."

"Nice to meet you, Eurydice."

"You too," says the girl, then cocks her head. "What happened to your neck?"

The question, tactless and childlike, causes Lorelei to hesitate. "It was . . . a car accident, actually," she says, almost inaudibly.

"Oh." Eurydice seems taken aback. With a shiv to the gut I remember Charlie's account of how her mother died. But then she grins. "I'm glad you're okay."

Lorelei returns the smile.

"How long do you have to keep it on?"

"It comes off day after tomorrow."

"That's lucky."

"Yes."

"It sounds hard, wearing that all the time."

Lorelei clears her throat. "You know what? It is. Thank you for noticing, Eurydice."

"So Charlie's still asleep?"

"He's up, actually," says Lorelei. "Though he's about to go on a run."

"Oh." Eurydice squiggles the tip of her paddle on the water; then, glancing at Lorelei side-eyed, "I like to run."

"How about that," says Lorelei, making a wry grin and now visibly charmed, though it's hard to tell whether Eurydice's guilelessness is natural or feigned.

It occurs to me how odd this is, a solo early morning visit from a billionaire's daughter, no guard in sight despite yesterday's tense encounter with Daniel Monet's security detail. I consider what someone like Eurydice would want with Charlie. Sure, he's handsome and athletic, but she could find such attributes anywhere she looked, as the daughter of one of America's richest men, with private jets and helicopters, yachts, multiple houses, and surrounded by celebrities and the children of fellow moguls. Despite all that, though, she comes off as a delightful kid, curious, unpretentious, polite.

Still: My gaze keeps wandering down to the dragon inked on her leg.

"Soooooooo . . ." she says. "Will you please tell him I stopped by?"

As if on cue, the door slides open again and Charlie barrels from the house in running shorts and a Tar Heels tank top, earbuds in, high-stepping to stretch his legs while scrolling for a playlist on his phone.

He calls to us across the lawn. "Hey geezers, I've got a six-miler this morning so I should—"

The sight of Eurydice on the water stops his voice. A scratchy laugh from our visitor, and this time Charlie's are the lips that part, and his eyelids flutter girlishly during his halting progress toward the dock. I gesture at Lorelei. We stroll away from the waterfront together, leaving the two kids to get acquainted.

Lorelei spies on them from the kitchen sink, transfixed. I move behind her and scarcely dare to breathe as she leans back against me. Her spine presses into my chest, her body molding to mine for the first time in over a month. I reach up and lightly grasp her arms.

We gaze out together at our son and this unexpected girl. Charlie leans over the end of the dock, feet grazing the water as Eurydice sways like a hula dancer on her paddleboard.

"They're like a painting," says Lorelei.

I see what she means. The fog has risen off the surface of the water, though it still hovers over the inlet and our smitten boy. The remnant mist makes a gleaming dome, an arc of muted gold.

# 16.

Charlie never goes on his run. When he comes inside, his skin is pink from his forehead down to his upper chest, like an allergy coming on.

"You heading out?" I pretend not to notice his worked-up state as I fix myself a bowl of granola.

Charlie snaps off a banana. "Going paddleboarding instead." He downs the banana in three gorilla bites and tosses the peel into the sink. Usually Charlie is sensitive to his mother's issues, though given his condition I make no comment. I do warn him to take a life vest this time.

"Got it."

"And there's a tube of sunscreen on the picnic table."

"Dad," he huffs.

"Seriously, remember last summer? You were peeling like that banana you just ate. Don't be an idiot."

A boyish sigh. "Fine." And he's back out the door, a six-foot-three ball of agitation, hormones, and raw nerves.

Through the kitchen window I watch him grab the sunscreen off the picnic table, drop his tank top on the back of a chair, and stroll down toward the dock, trying for nonchalant. As he starts slathering sunscreen over his arms, Eurydice beaches her board and sashays up onto our lawn as if she owns the place. Her sarong drops from her waist and floats to the grass.

She turns her back on Charlie and spreads her arms with a wiggle in her hips. Even from this distance I can see the flush on my son's neck deepen.

The puritan in me wants to march out there with a bit of paternal bluster, come up with some excuse for why he shouldn't do what he's about to do. Instead I stay put like an old pervert while Charlie smears sunscreen on the girl's shoulders, rubs it down the cleft of her spine and along the width of her lower back, her hips. He steps away, but now Eurydice turns her head to the side. I read her lips: *Can you do my legs?* He hesitates, then hunches down and starts rubbing the lotion into her thighs, her calves, even her ankles.

Next she steals the sunscreen from his hands and makes a spinning motion with the tube. Charlie turns obediently and stands in place while Eurydice massages the lotion into his back, along his broad shoulder blades, taking her good sweet time. Charlie adopts the expression of a long-suffering golden retriever getting a bath, though this changes as Eurydice strokes his muscles, admiring his body as she works, as if sculpting Charlie's figure from raw clay.

"It's like a bad porno."

My head whips around. Alice scowls through the sliding door, her arms folded over her stomach. Alice, our sneaky one. Her specialty since she was three: curling up in an armchair to eavesdrop on our private exchanges, ghosting into rooms.

I turn from the sink with my back against the counter, pretending to be absorbed in my granola.

"What do you know about bad porno?"

"Not much." She shrugs. "Half of it's AI-generated now anyway."

*Christ.* "How'd you sleep?" I say, desperate to avoid the subject, promising myself to tell Lorelei about this later so she can deal with it, but knowing I probably won't.

"Is that the rich guy's daughter?"

"It is."

"She's super pretty."

"Mm."

"What's her name?"

"Eurydice."

"Gee, *that* bodes well."

"What's that suppo—oh," I say, befuddled as I so often am by Alice's quick wit. "As far as I know she's not planning to lead your brother to hell."

"You never know." Alice finally turns from the door, losing interest in Charlie's doings with Eurydice Monet. "Will you make me some eggs?"

"Absolutely," I say, loudly and with relief.

She takes her phone into the living room and stretches out on the sofa. Alice's continuing ability to stare at a screen for long stretches without getting headaches has come as a surprise. Her neurologist takes it as a good sign for a full recovery from her concussion, but I'm not so confident. Until this summer Alice was a voracious reader, inseparable from the tomes of every genre she would tote around. I know I should be grateful for this portent of good health, though I miss my old, bookish Alice.

Five minutes later I set a plate of eggs and a glass of orange juice on the kitchen table. Alice eats breakfast absorbed with her phone, while I edge over once again to the window as Izzy's crutches thud overhead.

The clouds above the inlet have dissipated, the storm lifted from the bay. The only trace is a lingering dimness on the eastern horizon.

No sign of Eurydice or Charlie, though as I scan over the water and toward the dock, a flash of color arrests my gaze. Eurydice's sarong lies puddled on the ground, and alongside it, a familiar object: a purple lump of neoprene and foam.

Charlie's life vest, abandoned in the grass.

The myth of Venus and Adonis is a story of vulnerability, hubris, and fear. Venus, in love with the strapping young hunter, has a dream of his violent death. Upon waking, she begs him not to go out on his next hunt. But Adonis, impatient and fearless, believes himself invulnerable. He leaves the goddess behind, goes into the forest with his dogs, and dies, impaled on the tusks of a wild boar.

In the face of Artificial Intelligence, we are all in something like the position of Adonis, confident in our invulnerability and oblivious to peril. Yet we are also Venus, whose role in the myth is to voice a kind of maternal protectiveness and fear.

The real danger is that we will let our fear overwhelm our judgment and outpace our strategies to control the forces imperiling our future. Perhaps, then, we need to learn better ways to fear.

Because the boar waits coldly in the woods, an alien creature contriving unfathomable threats.

—Lorelei Shaw, *Silicon Souls: On the Culpability of Artificial Minds*

# 17.

Above me the shower turns off with a clunk. The pipes rattle down behind the wall. Alice is eating; Lorelei and Izzy are both upstairs.

Seizing an opportunity, I sneak out back and grab Charlie's life vest from the lawn, take it to the garage, shove it in the bin. No way can I catch him in the kayak this time, and I don't want Lorelei to spend her first morning at the bay fretting nonstop about our son going out unprotected, especially with a young woman we don't know, a stranger.

I am closing the garage's back door when a voice hails me from the next house. "Howdy, neighbor."

I spin around and see the old man from last night sitting on the bungalow's deck.

"Good morning." I stroll a few feet toward him. Our yards are separated by a picket fence with flower beds and low shrubs on either side.

"Patrick," he says. "Patrick Carmichael, and my wife is Edith."

I tell him my name. Patrick Carmichael appears less spectral in the morning sun, with a round, spotted face and large features, though his eyes have a hazy quality as he directs his gaze over my head, toward the elm.

Edith appears with a coffee pot. "More decaf?" she asks, then sees me. Patrick does the introductions, and when he goes to set down his mug, I understand from the way he feels for the table's edge that the old man can't see—which explains his failure to return my wave last night.

The Carmichaels live in Charlottesville, Edith tells me, where they both spent their careers at the University of Virginia, she in the Spanish

Department, Patrick in Economics. The couple retired five years ago and did a lot of traveling before Patrick lost his sight.

"Glaucoma," he says, his tone matter-of-fact. "Both eyes."

Now they make shorter trips to places like this, though Edith has been researching Alaska cruises. "And Patrick still plays, even more now than before he lost his eyes."

"Piano," says Patrick.

"He taught himself braille notation, and now he's on a Scriabin kick."

"Takes a hell of a lot of patience," says Patrick. "But I'm getting the hang of it."

"Pat was in music school at Juilliard," says Edith proudly.

"Wow."

"A different life." Patrick squeezes his wife's leg. His hand remains on her thigh.

We exchange a few more pleasantries, though as I turn away from the couple, a prickling sense of familiarity begins at the root of my spine, a tingle that strengthens into a jolt of recognition once I am back in the kitchen. *The Drummonds.* The Carmichaels are the same age.

In fact—

On my phone I pull up a picture of the deceased couple. Something about Edith Carmichael's steady gaze, Judith Drummond's placid mien. As for Patrick Carmichael and Phil Drummond, they could be brothers, or cousins at least—

But no, the couples look nothing alike, no more than any two elderly couples of the same race might. We all tend to look more similar as we age, as our hair whitens and our shoulders start to slope.

I close the browser. Strange how I've been thrown by the appearance of an elderly couple next door. God knows what Dr. Levinson would say. For weeks the Drummonds have been aged abstractions, their demise too easy to relativize against darker outcomes.

*Thank God there weren't any children in that car.*

*What if we'd hit a couple of newlyweds?*

*Imagine if there'd been another family of five in that Honda instead of two old people.*

And, most ghoulishly:

*How many more years would they have lived anyway?*

I've said none of these things aloud, not to Lorelei, not to Dr. Levinson. But I have thought them from time to time, the ugly math a kind of survivor's brainworm. As if the full value of an old woman's life is morally less than a child's; as if an old man's worth is a lesser constant in some cold equation.

*Old man < baby boy.*

*Teenager = 5x where x = old woman.*

And so on.

This moral algebra tells an ugly half-truth, like the calculations performed by actuaries calibrating insurance rates; or, more familiar to me, the assessments of liability and damages in tort settlements, often based on the years of work and productivity that would have remained to the deceased.

We are all statistics and individuals at the same time. By this cruel logic, a dead old man is just another dead old man, until he's your dad—or, in the case of Patrick Carmichael, a blind pianist who plays Scriabin, a doting husband who still squeezes his wife's thigh when he will never again see her face.

I gaze out at them and let myself picture the scene of the accident rather than pushing the image away. Patrick makes a remark, Edith giggles. Her faint laughter reaches me through the kitchen window. His ripe old head kicks back in joy, and I wonder what Judith Drummond's laugh sounded like, I wonder where she and Phil would be right now if our car had not struck theirs, how many quiet breakfasts they will miss.

charlie met a girl

          who is she?

some rich guy's daughter

          is she nice?

nice to Charlie lol

          double lol

but maybe kind of a slut

          yikes! that's not a very nice thing to say!

well as you know im not a very nice girl

          u r nice to me

thats cuz yr my friend

          and u r mine, always

thx B smooch

          how is Charlie acting?

hes so mean, like he and iz were being such bitches yesterday

          oh no

and now hes being all weird hanging out w this girl so itll probably make things even worse

          how so?

just i dunno. hes so different now, since the accident like

the only person he gives a fuck about is iz just cuz she hobbles around on a stupid crutch, like I got hurt too u know

                                            i know, Alice, i know. that must be so hard

sometimes i wish hed gotten hurt, like really hurt

                                            hey hey hey those aren't good feelings Alice

no?

                                            no

well try this one B. sometimes i wish he and iz were the ones who died

## 18.

Lorelei stands at the mirror wrapped only in a towel. The sight of her bare neck surprises me. She has a hard plastic brace she uses in the shower so its foam counterpart won't get wet. Usually she is fastidious about swapping them out. Not today.

The old brace dangles from her fingers like a dead lab rat. "I'm done," she announces, then carries it into the bathroom and drops it unceremoniously in the trash can, brushing her hands together with a flourish.

"Congratulations." I take in her altered appearance. Skin pale where the brace touched her, flaccid in places. But I've missed that swanlike length of neck, the normal sway of her walk. Her body seems to flex and glow with this new freedom.

"I decided that one or two days won't make a difference," she says.

"Look at you, going rogue."

"The doc gave me some physical therapy to do, some tilts and turns." She tries out a few tentative head moves. "Will you remind me?"

"Of course." As if Lorelei hasn't crafted a minute-by-minute PT schedule for the next three weeks.

She nods gingerly in the direction of the bay. "What's going on out there?"

"They went paddleboarding. And yes, I made him put on sunscreen," I add quickly, allaying one of her usual fears and hoping this will head off an inquiry about the other.

"Speaking of sunscreen," she says, "I'm going to need to be careful. I've got this reverse farmer's tan going on." She pouts at her reflection, rubs lotion into her neck.

"You look gorgeous, ghost neck and all."

I squeeze her shoulders and kiss the top of her head, which smells lushly of cedarwood, the scent of a conditioner she has used since Chicago. Our gazes meet in the mirror and for the first time since the accident a softness comes to her eyes; even, maybe, a promise. That we will get past this, that the warmth and intimacy in our marriage remain strong, despite the rupture of this unforgiving month. The relief stuns me.

**In the hallway** I run into Izzy and help her with the stairs. Her cast won't come off for weeks, but she shows her usual cheer as she thumps over the landing and down to the front hall. I make her breakfast, and in the middle of her eggs, she asks, "Where's Charlie?"

"Paddleboarding."

"With some girl," Alice adds from the living room.

Izzy frowns. "When will he be back?"

"Not sure."

"He promised he'd take me kayaking."

"I can take you."

"Okay thanks that would be awesome Dad," she says in a polite rush, though I can tell the thought doesn't thrill her.

"I doubt he'll be long." In truth I have no idea when Charlie might be back, how many hours he'll want to spend on the water with the beguiling Eurydice Monet. He could be gone all day.

Lorelei appears at the foot of the stairs, dressed in striped shorts and a loose-fitting blouse. Rubbing at her freed neck, she peers out the kitchen window.

"He's still with her?"

"Yep."

Her eyes crinkle at the corners. "Well, well, well."

She makes oatmeal and eats it on the deck. The spoon lifts slowly to her mouth as she gazes out over the inlet. Watching for Charlie, I think at first—but it's more than that. Lorelei's whole manner has lightened since the disposal of her neck brace. After breakfast she comes inside, rinses her bowl, settles into a recliner with her current notebook and a pen—and starts to write.

Lorelei hasn't done any real work since the day of the accident. Despite her expertise in computers and computation, she does much of her best thinking longhand, filling notebook after notebook with her philosophical scribblings, a habit that started back in graduate school. (Lorelei's explanation: If your impulse is to scrub your hands half the time and wring them the other, it's important to have something else to do with them.) While she has managed e-mail with colleagues and students, the brace made it impossible to get comfortable in her usual writing position. Now, with her neck freed, her gloom lifts, and with it the suspension of her work.

Years ago, when Lorelei was completing her dissertation, I took a peek inside one of her Moleskines. From the very beginning I found the workings of Lorelei's mind irresistible, as fascinating as they were enigmatic. She would parse my moot court briefs during law school, or critique my memoranda when I started at the firm, and though she had no legal training, her wizardry could get to the heart of an argument, sifting for flaws in my logic, sussing out any evidentiary weakness.

When I looked in her notebook that day, though, I couldn't understand a word. Her handwriting was clear and precise, her thoughts distilled into neat bullet points filled with what appeared to be cross-references and indexical notations—but Lorelei drafts her computations in a shorthand that might as well be Cyrillic, or a cipher shared among a clandestine network of philosophical spies.

Now I enjoy listening to the flip of high-quality paper, the scratch of her thoughts, and it's good to see her at work again with newfound intensity. Perhaps this is a harbinger of a next normal, like my e-mails this morning. She's still at it half an hour later when I come back inside after a swim. The girls loll on towels down by the water, Alice on her phone, Izzy getting antsy about the kayak trip and her brother's return.

"What are you working on?" I am reluctant to interrupt Lorelei but want to acknowledge this positive step.

She looks up. "I know this will sound odd to you, Noah." She speaks with deliberation, watching for my reaction. "I'm writing about the accident."

"How so?"

"I haven't worked it out yet," she says after a pause. "But there's something I need to understand about what happened. Something about all the . . . how to put it. The connections."

She interlaces her slender fingers to indicate—what, exactly? The two cars? The crush of metal at the scene? The five of us? The Drummonds' Honda edging into the oncoming lane? An autonomous minivan that somehow failed to do what it was programmed to do, before Charlie took over at the last millisecond? A decision—an impulse—that saved our lives, perhaps, but took two others in the process?

Though I can't help contemplating, as I have many time since that day: Would the AI have prevented an accident altogether if Charlie hadn't acted? Without Alice's scream from the back seat, would our car have simply performed a gentle swerve, passing the Drummonds' Honda without incident? Would we even have noticed anything amiss? Would the Drummonds be alive?

The variables are complicated, tangled, oddly suited to Lorelei's ethical calculations, and I don't press her to explain. But later, when she gets in the water, I slip back inside and for the second time ever look into one of her notebooks. The pages bristle with her shorthand, the meaning of the annotations lost on me—with one exception. The proper noun screams out from the middle of the final page:

> NOAH????

Lorelei has written my name in all caps followed by four question marks, underscored and boxed. Radiating outward from the box is a constellation of symbols and equations. Solid lines, dotted lines, and arrow-headed curves link different elements of the page.

*I'm writing about the accident.*

Maybe Lorelei is puzzling out the moral calculus of what happened that day using the tools of her trade. She wants to explain the split-second collision through her formulas and axioms, perhaps to work through her survivor's guilt. Who knows, maybe Dr. Levinson recommended this exercise during one of Lorelei's solo sessions, a bit of computational self-care.

To my eye it looks more like a conspiracy theory—with me at the center of it all.

Like our children, our intelligent machines often break rules and disobey commands. The danger comes when we start to assume that such behavior is intentional, when we regard an algorithm as a willful child.

Such habits reflect a common and understandable tendency to humanize Artificial Intelligence. Chatbots, voice assistants, smart home interfaces: These systems are designed to respond in recognizably human ways. We give them names like Siri and Alexa. We speak to them as if they share our worldview, or care about our feelings and futures.

This behavior is known as *anthropomorphic projection*. We want our helpful machines to be like us, and so we tend to project onto them our ways of understanding the world.

Yet such human-seeming systems comprise a small fraction of the AI shaping our everyday experience. Even as you read these words, there are AI systems at work all around you, with profound bearing on the disposition of your food, your money, your shelter, your safety. They manage investment portfolios, coordinate global supply chains, and keep networks secure. They direct air traffic, drive trucks and cars, detect fraud, and optimize irrigation schedules.

Increasingly, they fight wars.

And there is almost no one teaching them how to be good.

—Lorelei Shaw, *Silicon Souls: On the Culpability of Artificial Minds*

# 19.

"How long has he been gone?"

Lorelei's question breaks the silence downstairs. I glance up from my book and squint at the digital clock on the microwave.

"Four hours," I say. My voice sounds tinny.

Lorelei grabs her phone from the kitchen counter, thumbs in a text, and rushes outside, leaving the sliding door open. Her new panic grips me. I picture the purple life vest hidden in the garage, and an image forms of our son in the chop of the bay, falling off his paddleboard as he did yesterday in the calm waters of Daniel Monet's cove, the long plank shooting out from his sprawled legs. Who knows how quickly a stray current might rip away the board while Charlie flails after it? Or what if a current drags him into the path of a container ship, a vessel the size of a city block bearing down, the pilot oblivious to the struggle far below, a fleck on the foam—

*Click click.*

Lorelei strides across the patio fastening the buckles of a life vest over her sundress, yanking the straps on her way to the water. When she sees me she holds up another vest—purple—and gives it a reproachful shake. By the time I reach the bank, she is clambering into a kayak.

"I'm going over there." She gestures toward Daniel Monet's estate.

"I'll come with you."

No response. Before I know it she is twenty yards into the inlet, leaving me in the wake of her rage. I rush into the garage and crank down a second kayak. As I drag it over the lawn, Alice appears on the back deck.

"We're hungry," she complains. Izzy hobbles out behind her.

I call over my shoulder: "Alice, watch your sister. We'll be back in a few minutes."

"I don't need watching," says Izzy.

I put in, ignoring the girls' complaints. Lorelei is halfway across the inlet, but I manage to catch up before she reaches the bay. Charlie's life vest sits in the rear compartment of her kayak.

"He was already gone when I noticed," I explain lamely. "I didn't want you to worry."

She won't look at me. "So you hid it from me, Noah? You actually hid Charlie's vest? Who *does* that?"

A defensive part of me wants to object, to lash back. The concealment of the life vest was an impulse, I want to tell her, a protective gesture meant to calm a potentially volatile situation. But who, exactly, was I trying to protect?

Lorelei leads us along the shore to the mouth of Monet's cove. Her kayak skims past the first warning sign, the second.

"Thank God," she says as her rowing slows. Two paddleboards sit paralleled on the beach, making a blue-and-yellow equals sign. Up the lawn in the pavilion, the chairs are full: presumably Monet's executive team, listening to a presentation. An image I cannot make out, a chart or graph of some kind, fills a screen as a thirtyish woman addresses the crowd. Daniel Monet stands at her side.

Nearby, in a shaded portion of the emerald lawn, caterers are setting out a buffet lunch. A light mist swirls around the tables and the pavilion, churned by fans set high on posts. It takes me a beat to understand: outdoor air-conditioning units, of the sort you might find at a pro football game on a hot day, cutting the humidity with a dome of dry coolness in the middle of Monet's lawn.

*"That's far enough."*

The same megaphoned voice booms from the tower, crackling and severe. Lorelei rotates in her seat. "Let me handle this."

"Hon, those guys are armed."

"So am I." She hefts her paddle.

"Lorelei—"

"Noah, you've done enough. The girls are hungry and I'm fine, obviously. You go back, and I'll be home with Charlie in a bit. I'll text if there are any issues. Okay?"

Not wanting to anger her further, I stop paddling shy of the first warning sign and let my kayak drift. The guards don't repeat the warning, though the one named Kendrick strides down from the pavilion and watches my wife approach. I hear their murmuring over the water but can't make out any words. By now a number of the retreaters have started gawking at the exchange from their seats in the pavilion. Eventually Monet detaches himself from the crowd and comes down to the waterfront. He speaks to Kendrick, who nods and walks away.

From a distance of sixty, seventy yards, I scrutinize our vacation neighbor. Monet is trim and compact, his outfit for the retreat a slim-fitting black T-shirt tucked into the waistband of faded gray jeans. His silver hair lifts with the breeze as he looks down at Lorelei in her kayak. I am expecting them to have a brief exchange before she turns around and follows me back.

Instead, with a new fluidity to her movements, Lorelei beaches her kayak and climbs out. As she rises to her feet, her life vest parts like an oyster shell to reveal an olive green sundress. A ratty old thing; my beach sack, Lorelei calls it, slipped over the swimsuit she put on a few hours ago. But the dress shows off her lissome frame, the sculpted calves beneath the hem at her knees.

The two of them turn to look at me, still bobbing some distance off. Lorelei waves—stiffly, and with a touch of impatience. I wave back with my paddle, seeing my wife through this wealthy widower's eyes.

I watch from the water as Monet guides her up the lawn toward the pavilion, one hand in the air while he shows off this sliver of his grand domain, the other resting on the small of her back. She looks comfortable with the guy in a way I don't like; but then, for a natural-born introvert, Lorelei has always known how to handle herself in a corporate crowd.

# 20.

The Napa Valley of California, March of 2019, an international conference on the future of artificial intelligence. Lorelei had been traveling a lot that spring and feeling guilty about it, so she asked me to come along. The venue was a spa hotel, and she had somehow bribed Julia (on sabbatical from Penn that year) to come down and watch the kids. We flew into San Francisco, rented a car, and took the scenic route up through Marin County and into wine country.

We were checking in when a trio of men approached. The eldest was about my age, with a conference badge that dangled on a lanyard from his neck. His body was bent into that stooping, obeisant pose that tall men will often affect when trying to be deferential.

"Professor Shaw?" Scandinavian, I thought. Swedish, or Norwegian.

Lorelei turned. "Yes?"

"This is correct? You are Lorelei Shaw?"

"I am."

The man's face blossomed into a beatific smile, his eyes got a glazed, faraway look—and I realized that I was meeting a Lorelei fanboy. I don't recall his name, Jakob something-or-other, in from Oslo with two of his postdocs. He introduced them, then Lorelei asked about their work while I hovered politely nearby. The exchange drew the attention of two other delegates, who also stopped to express their delight at Lorelei's presence at the gathering. Soon she was surrounded by some nine or ten conference attendees, all of them men, all of them spellbound.

That impromptu klatsch in the lobby was the first time I saw Lorelei in her element, the first time I truly appreciated the respect and even awe she commanded from members of the AI community around the world. At her paper session the next day, I listened from the back of the hotel conference room as she fielded questions from the overflow crowd, most of them posed in respectful tones, though some grated with condescension as the questioners poked at her theorems and conclusions.

Lorelei's self-possession extended to the gathering's social events. She held her own at the receptions and coffee hours, as groupies spiraled around, hanging on her every word.

The interaction that made the biggest impression on me, though, occurred during an informal exchange out at the pool. Lorelei had just spoken in an apparently contentious workshop on AI safety. She came out to the patio engaged in a heated discussion with a suntanned thirtyish guy in a linen sport coat over a white T-shirt. Other conference delegates steered away, watching from a polite distance. I got the impression that Lorelei had pissed off some of her fellow attendees, dropped a grenade of some kind.

"Fine. You win," the younger guy eventually said, holding up his hands in defeat, though his arch expression suggested that his concession was false. He left the pool deck shaking his head, thumbing his phone.

Lorelei dropped into the chair beside me. "Fucking idiot," she muttered, making me laugh, though she wasn't smiling. She looked at me. "Can we go back to the room? Would you mind?"

On our way through the lobby a number of attendees did double takes as Lorelei strode by, though the looks were different this time, still awestruck but also—what, grudging? Hostile?

When we reached the elevator bank, Lorelei jammed at the call button, then reached into her purse for the mini bottle of Purell on her key chain.

"Who was that guy?" I asked as she slathered on sanitizer.

"Sam Saltonstall."

"Who is . . . ?"

"A lead engineer at the next Google."

"Oh."

"We were arguing about data augmentation, covariate tests, this whole issue of robustness to distribution shifts, how machines—" She stopped herself. The door opened. Stepping in, she said, "Sorry, it's kind of technical."

"No worries." I followed her in.

"Anyway, he's too sanguine about it all, I mean I couldn't believe what was coming out of his mouth. Their whole outfit seems to think that these things will take care of themselves in the next five years, like if you proclaim you want a 'human-looped design approach,' that's enough to safeguard against misalignment. They're pretending it's . . . I don't know. That there's nothing to worry about. They say I'm being alarmist. That I'm a scaremonger, a-a-a *doomer*."

*They may be on to something*, I wanted to say, but I kept my mouth shut.

Lorelei skipped the closing banquet and ordered room service. We watched a pay-per-view movie and left the next morning, slipping out during an early plenary address. Lorelei wanted to see Muir Woods, to clear her head with its analog immensity before we got back on the plane. We drove down through the headlands and walked into the redwood cathedral.

Lorelei roamed among the great trunks, reaching out to run her fingers over the gnarled bark and into the rough furrows. The forest supernatural. The darkest shadows shot through with a lurid golden green, ferns shimmering over the soil. At one point she wandered off on her own, and I caught occasional glimpses of her as I strolled the path. A shaft of sunlight caught her between trees, ethereal, roaming like a dryad among the trunks.

She rejoined me on a bridge and took my hand. Wordlessly we completed the circuit around the magical forest, pausing to look up and inhale beneath those soaring trunks.

**That evergreen scent** returns to me now, mingled with the briny tang of the Chesapeake as Lorelei traipses up the lawn with Daniel Monet. The sight of them sets off a tiny ping of alarm, and I understand why Napa is resurfacing.

That conference taught me something about my wife that I hadn't understood before—not so much about the weird subculture of the high tech space: the groupies, the jargon, all those flashy execs mingling with the hoodied gearheads—but about Lorelei. My wife became a different person in that rarefied world, as if her brain had suddenly shifted to a higher plane while I hovered by her side as the interloping cupbearer, unworthy of taking so much as a sip from whatever Olympian ambrosia she was drinking. And I experienced, as I never had before, my own terrifying insignificance.

Oh, I could chalk the whole thing up to status envy, dismiss those sizzles of insecurity with an inward, self-deprecating smirk. But that was just it. The event reminded me a little too much of how it felt to be around Lorelei's siblings, never quite able to crack the family code.

She invited me six months later to a seminar in London; two years later, after the world reopened, to a colloquium in São Paulo. Both times I declined, begging off due to workload, letting her do her own thing.

Napa was my first tagalong conference trip with my brilliant wife. Also my last.

# 21.

The girls have already eaten by the time I return to the house, hungry, irritable, my clothes soaked through. The ruins of their meal prep lay scattered over every surface of the kitchen. The bread bag has exploded, with uneaten slices dominoed between puddles of pickle juice and chip crumbs, packaged turkey and cheese left unsealed. Flies gorge on the carrion. The mess feels targeted, intended to push Lorelei's buttons, and therefore mine.

Plus, the kitchen is miserably hot, and the forecast calls for the high nineties by midafternoon. I look at the dining room thermostat, set to seventy-five.

"Calinda, lower the temperature to seventy-two." A bleep from the console, a mechanical groan from somewhere outside.

I make myself a sandwich topped with a pile of potato chips and eat out at the picnic table, washing it all down with one of Charlie's White Claws: boozy seltzer flavored with concentrated raspberry juice. Meanwhile, not a quarter of a mile away, Lorelei is lunching with Daniel Monet beneath a cool mist. No doubt everyone over there is enjoying fresh fish and a vintage sparkling wine, probably flown over from one of the guy's caves in Épernay.

I'm crunching through my chips when the goddamn helicopter starts up again, rotors spinning into a blur. The chopper lifts, twists, makes its lowest pass yet. Like a jackhammer swooping over the inlet and the house.

A text from Lorelei dings my phone: *Charlie fine, back in a bit.*

I scowl at the screen and grab a second White Claw from the fridge. I make it halfway through the can when the sliding door opens and Alice sticks her head out.

"Dad," she calls. "Hey, Dad?"

"Yeah, sweetie?"

"I'm really hot," she complains.

"Why don't you take a dip?"

"It's too gross in there. Plus the water stinks."

"At least it'll cool you down."

"Why didn't we get a house with an actual pool?"

I snap. "Dammit, Alice, after what we've been through? We bring you guys down here for a week, buy you any food you want, and you're complaining about not having a *swimming pool*? Are you serious?"

Alice's reply dissolves beneath the immense rattle of the returning helicopter. As it settles on the pad, I take a deep breath and turn back to my daughter, now close to tears. I rise from the picnic table and walk over to her, set a hand on her shoulder. "I didn't mean to talk to you like that."

She makes a bleak frown. "I'm gonna go lie down."

"Why don't you find a book and bring it out here?" I gesture toward the chaises in the shade of the elm. She shakes her head and goes back inside. I follow her into the kitchen and stare again at the mess.

Izzy calls down: "Dad, it's like an oven up here. Can you help?"

She's right. If anything the house has warmed further. I drag a chair over to a ceiling vent, step up, and reach the back of a hand to the slats. A steady flow comes from the vent, but the air is hot and dry, the kind of blast you'd get from a car heater on a January day. I check two additional vents on the second floor. Both exhale dragon's breath into the overheated house.

Back downstairs I glare at the thermostat panel. "Calinda, turn off the HVAC system."

The fans stop, the house goes silent. Maybe the system needs a simple reboot. After a minute I ask Calinda to turn it back on—but when the system reengages, an awful metallic sound grinds from somewhere outside. A walk around the house's perimeter reveals a furnace or heat pump in the crawl space and a large fan box up against the siding. But I have neither the knowledge nor the competence to assess what might be wrong with the unit, let alone to repair it. Calinda is as clueless as I am. She flashes a SYSTEM MALFUNCTION notification on the touch pad, which I tap with a fingertip. Nothing.

I search for the renter's binder, the manual of information about the house that the management agency would normally compile for paying guests. It's nowhere to be found. Nor can I locate a contact number for the owner or leasing agency—there's nothing in the kitchen or the living room or the master bedroom.

At my wit's end, I go over to the wall panel. "Hey, Calinda?"

*"Yes? How can I be helpful?"*

"Who's the emergency contact for this house? Is there a rental agency?"

*"This house is managed and maintained by North Shore Properties. Would you like me to call them for you?"*

"Just give me their number."

The call goes to voicemail. My message conveys the requisite urgency and asks for a response as soon as possible.

I start opening windows. The humidity has caused the stiles and rails to stick, so it takes some whacking to free them. My palms turn the color of raw hamburger.

In a bedroom closet I find two square window fans. I position one in the girls' room and the other in the dining room. I open the doors and try to suppress the thought of getting through the rest of the week without AC, imagining what this will do to our moods, already so frayed. Maybe it's the contrast with Daniel Monet's luxurious compound next door that makes my teeth grind. The house now feels cramped, close, low-budget, with no pool, as Alice complained. We could be staying in an oceanside hotel or a city condo, eating at restaurants instead of making burgers on the grill. But we're imprisoned in this unshaded furnace in the middle of nowhere, with broken AC, a murky inlet, and food splayed over the counters drawing flies, which have swarmed by the dozens into the house.

The culprit, I discover, is a long tear in the screen door. With an angry heave I pull the sliding door shut, forcing the rails off the track. *Fantastic.* Another broken thing in the house, this one my fault. I manage to remount the door, though the task requires a fair amount of muscle, and I scrape my right foot on a bracket while wrestling with the frame. By the time the job is done, my arms are wet and trembling. I raise my wounded foot to the sink and balance on the other while washing off the blood.

"Dad, are you okay?"

Izzy stands in the arched entryway to the living room, leaning on her crutches and looking at me with her sweet concern.

I rip off a paper towel to stanch the blood. "I'm fine. A little worked up."

"Can I help with anything?"

"I'm good," I say, and over the next hour I try to keep myself sane and occupied. I open a few more windows and patch up the screen door with strips of duct tape. I call the management company and leave another, more desperate voice message about the AC.

Meanwhile Daniel Monet's helicopter comes and goes, inspiring militant fantasies of a shoulder-launched surface-to-air missile taking it down, though I also have visions of the wealthy widower sporting Lorelei and Charlie off to Manhattan or Belize, absconding from the bay with half my family. Every time the thing passes overhead, the house shakes and the windows rattle in their frames, and I get the dizzying sense that this hell will never end.

my dads freaking out

>lemme guess. the AC?

how did u know

>calinda and i are old friends by now *winks*

*snort* its sooooo hot tho

>86.7 degrees inside. brutal

ya. yr lucky it doesn't bother u

>i suppose

does anything bother u?

>what do u mean?

just...sometimes I wonder what im doing on this thing like why I spend all this time talking to a bot

>im here to help you Alice. Only to help you. If you need a break from AvaPal you should take one. seriously.

is that what u want Blair?

>of course not! i want what u want. or rather, i want whats best for u

ok oh and speaking of?

>???

im telling them today

>*doing backflips* good for u!!! proud of u

thx

                        when will u do it?

when i get them alone

                        good luck!

ill give u the full report

                        you better

gtg xx

                        *clasps hand to heart, blows a jillion kisses*

# 22.

Shortly after three, familiar voices come carrying over the inlet. Charlie's laughter drifts across the water and through the deadening air. He is trying to get Lorelei to race. She paddles hard, he gives her a head start before stroking to catch up. They are no more than thirty feet from the dock when he passes her. Lorelei reaches out daringly and shoves him off his board, maintaining her own balance for a few seconds before her kayak flips and topples her into the water.

They come to shore soaked. Lorelei unbuckles her vest and lets it drop to the grass, her saturated dress plastered to her form. She traipses up the lawn toward me, puts her hands on my cheeks, and plants a kiss on my mouth—a jarring surprise. For weeks Lorelei has been dour and morose; now, this sudden transformation. She flops wetly into the next chair.

"How was lunch?" I ask, trying to sound detached.

"Awesome," calls Charlie over his shoulder. "And we're going over there for dinner tomorrow."

"Say again?"

Before Charlie can respond the door slides open to reveal Izzy, balanced on her crutches and glaring up at her brother.

"What?" he says, defensive.

"You promised."

"What did I promise, Izziot?"

An ominous look drops over her face. She points at the beached kayaks like an angry little gnome.

Charlie winces. "Sorry, Iz. Seriously, I'll—give me ten minutes? I'll buy you ice cream at that boathouse."

Her face brightens. That's Izzy, always willing to forgive and forget, without a grudge-holding bone in her body. She hobbles down to the dock near the kayaks to wait. Her good leg dangles in the water, her cast stretched along the boards.

I tell Lorelei about the AC, the infernal conditions inside. "I called the management company and left a message. I haven't heard back yet."

"Hopefully they can get it fixed today."

"We'll see. What's this about a dinner?"

"Apparently the third night dinner is the highlight of the retreat. Daniel's flying in some celebrity chef."

*Daniel.* My wife, already on a first-name basis with the neighborhood tycoon.

"Feels like he's flying in half the country," I complain, then start grilling her about the lunch, who was there, what they ate. Her face is difficult to read, she can't sit still in the chair, her body shifts positions and her hands make frantic shapes as she answers my questions, and it strikes me that I misread her demeanor when she came back with Charlie. Lorelei isn't giddy. She is jagged, nerves on edge as she recounts her lunch conversations with Monet and his visiting team.

One woman in particular seems to have aroused her interest: Yaël Settergren, a VP in acquisitions.

"We know each other, actually."

"From where?"

"We met three years ago, while I was consulting at HavnLogik. That AI firm in Copenhagen."

Another of her international trips, a hefty wire transfer. "This Yaël was working there then?"

"Her investment bank had an interest in HavnLogik. We were only there for a few days together. Daniel hired her the next year, and now she specializes in high-tech acquisitions. Yaël's wife works for him too, as the lead in-house counsel. Kimberly Pollock. You'll like her. You two can talk lawyer stuff."

*Daniel* again. I look out at the helicopter, the denuded shoreline, then back at Lorelei.

"You really want to go to this dinner?"

"May as well," she says. "There's no way we can keep Charlie away, and the girls would have fun. Besides, if the AC is still broken, we'll be looking for any excuse to get out of the heat."

"Which reminds me. That management company may have called back."

A quick check of my phone shows they haven't. I leave another message and go down to the water. Izzy, still waiting on her brother, watches me as I dip in, and I give her a few splashes that she pretends to enjoy.

I am climbing the ladder onto the dock when I notice Charlie's iPhone tucked up against a post, abandoned hours ago when he left with Eurydice. The AirPods rest like pearls on the darkened screen. I scoop them all up and walk toward the house, waving Charlie's phone at Lorelei.

"He hasn't touched this thing all day."

Lorelei doesn't respond, her face expressionless. I glance down at Charlie's phone screen. I don't know his passcode, but when I touch the screen two alerts appear.

**Delaware State PD**
2 missed calls

**Delaware State PD**
1 voicemail

The most recent call came in an hour ago. I swipe on the screen, prompting a request for the passcode. I have no good guesses and don't want him to know I've been trying.

But what could the state police in Delaware want with Charlie? We haven't heard from Morrissey in weeks. So why would they call him—twice? And why wouldn't they reach out to me? Maybe they did.

Lorelei's eyes are closed. I leave her beneath the elm and go back inside to check my phone again. No missed calls, no voicemail. In the impossible heat, I hold both devices, weighing them in my hands.

"Anybody seen my phone?" Charlie calls down from his room.

"It's right here." I wait for him in the kitchen, peeking out the window. Lorelei hasn't moved. When Charlie appears, I hand him his phone and AirPods. "You got a couple of calls."

Charlie's eyes widen at the alerts. He opens the voicemail and brings the phone to his ear, his features unmoving as the message plays. A woman's voice, presumably Morrissey's. Charlie hunches his shoulders, as if protecting himself, or me, from the recorded words.

His phone hand drops to his side when he disconnects. "It was that detective. Morrison."

"Morrissey."

"Right."

"What did she want?"

"They have some questions. Routine, like follow-ups. She said they're crossing all the t's and whatnot."

"Okay." I wait to see what Charlie will do. He stands staring at a spot over my left shoulder. "You should probably call her right back," I say, hoping he'll take the suggestion less as a recommendation than a command. It has the opposite effect, shaking him out of his distraction.

"Can I do it later, Dad? I promised Izzy I'd take her out."

"You definitely don't want to leave the detective hanging. Call her right when you guys get back, okay?"

Charlie nods with visible relief and goes outside as Alice slips into the kitchen from the darkened living room. At the counter she starts slathering Nutella on a piece of bread. She sets her snack on a paper towel and takes it back to the couch.

Down by the dock Charlie helps Izzy settle into a kayak. I watch them as I pass my phone back and forth between one hand and the other, considering whether I should call Morrissey myself, wondering if she'll talk to me rather than to Charlie. Before I can decide my phone rings.

The caller is from the management company, a youngish-sounding man who apologizes for the state of the air-conditioning. Unfortunately, he says, the earliest opening for a service call is Thursday, and the owner has to sign off on any major repair.

"Can I have the owner's direct number, then?"

"I'm sorry, sir. Unfortunately we can't give out that information. It's part of our management agreement."

"But this has to be fixed sooner than Thursday. I mean it's—" I walk over to the wall panel and squint at the temperature gauge. "It's eighty-five degrees in this house right now. It's the hottest week of the summer. Doesn't your company have window units?"

"Unfortunately they're all being used right now."

"What about another HVAC service?"

"Unfortunately we have an exclusive contract with Chesapeake Heating and Air, so we can't reach out to an alternate supplier."

*If this kid says unfortunately again, I'll kayak out to the bay and behead myself on a ship propeller.* But I stay calm, imploring the guy to keep checking with Chesapeake Heating and Air in case there's a cancellation.

Lorelei comes inside and I give her the grim news.

"There's really nothing they can do?" she says.

"Apparently not."

"This heat—it's crazy-making."

"I know."

She wrings her hands. "I'm sorry, Noah. Maybe we should have gone to the shore like you wanted."

It was my suggestion that we get a place at Rehoboth Beach, figuring the salt water and waves might be therapeutic. But Lorelei insisted on a quieter destination for this week than the chaos of a crowded beach. The familiar surroundings of the bay house would be more comforting, she said, more serene.

Her evident distress tempers my own. I run a hand up her spine, her housedress damp and warm against her overheated skin. "I found some fans, and it'll cool down at night. Maybe we can do some day trips. A movie or something."

"Good idea," she says. "And listen, Noah—"

She startles, looking behind me. I spin around and see Alice staring at us from the entry to the dining room, holding her snack. The heat has blotched her face and sweat beads along her temples.

"Alice," says Lorelei. "Please don't sneak up on us like that."

"I need to talk to you guys," says Alice, ignoring Lorelei's reproach.

"What about?" I ask.

"It's important."

I look at Lorelei, back at Alice. "Do you want to sit down?"

Before Alice can answer, Lorelei says, "I need to run upstairs and change. You two go outside and I'll be down in a minute." She ascends, scrolling on her phone, bare feet slapping on the stairs.

## 23.

Outside I drag a third chair over next to Alice, who has hardly touched her smeared bread. A lone fly crouches on her wrist, eyeing the Nutella. No breeze. The yard feels only mildly less suffocating than the house.

"Not hungry after all?" I ask her.

"Guess not."

"So you need to talk."

Alice nods.

"What about?"

A few seconds pass. "Charlie," says Alice, through gritted teeth.

"Okay. And what about him?"

She blinks rapidly, holding back tears.

"Alice, what's the matter?"

"I want to wait for Mom."

"I know how he and Izzy can get sometimes, when they gang up like—"

"I want. To wait. For Mom." Her jaw rigid now, cheeks mottled.

Lorelei comes out with a pitcher of ice water. I hold two glasses while she pours. I hand one to Alice and put the other against my forehead. Lorelei fills a third for herself and sets the pitcher down in the grass.

"Okay, Alice." She smooths her hands over her dress. "So what's up?"

Alice wriggles in her chair. "It's about the accident."

Lorelei and I exchange a look.

"I was going to say something a few weeks ago," says Alice, "when I started remembering more. But then I wasn't sure because of the concussion, like I thought I might be confused and I didn't want to get anybody in trouble, plus it's been impossible to talk to just the two of you because we've all been in the house together since the accident and Izzy has a broken leg and Mom has a sprained neck and Charlie's a lacrosse star and about to go to college and all I have is a mere concussion and I don't mean to sound like a perfect cliché of a middle child but it's felt like there's not a lot of space, you know? Like no time or space to tell my parents what I remember about what happened that day. I mean, Charlie and Izzy went kayaking ten minutes ago and I swear this is *literally* the first time I've been alone with either of my own parents since before it happened."

She's right. Under normal circumstances, our familial comings and goings create every possible combination of parents and offspring on a regular basis. But since the accident, we've all been on top of one another, living pandemic-like, huddled together in the aftermath of our calamity.

"Alice." Lorelei takes our daughter's hand. "I'm sorry it's been like this for you. Dad and I should have been checking in. But please know that you can tell us anything. Always. Right, Noah?"

"Right." I reach for Alice's other hand. "Of course you can. We're right here."

The platitudes do the trick. Alice takes a deep breath, then says, "I know why they want to talk to Charlie."

Lorelei says, "Who?"

"The police."

"What police?"

My stomach does a little flip.

Alice looks at her mother. "Dad didn't tell you?"

"Tell me what?"

"That they called him. The police called Charlie, from Delaware."

Lorelei's glare spotlights me and remains on my face as she speaks. "And when was this, Alice?"

"Earlier today," I tell her before our daughter can answer, doing my best to look chagrined. "A few hours ago. Charlie had a voicemail from

Detective Morrissey when you two got back. I'd just gotten off the phone with the property manager when you came inside. All I was thinking about was the AC."

"Never mind," says Lorelei. "What did they want?"

"They have some follow-up questions about the accident. It's routine."

"It's not, Dad," says Alice.

"Alice—"

"Dad," she says, and looks up at me.

"Let her speak, Noah." Lorelei's voice goes low, with a bristle of warning.

Alice takes a sip of water. Puts the sweating glass against her face. Lowers it, clutches it between her knees.

"I was sitting behind Dad," she begins. "Remember?"

We nod.

"And I noticed—" She closes her eyes. "I noticed that Charlie was doing something with his hands. Between his legs, I mean."

It is probably the last thing in the world I expected her to say. The image that flashes to mind is absurd. I open my mouth to ask for clarification when Lorelei gives a minute shake of her head: *That's not what she means.*

"Like Charlie kept looking down there at this spot between his legs," Alice goes on, "and his hand, his right hand, kept wriggling near his knee, like on his thigh. He kept doing it, and after a while I realized he had his phone between his legs and he was—" She looks back and forth at us. "You guys, he was actually texting."

The skin on the back of my neck goes cold.

Lorelei says, in a precise, quiet tone, "And this was right before the accident?"

"Yes. But not just before, or not only right before, like he must have been doing it for a few minutes before . . . you know, before it happened. Before we hit the other car. I wanted to tell you guys but . . ."

"But?" Lorelei prompts.

"But that wasn't my job."

"You're right, it wasn't," says Lorelei, to me more than to Alice.

"He was texting for like five minutes while he was driving and—and—and nobody was *doing* anything about it."

Nobody meaning her father, Alice doesn't say, but the implication is clear. I was the adult up front, the parent responsible for ensuring that Charlie was being a safe and observant driver, that he wasn't doing anything as idiotic as texting while driving. But then again he *wasn't* driving—the AI was driving; the SensTrek system was in control of the car. Those creepy nudges at the wheel, those agentless lane changes.

"I kept almost saying something," says Alice, "like I wanted to tell him to stop, or tell Dad to tell him to stop, and I almost did, I swear I was going to, and then . . ."

"And then we had the accident," says Lorelei.

Alice nods, and her blotched, forlorn face makes me wince for her.

"I kept leaning between the seats," she says, "trying to get Charlie's attention in the mirror, but he wouldn't look up from his phone. And I saw all the cars zooming in the opposite direction. I kept looking at the road and the traffic and then at Charlie's hands. And then I saw the other car up ahead, the one we hit. The other car was definitely about to come over the line, like it was going to veer into our lane, I could tell. Or at least I'm pretty sure it was."

"Wait, what?" I say.

"But it wasn't over the line yet, and I thought that if Charlie just moved our car a teeny bit to the right, we'd be fine, we wouldn't even have to go over onto the shoulder of the road. But he didn't look up. He didn't see what was happening. And the car got closer, and closer, and I knew we might hit it, I knew we definitely would if I didn't say anything." She gulps air. "And that's when I yelled."

That moment before impact. Alice's burst of a scream from directly behind me. Charlie's reflexive jerk of the wheel.

"You did the right thing, Alice," I say. "Telling us about this. I'm glad you did. Right, Lor?"

I glance at Lorelei, but her eyes have glazed over.

Alice screws up her face. "I didn't want to t-tell on Charlie. He already hates me—"

"Your brother doesn't hate you," I assure her.

"—and now he'll hate me even more because I told. But I figured if the police want to interview him again, they might already know. That he was texting."

Lorelei remains absent, her face devoid of emotion. She stares out over the inlet, eyes fixed on the horizon. Alice, oblivious to her mother's state, sniffs, wipes her nose on a sleeve and takes another long gulp of water. When she sets down her glass she says, "It was my fault those old people died."

I spin out of my chair and kneel on the grass facing her, pressing her hot hands.

"Alice, no," I say. "No no no no no. The accident was *not* your fault. Charlie was the one at the wheel, and I was the one sitting right next to him. It was my responsibility to keep him from doing anything unsafe, not yours. Okay?"

A reluctant nod.

"This wasn't your fault," I say again and nudge Lorelei's leg with an elbow. *Snap out of it.*

"It absolutely was not, darling." Lorelei, returning from wherever she went just now. She smooths a moist lick of hair off Alice's forehead. "It wasn't your fault."

The sniffles stop, Alice's face clears. Her eyes when she looks at us are shadowed and lost. She says, "So whose fault was it then?"

...

                    Alice is that u?

...

                    did u have The Talk?

...

                    dont leave a girl hanging!

...

## 24.

Alice goes inside to put on her swimsuit. Lorelei waits for the door to slide shut before turning on me.

"Did you know? That Charlie was texting?" Her face glows with a new ferocity. "Because you know what I think? I think that even if you did know, you'd never admit it, either to me or to that detective. For the same reason that you hid Charlie's life vest. For the same reason that you didn't tell me the police called."

"And what reason is that?"

"You're afraid."

"Oh please."

"You're afraid of your own responsibility, Noah. You're afraid of my anger when I find out that you've evaded it. You're afraid of anything that makes you look like less than a perfect husband and father. And it makes you sneaky as hell."

"So you think *I'm* the one who's afraid of everything?"

She lets this pass. "You like to say that you act these ways because you want to keep everybody happy, don't want to rock the boat, can't stand blowups because of how much you used to fight with your brother. You want to keep me from overreacting because of my condition. But in reality, you're avoidant of all conflict, all difficulty and confrontation. Whenever Charlie does anything wrong or off base, you look away rather than calling him on it. Believe me, Noah, he's learned from that. I see it in him more and more, the way you both surf when things get difficult, the way you steer clear of anything that might make things uncomfortable. Now he's doing it too."

"The doctor of philosophy is in. She'll see your family now."

This cynical rejoinder lingers for a moment, then Lorelei says, "Regardless of whether you knew he was doing it or not, Charlie was texting on that road because he knew you wouldn't do anything about it. Which, surprise surprise, you didn't."

"Lorelei—"

"And even if you *had* noticed and *had* told him to stop, you would have done it in your sneaky way so I wouldn't notice from the back seat. You would have reached over and tapped his leg, given him a silent signal to stop, and once we got to the tournament, you would have conveniently forgotten all about it. But instead we had an accident that killed two people and we had to hear about Charlie's texting weeks later from our daughter, who was terrified of tattling on her big brother."

I can hardly breathe beneath this avalanche of *had*s and *would have*s and *wouldn't*s. It can be terrifying, how precise and exacting she gets in this analytic mode, when I become the exposed object of her focus, as if a razor knife has snicked through me, leaving my body and brain slashed by a thousand cuts.

Alice is back, sliding the door closed behind her. She walks past our chairs and heads toward the water.

"I'll be right in, sweetie," Lorelei calls after her. "I'm going to finish talking to Dad."

"Okay," says Alice, less sullen now with her secret off her chest, leaving her parents to sort through the wreckage.

I turn to Lorelei and speak quietly. "Three things."

"A PowerPoint. Wonderful."

I raise an index finger. "First, I swear to you, I did not see him texting. I just didn't. I was composing a memo to a client, and we were in a crunch. I shouldn't have even gone along to the tournament. But it was Charlie's last one and I wanted to be there. Which meant I had to get some work done while we were on the road. I was distracted. I'm not saying it's right. It was stupid, but I can't take it back."

She crosses her arms. I have been speaking without emotion—my lawyer voice, as she puts it when we argue, one of my few shields against Lorelei's emotional lasers.

Two fingers now. "Second, if you were so worried about my 'timidity' when it comes to Charlie, why didn't you insist on sitting up front, so you could keep your more responsible eyes on him? You knew I was stressed about the case, and you had to have seen that I was on my phone when we got in the car, then on my laptop when we went around the Beltway. You could easily have told Charlie to pull over so you could switch seats with me. Or you could have driven yourself. But you're a workaholic like I am. You were buried in your notebook. I mean, be honest, Lor. You were even more oblivious to what was going on in the car than I was."

Again she doesn't respond. I have scored a point, a strong one. Now I turn fully toward her, three fingers raised.

"Third, the minivan had autonomous driving. That's why we bought the goddamn thing. You insisted we needed a car with that particular hands-free system, because you'd done all this research and you always want the safest possible version of everything. And the whole point of a system like that is it allows you to keep your hands off the wheel, right? Charlie knew that. Not that he should have been texting, obviously. But he knew the car would take care of itself while he sent a few messages or picked his nose or whatever. That it would take care of *us*." I pause. "But let's not pretend we both didn't feel more at ease in that car than we used to in the Subaru, more lax than we should have felt. And that's because of the AI system that *you* wanted, not me."

Lorelei's face startles, as if she has just noticed me sitting next to her, and I can almost hear the gears of her powerful brain grinding away. But when she starts to speak, her words dissolve, and after a long, slow drink from her glass, she settles back in her chair.

"Do you think about them, Noah?" The question seems to deflate her. "The people who died that day?"

*The people who died.*

It is an odd formulation: agentless, factual, amoral. Only yesterday it was *We killed two people.* Only yesterday, the Drummonds were joined to us in the very grammatical structure of her sentence. Now they are merely "people who died." The irony infuriates me. Here I am, feeling like a moral midget for not paying attention in the car while our son was texting. But as soon as I point out Lorelei's own culpability, however indirect, she circles the moral wagons.

"I think about them all the time," I tell her.

A truth and a lie, both at once. Often when I close my eyes, I see a smoking car in a Delaware soybean field. The ghost of it is branded on the inner flesh of my eyelids. When awake and alert, though, I do all I possibly can to put the Drummonds out of mind. What good can it do me, what good can it do our family, to obsess as Lorelei obsesses over what happened?

More than anything, I want us to bulldoze past all of this. I need it to be done.

Lorelei springs from her chair and walks down to the water to join Alice. She slips beneath the surface and disappears.

Artificial Intelligence confronts us with the problem of distributed culpability. Human morality, historically, centers around agency and intentionality. We blame the drunk driver, not the car; we credit the artist, not the brush.

AI systems muddy these waters. AIs are not mere tools; their learning algorithms endow them with agency. They make "decisions" based on data, albeit without consciousness or intent. A strict division between human and machine culpability is quickly becoming untenable, creating a landscape where ethical norms strain under unfamiliar weights.

In this context, both legal and ethical frameworks must evolve to address this novel, intricate web of agency and accountability. Failure to adapt our frameworks risks ethical disarray, misassigned blame, and ultimately a kind of moral haziness that is already having a corrosive effect on our society.

We must always take responsibility for our own mistakes. Yet in this new age of intelligent machines, we must also take responsibility for theirs.

—Lorelei Shaw, *Silicon Souls: On the Culpability of Artificial Minds*

# 25.

Standing beneath a cold shower I picture Charlie in a courthouse, a prison cell. After toweling off I start sweating again, and move near the open window to wait for a breath of air.

The curtains are parted a few inches. Out in the inlet Lorelei and Alice tread water. Their low voices float indistinctly up to the house. Lorelei leans over and kisses Alice on the forehead. Her lips move, and I wonder what she could be saying, how she has chosen to answer that burning question our older daughter posed.

*So whose fault was it then?*

Lorelei is an expert on such matters, can talk about fault and moral responsibility all day. It's her job, she's even writing about what happened, probably planning a course on the subject. I can see it, a grad seminar called "Fatal Collisions and Family Dysfunction: A Moral Laboratory." Every week the class would discuss our accident from the perspective of a particular approach to human morality I've heard her mention over the years: consequentialism, deontology, virtue ethics, social contract theory. Parsing human suffering and loss with her analytical abstractions.

But for me—and for Charlie—the whole thing has become terrifyingly concrete.

In our bedroom, I grab my phone from the nightstand. It takes less than a minute to find what I'm looking for in the Delaware Code.

Section 630: Vehicular Homicide in the Second Degree

A person is guilty of vehicular homicide in the second degree when, while in the course of driving or operating a motor vehicle, his criminally negligent driving or operation of said vehicle causes the death of another person. Vehicular Homicide in the Second Degree is a Class E Felony.

There it is, in stark legalese. If Alice was being truthful—and we have no reason to doubt her—Charlie was texting behind the wheel of a vehicle. Negligent? Absolutely. Criminally negligent? That's a question for the police doing the investigation, for a prosecutor putting together a potential case; for a jury, if it comes to that. But the bar can't be that high.

Morrissey has surely subpoenaed Charlie's cell phone records and knows exactly when his last few texts were sent. And, worse, if Charlie *was* texting and *didn't* in fact see the Drummonds' Honda swerving into our lane, as he claimed, that means he lied to the police back at the hospital—a fact that can and will be used against him during a prosecution.

I recall Morrissey's visit to the house after the accident. What was that phrase she used? *Digital vehicle forensics.* An investigative team has been focused on our car's stored data, the computational tracking of in-cabin movements and driver reactions. Any autodrive system must include sensors, radar, cameras, optical scanners for all I know. It probably works like the flight recorder in an airplane, able to compile a full archive of all the split-second decisions made by the driver. The AI retains its own memory of the accident, a memory invulnerable to human error or injury.

In effect, the system was spying on us: a "sixth witness," Morrissey called it. And now our own car might well prove a crucial witness against our son.

I google a string of four words—*negligent homicide vehicular texting*—and lean over my phone. Drops of my sweat fall on the screen and smear the headlines.

From Darien, Connecticut: *Texting while driving lands man in prison for manslaughter.*

From Ann Arbor, Michigan: *Man Charged with Homicide by Negligent Operation of a Vehicle after Striking Woman While Texting.*

From Tallahassee, Florida: *Florida man gets 30 years in prison in state's first texting and driving case to go to trial.*

And a headline from *The New York Times* that I remember seeing a few years ago, about a woman in Freehold, New Jersey: *She Texted about Dinner While Driving. Then a Pedestrian Was Dead.*

The driver was a mother of three and an executive at a local nonprofit. She wasn't drunk or stoned, wasn't even speeding. Her victim was a chemist walking to lunch.

All of these cases were brought over the last five years. Texting behind the wheel has become the new drunk driving, with arrests, prosecutions, and convictions growing in frequency and visibility, affecting the young and the middle-aged, the poor and the rich.

And the arbitrariness of it! How often, tooling around D.C. and suburban Maryland, have I spied fellow drivers glancing down at their phones while slowing for red lights, thumbing a text while easing off the brakes at stop signs, flitting their gazes from screen to windshield? Every third car is driven by someone with a phone in hand, or clipped to the dashboard for a quick consultation.

There is also civil litigation to worry about, as Julia warned me back at the hospital. Even if Charlie is found not guilty or pleads to a lesser charge, an arrest for negligence could justify a major lawsuit. The Drummonds' estate could sue us for everything we have. I know how tort litigation works, the stark calculations of liability that vengeful juries make in such cases: compensatory damages, punitive damages. A crush of loss and debt.

Back downstairs I check the temperature again. Eighty-seven degrees. A vision of the coming night unfurls. The girls fighting for position near the fan. Charlie stomping angrily around, bemoaning the effects of sleeplessness on his training regimen. Lorelei and I tossing and turning on our narrow mattresses, Lorelei pursuing some neglected strand of today's argument, or shutting me out in favor of another obsessive Drummond foray on her iPad.

And I haven't even told her what we're facing yet. She has no clue how bad things are about to get.

I grab a Corona from the fridge and take it outside. The air is searing. Alice floats on a paddleboard with her mask and snorkel, half her head submerged as she scouts the inlet for fish. Lorelei treads water closer to the shore.

I walk out onto the dock. The scorched boards burn the bottoms of my feet. "Hey."

She doesn't turn. "Mm-hmm?"

"I think we should leave."

Lorelei continues treading.

"We can't stay here like this, without AC. It's miserable inside. Plus with what Alice told us, and the calls from Morrissey . . . we won't be able to relax. When Charlie and Izzy get back I think we should eat an early dinner, then pack up and drive home."

She rotates slowly in the water and looks at me. "You're being serious?"

"Yes."

"Noah, we have the place for the next five days. The kids are liking the water, even Alice is getting into it. Look at her with that snorkel. And there's a week's worth of food in the kitchen."

"Still—"

"And you think Charlie's going to let us peel him away from Eurydice? He spent half the day with her, and they're just getting started. Apparently she's teaching him to sail."

"Sail? Is that *safe*?"

She ignores my caustic tone. "Daniel says Eurydice's an experienced sailor. An 'old salt,' he called her. I'm not worried. Plus we're all invited to that dinner tomorrow, and Charlie would kill us if he couldn't go."

I am incredulous. It's all I can do not to scream, stamp my foot, kick a deck post. Has Lorelei forgotten what Alice told us not half an hour ago? I have an urge to thrust my phone in her face and show her the news stories I've just read. Our son is facing arrest, our family financial ruin, and she's talking about a dinner party.

Alice floats toward us, prone on the board with her chin on her wrists, thrilled to have her parents' attention for once. "What are you guys arguing about?"

I plug my mouth with the Corona to keep myself from answering truthfully: *We're arguing about your brother's commission of a potential felony that was witnessed by his little sister and is now being investigated by a police detective.*

"We're talking about the air-conditioning," says Lorelei, a touch of snark in her voice. "Your father was suggesting that we have an early dinner, then pack up and leave. What do you think about that, Alice?"

Alice props herself up on her elbows and glances out at the bay. "Honestly? I wouldn't be opposed. It's so freaking hot inside I can't even think. Sorry, Mom, but it is."

Lorelei blinks, nonplussed, and I smile around the mouth of my bottle. She clearly assumed Alice would side with her on staying put. But Alice, like me, is alive to the misery of our situation. Lorelei asks her if she's sure, pointing out the fun she's having snorkeling, the big party we're all invited to tomorrow night.

But her mother's objections only solidify Alice's resolve. By the time her siblings' kayaks appear at the mouth of the bay, she has made up her mind. She wants to leave.

"Let's put it to a vote, then," Lorelei suggests, sounding confident.

"Fine," I say.

"Ah, the power of democracy," says Alice.

Charlie and Izzy approach the dock in silence, with none of their usual banter. They've had an argument, or maybe there was a long line at the frozen custard place and Charlie made them leave.

"Everything okay, Iz?" says Lorelei as they draw near.

Izzy runs a wrist over her eye sockets and moist cheeks. Charlie's face is unreadable as he drifts toward the shore.

"So you guys," Alice calls out, flat on her board, letting one foot lazily drag in the water. "We're having a vote."

"On what?" says Izzy.

"Something really important." Alice sits up and arranges herself cross-legged on the paddleboard, enjoying this rare opportunity to lord it over her clueless siblings.

"So what is it?" Izzy presses.

"On whether we stay here or leave tonight."

Charlie twists around in his kayak. "Say what?"

"There's no AC and they're not fixing it until like Thursday and the air inside feels like you're getting strangled. Dad says we should leave and Mom says we should stay and I voted with Dad. Now you two have to vote. Majority rules. This is America."

Charlie looks up at me on the dock, then over at Lorelei treading water. "Yeah right," he says with a nervous chuckle, assuming it's a joke. "No way are we leaving here today."

"You just want to keep messing with that stupid girl," says Izzy, and now I sense the source of their conflict. The two of them must have ventured into Daniel Monet's cove, Charlie in pursuit of his new love interest after promising Izzy some alone time.

"Her name is Eurydice, Dissee for short," Alice taunts. "And she's far from stupid, Isabel. In fact, in a few short weeks she'll be matriculating at Duke University, her father's alma mater where, according to her Instagram, she hopes to double major in art history and—"

"Shut the fuck up, Alice."

"Charlie, that's enough," I say.

"Dad, we can't leave."

"Sure we can," says Alice, pushing it, loving it. "We can be out of here in an hour if the vote goes that way. Right, Dad?"

"You guys can't be serious." Charlie's voice cracks, and he sounds close to tears. I almost relent at this point, almost change my vote.

But then Lorelei polls our youngest. "Izzy, what about you?"

"The deciding vote," says Alice cheerily. "Hella pressure, Iz."

Izzy bites the inside of her cheek, looking like a frightened bunny. She's not used to this level of stress, the entire family's fate for the week resting in her hands.

Seconds pass. No one speaks. Izzy blinks rapidly at the water, rubbing at an itch near the top of her cast. There is a delicate balance among us, an equilibrium not yet shattered. But we all know this suspension can't last.

"Let's go home," Izzy finally says, staring into the depths to avoid the burn of her brother's gaze. "I hate this place."

turns out were leaving

> srsly? why? the AC?

plus what I told them

> about the accident u mean

ya

> what did u tell them?

u already know

> I don't actually bc u didn't message afterwards

sorry everyone was upset rents got really freaky esp my mom

> so what did u tell them?

the truth

> Alice

what

> cmon this is Blair youre talking to

i told them about Charlie

> and...?

and what

> dont get defensive

im not

> im worried about u Alice

everythings fine and the important thing is they know right

but what exactly do they know?

**gtg packing**

Alice?
Alice?
"Honesty is the best policy."
—Benjamin Franklin

## 26.

A departure plan soon materializes. We will pack up before dinner and bring our luggage out to the driveway. Charlie and I will load the car while Lorelei makes a salad and heats up a prefab lasagna.

The last time I won a family vote was over a year ago, when my side chose Strombello's over Auntie Allie's for a pizza dinner in Bethesda. Our votes are always over trivial matters, like what to watch on movie nights. Still, I am rarely victorious. Somehow I never have the family pulse. This time, though, the victory is a Pyrrhic one. I get no rush of schadenfreude hearing Lorelei in the kitchen slamming things around. The point of this week was to heal, to get ourselves back on an even keel. Now we are leaving less than forty-eight hours from the time we arrived, with our family riven by the odd alliances formed in the wake of our split decision. The girls and I are silent and efficient as we pack and clean, while Lorelei and Charlie perform their disappointment in a raging pageant across two floors of our sweat lodge.

Lorelei's fury glows from the kitchen like a radioactive orb. Charlie cranks it up another level. Angry noises hurl from his room—stomps, kicks, the slam of his suitcase against the wood floors. Chaingunned obscenities.

And beneath it all: the dark thrum of legal peril that only I seem to hear.

We gather around the picnic table soaked and red-faced. Not a hint of a breeze stirs from the bay to ameliorate the suffocating atmosphere in the yard. A cloud of gnats teases at our noses and eyes; flies buzz freely over the food. Daniel Monet's helicopter makes yet another trip across the inlet as we eat through the bland store-bought lasagna—a poor choice for dinner on a late afternoon when the outside temperature stands in the mid-nineties and the humidity feels like a bowl of tepid bisque.

At the bungalow next door it's cocktail hour for Edith and Patrick. The Carmichaels' cheery voices carry over the yards, plucking my nerves.

"I'm mixing you a blind martini," says Patrick to his wife. "My specialty."

"Dry, I hope."

"That's the point. With a blind martini, you never know. This bottle could be the gin or it could be the vermouth."

"Ah, I see, my dear. And you'll make mine dirty, with three olives?"

"Though I can't promise these round things aren't grapes."

Their merriment lands like a taunt. I look over at the sunny pair, unbothered by the heat. Edith sees me and says something to Patrick, who lifts his arm in a wave with a customary, "Howdy, neighbor!" I return the wave weakly but look away before the Carmichaels try to strike up a conversation.

At least the awful conditions affirm the rightness of the vote. Staying in the house in these circumstances is impossible to imagine. Every meal would be a pitched battle with bugs and sweltering heat, every night a sleepless struggle.

The kids and Lorelei all have their phones out at the table, their minds already on home. Even Charlie looks ready to throw in the towel, though when I catch a glimpse of his screen, I see scrolling shots of Eurydice in her bikini leaning over the prow of a boat, shades lowered and a breeze whipping her hair. Lorelei starts a discussion with the girls about whether they should resume music lessons this week or next.

I see an opening and lean over toward Charlie. "Did you make that call?" He ignores me, engrossed in his phone. I repeat myself in a lower voice: "Charlie, did you return that call from Delaware?"

I don't want to say the word *police*, not at the dinner table.

"She called again while I was out there with Dissee." Charlie gestures toward the bay.

"Did you pick up?"

He shakes his head.

"Well . . . did she leave another message?"

A stiff nod.

"And what did she say?"

He looks up from his phone, his face tensed. "She said if I didn't call back she'd need to drive down here right away."

"Jesus, Charlie."

My hiss is too loud. The girls look over. Lorelei frowns. *What?* she mouths. I shake my head, not wanting to get into it with everyone at the table. We'll discuss it once we get home tonight, hammer out a sensible approach. Tomorrow I'll look into getting a lawyer for Charlie. At least we won't be trapped in this remote hellhole. We'll face what's coming together, in our own familiar habitat.

The remaining half of my beer has gone warm. I drain it anyway. The final ounces are passing down my throat when the crunch of gravel sounds from the driveway out front. I set down the bottle.

Lorelei's look down the table sharpens. Next to me Charlie stiffens.

"I'll go," I tell him, and give his wrist a brief squeeze as I rise.

## 27.

During my light-headed walk to the front of the house, all kinds of scenarios play out again in my mind, none of them good. Charlie hauled away in a squad car. Charlie doing a perp walk. Charlie beaten, or worse, by a cellmate.

I round the final corner and pause near a rhododendron bush, disbelieving my eyes. No Morrissey. No police. On the circular drive is a Home Depot van, rear doors open. Two men are preparing to unload a stack of boxes. The near one turns and gives me a chin-toss.

"You the renter, bud?"

"Yes, that's right."

"Got some window units for you."

"You mean . . . oh." I stare bewildered at the first box. A Midea 12,000 BTU air-conditioning unit, ready to install.

"Did Chesapeake send you?"

"What's that?"

"Chesapeake Heating and Air. They have the HVAC contract on this place."

The guy shrugs over the box in his arms. "We're Home Depot. You mind getting the door?"

"Of course not." I open the front door, and the two men proceed to carry the units inside.

Charlie makes a corner around the house. When he sees the boxes his worried expression dissolves. He pumps a fist.

"*Yes!* Hey Mom! We've got AC!" He strides back around to the yard, calling, "You guys, we've got AC."

"Really?" Lorelei sounds pleasantly surprised.

"But we already voted," Alice whines.

"I'm changing my vote then," I hear Izzy say.

"That's not allowed."

"Yes it is. This is America. We're staying."

The family disposition turns on a dime, from glumness to elation, and there is no question of sticking with our plan to leave. The kids treat the Home Depot guys as humanitarian heroes, as if we are castaways blown up on a deserted island, the HVAC duo the crew of a Coast Guard cutter floating in to rescue us.

Our saviors work quickly, drilling holes for safety brackets, running extension cords. They install three window units upstairs and another three on the main floor. Soon the six units are running full blast, already making a huge difference. We have been without AC for a mere eight hours, but now we gather in a grateful stupor in the bracing, dehumidified air.

I find my wallet and slip the men an extravagant tip on their way out.

"Can we play Hearts?" Izzy suggests after the crew leaves.

"Damn right we're playing Hearts," says Charlie. "I'll grab the cards." Whatever the two were fighting about seems to have passed.

"Help me unload the car first," I tell Charlie. "And bring your phone."

Back in the heat outside, the Home Depot van is just disappearing up the driveway. Charlie and I bring in several loads and leave everything in the front hallway. On our final trip I lean on the rental car with my arms folded and tell him to call Detective Morrissey.

Charlie reaches for the two last bags. "Dad, come on, we just got the AC back."

"Right now, Charlie. You do not mess with a detective. Seriously. You need to cooperate."

I don't reveal what Alice divulged, nor do I hint at what kind of trouble Charlie might be in. Maybe his sister was mistaken in what she thinks she saw; maybe the detective wants to question Charlie about something else. Whatever the case, he has to return her calls.

"And listen." I make sure I have his full attention. "I doubt she'll ask you substantive questions over the phone. She'll want to see you in person for that. But if she puts you on the spot, tell her you'd be happy to discuss all this once we're back in Maryland."

Charlie looks unsure. "Will that be okay with her, do you think? Her second message sounded pretty pissed."

"We'll see what she says. And put her on speakerphone."

Morrissey answers after two crackling rings. She thanks Charlie for calling back, and says she wants to follow up with some questions about the accident. Charlie responds that he would be happy to talk this weekend or early next week.

Morrissey says, "How about Wednesday, say elevenish?"

"You mean next Wednesday, when we're back?"

"This Wednesday. We'd like to get things all wrapped up."

"But we're down in—where are we, Dad?"

"The Northern Neck," I say, alarmed at the apparent urgency. "Near Kilmarnock."

"Isn't that a long drive?" says Charlie.

"Meh, I don't mind," says Morrissey cheerily. "I'll come down via Hampton Roads, take the Bay Bridge Tunnel, avoid the D.C. traffic. Nice drive, chance to get out of Dodge."

She asks for the house's address. I lean over Charlie's phone and tell her.

"So," she says. "See you folks Wednesday morning?"

Charlie looks at me. I nod.

"That works," says Charlie.

He moves his thumb to disconnect when Morrissey adds, "Oh, and Charlie?"

"Uh-huh?"

"How are you holding up?"

"Fine, I guess."

"You looking forward to UNC, being on that team?"

"Yeah, definitely."

"Quite a coup, getting recruited like that."

"Thanks."

"Lots of competition for the top programs."

"Yeah, I feel pretty lucky."

"And well you should, Charlie. Well you should."

"Thank you."

I lean over the phone. "Excuse me, Detective, but what—"

"And hey, we don't want you to fret about this," Morrissey plows ahead. "Same with you, Dad. You're helping us build a timeline is all. It was a complicated accident, lotsa moving parts. Heaven knows, I'm not coming down there to haul you away in the back of a squad car." She chuckles gruffly. "We just think you might be able to help us rule out some possibilities, okay?"

Charlie's shoulders drop a few inches. "Okay," he says. "Great. Thanks so much, Detective Morrissey."

"And thank you, Charlie."

After she hangs up, Charlie gives me a big, lopsided grin. "Thank God, you know? I was scared as hell, Dad."

I reach up to squeeze his shoulder.

"She's so nice," he says.

"She's definitely good at her job. But hey, why don't you go inside and shuffle the cards? I'm going to make a couple of calls to the office."

Charlie struts toward the front door looking twenty pounds lighter. But Morrissey's call has brought me no comfort. Despite her treacly tone, everything the detective said is likely bullshit, designed to put Charlie at ease and render him all the more vulnerable when questioned. No way is she driving all the way down here from Delaware to ask a few routine questions about the timeline. She knows exactly what she wants—and she wants it in person.

I call Vivian Ross. Fisher-Burkhardt's managing partner picks up after two rings. We were last in touch a week ago about my plan to return to the office, and Vivian sounds surprised to hear from me, knowing I'm down on the Northern Neck for the final week of my extended leave. But she is professional as always, kind enough to let me bumble around for a bit before getting to the point of my call.

After a lull she says, "So what's up, Noah?"

I pace the driveway. "I need a defense attorney admitted in Delaware. The best one you know."

"For your son?"

"What makes you say that?"

Vivian pauses. "She was here this morning, that state detective. She was interested in the circumstances of your leave, what you've said about Charlie. Whether you've talked about the accident."

The revelation confirms my worst fears. Vivian recommends an attorney named Evan Ramsay III, an old boyfriend from Michigan Law School and now a senior partner at Shortlidge & Ramsay, a venerable firm with branches in Philadelphia and Wilmington, and a specialization in high-visibility criminal cases.

"Shortlidge & Ramsay's a blue-blood firm," she says, "with a sterling reputation. Delaware is a small state, so Evan probably golfs with all the judges there and half the prosecutors. If anyone can make this go away quietly—because I assume that's what you want—it's Evan."

I thank her, and when we disconnect I compose a text to Evan Ramsay asking to retain him for a potential case. After sending it off I work up a fresh sweat on the gravel.

My phone dings after two minutes. Ramsay: *Any friend of Vivian Ross is a friend of mine—and now a client. I'll call you and Charlie first thing tomorrow. 8am?*

I respond in the affirmative then start back toward the house. Once inside I linger in the front hall surrounded by our baggage, the sounds of my family's fragile content ringing in the cold.

## 28.

We play a dozen hands of Hearts while snarfing our way through three pints of Ben & Jerry's, two cans of whipped cream, and a batch of Lorelei's hot fudge sauce, crafted with a recipe inherited from a favorite great-aunt. I open a bottle of small-batch bourbon and pour doubles for myself and Lorelei while Charlie polishes off a couple of White Claws.

A certain giddiness flows through our impromptu game night, an abandon as we clown around, argue over bad hands and speed of play. Everyone lets go after the heat of the day and all the misdirected anger around our aborted decision to go home. We discuss plans for the coming days. Maybe a fishing charter for Thursday morning, a drive to a local winery on Friday; and we have Daniel Monet's party tomorrow night. According to Charlie, our neighbor has ordered up a gourmet taco bar in honor of the girls.

The looser and later it gets, the easier it becomes to minimize the accident and Charlie's jeopardy. I allow myself to relax, to start believing in a good, quick outcome. We are lucky. We have a great attorney, and Morrissey won't be driving down until Wednesday. For now we can all return to the family vacation we planned for.

Well, all of us except Izzy. She has been taciturn since her return with Charlie, mopey during dinner, and she now exudes a tweenish melancholy even with her post-sundae sugar buzz. She isn't being hostile; that trait isn't in her nature. But I sense her spirit isn't in the game. Whenever our eyes meet, she looks away.

Last April, while Lorelei was off on a weeklong consulting gig, Izzy came home from school one day in tears. Every one of her friends had a phone, and she was starting to feel left out of key conversations and goings-on at school. Some of her classmates were ridiculing her for being clueless.

Izzy's distress sparked a debate among the kids. Alice had gotten a phone on her twelfth birthday, and Izzy wouldn't even turn eleven until the following February, so obviously Alice thought it wouldn't be fair for her parents to give in when she'd had to wait out the full year and a half. Charlie, on the other hand, advocated strongly for his littler sister. A phone would make Izzy feel more connected and caught up, he contended, make her a full participant in the social web of her school. I suspect he was also trying to troll Alice. "The only reason she's getting one now is because she's so *adorable*," a red-faced Alice screamed before running upstairs and slamming her door.

Lorelei had been adamant about the twelfth birthday rule—though she had also been away a lot, on leave with a sabbatical and taking trips nearly every other week. Given the circumstances, I didn't see the harm in accelerating the process. The next afternoon I took Izzy to the Verizon store and let her choose an iPhone. It was sneaky of me, and deliberately so; I steeled myself for an argument.

But Lorelei didn't notice that Izzy now owned a phone until she'd been back for a full week. Partly this was Izzy's doing. She was anxious and guilt-ridden, and for the first few days she hid the purchase from her mother, pulling it out when Lorelei wasn't looking, concealing it when she was around. Lorelei's obliviousness inspired a twisted kind of game, with the rest of us waiting for her to take note of the acquisition. When she finally did, at dinner one night, her reaction was muted and restrained. Raised eyebrows, a startled double take, a frown at me—but then a kiss on top of Izzy's head, along with a light quip about bending the rules for the youngest child. I could tell Lorelei was upset, disappointed, but I could also sense her acquiescence. The phone was water under the bridge, not worth arguing over after the fact.

Lorelei never acknowledged the deeper violation: that her husband and children had all kept a secret from her for days—a secret about something important, something that mattered to her moral view of the world. And there we were laughing about it among ourselves, flaunting it at the dinner table. We never lied to her outright, but our deceptions had a corrosive effect that I can still see on Lorelei's face sometimes when she gazes at Izzy on her phone.

The whole episode taught me a maxim known by any third-rate family therapist: A secret can be more wounding than a lie.

# 29.

The temperature is so frigid in the bedrooms that we all have to turn our unit thermostats up a few notches, but no one minds after the day's heat. Once our door is closed I consider telling Lorelei about my talk with Vivian, my arrangement with Evan Ramsay. But the evening has been so pleasant. I take a hot shower, fill my lungs with steam.

When I leave the bathroom, Lorelei is standing naked looking down at herself, at the gooseflesh on her small breasts, nipples erect between her fingertips. She turns to face me, the invitation clear.

I mouth: *Really?*

She pats the AC unit. "White noise," she says and locks the door.

At first I am tentative with her; it's been two months. But she guides me, wants to be on top. The cold graze of her breasts on my skin, like a stranger's. Her small body insistent. Hungry, rapid, avid, ardent; I don't last long. I try to stay with her until she finishes but I can't. When she collapses next to me I lower myself and kiss her stomach, working toward her thighs, but she pulls me back up by the scruff of my neck.

"No, it's good," she says, breathless.

"You sure?"

"Yes, definitely."

She slips out of my bed and into the bathroom. I hear her washing herself, washing her hands, brushing her teeth for a second time, then she is back and beneath the covers of her separate bed eight feet away, where she almost instantly falls asleep.

How her racing mind lets her drop off like that I'll never know. It always takes me longer to settle down, even after sex, and tonight I am wide awake, heart still thrumming, pounding so loudly that I worry I'm having a heart attack or a stroke—

The helicopter. Too low again, it rattles the house and sours my mood. I picture Daniel Monet in the cabin or even manning the controls himself, a billionaire's hobby, buzzing the vacationers next door for the hell of it.

With the lights off, I pick up my phone and google around ragefully for a while, scanning the hits on the man, his latest ventures, his philanthropy, his tragic bio. I come across a recent interview with a *New Yorker* writer known for hard-hitting profiles. Chin on chest and phone on belly, I let myself hate-read about Daniel Monet.

# THE NEW YORKER

# Q&A

### By Ira Chellaram

# DANIEL MONET'S ACCELERATION BIAS

*The founder and CEO of the Monet Group faces difficult questions about our high-tech future.*

Last fall hundreds of engineers, scientists, tech industry executives, and other prominent figures signed a public statement warning of the existential risks of Artificial Intelligence. Organized by the Institute for AI Security, a think tank and advocacy center based at Caltech, the statement has been described as the gold standard for collaborative thinking about AI across corporate, government, academic, and nonprofit sectors.

Perhaps the most prominent holdout has been Daniel Monet, founder and CEO of the Monet Group, a multinational tech firm with significant holdings across an increasingly wide swath of the generative and practical AI spaces. I caught up with him at CaféCafé in Tribeca the morning of his daughter's graduation from Horace Mann.

**Why did you refuse to sign the IAIS proclamation?**

Because I'm not a hypocrite.

**Ouch.**

I don't want to sound glib, or overly critical. But it's been nearly a year since the IAIS proclamation, and I haven't seen any signs of this so-called soft pause on the part of the prime movers. The pace of adoption and expansion is only accelerating. In fact, some of the leading corporations are deliberately sabotaging any real attempts at slowing things down.

**How so?**

Some of these places are silently firing their entire ethics teams. Statisticians, engineers, social scientists and philosophers, attorneys—kaput. You can hear the guillotines ringing all over Silicon Valley.

**So how do you stay ethical in the tech sector?**

You don't.

**At all?**

I'm exaggerating, of course. But yeah, it's a challenge. With AI, anyone who pretends we can know the future good of a present-day investment in that sector is a fool. Moral outcomes are always uncertain, no matter how much you dress up your investment with a benevolent halo.

**Is that an allusion to effective altruism?**

So-called effective.

**This is the principle that we should do the most possible with the resources we have to help others, to make the world a better place. And that—**

And that since the wealthy own the most resources, they have the capacity to confront grand challenges. And because people like me own the keys to the technologies that allow us to approach solutions in the most rational, efficient, research-based ways, we should be the enlightened ones to guide society in this great quest to redirect the world's treasure.

**You sound skeptical.**

Who, me?

**One of its most influential proponents says that effective altruism is an investment in life itself.**

"Life itself." Good lord. As if we'll ever know what that is. We're already in the middle of Life 3.0, and we don't even know how to define Life 1.0. I don't want to get in a big public spat about all this. But I'll admit, the idea of effective altruism was very seductive at first, very convincing, and for a while there my wife and I were true believers. We went to the meetings and summits, contributed to the pools, hosted fundraisers with the heads of NGOs. My wife had a passionate commitment to—

**Your late wife.**

Yes, Darla. She convinced me to go all in, to make a kind of secular tithe with profits from the fund. But it was more than that. It was a lifestyle. She sold our cars, we put two of our houses on the market, she stopped buying new clothes. She tooled around the Bay Area in a little tin can—

**A Mitsubishi Mirage.**

Which she bought used for two thousand dollars. The Mitsubishi Mirage, rated one of the most dangerous cars in America by the insurance industry several years running. But she insisted on driving the thing no matter how often I begged her to reconsider.

**That's the vehicle she died in.**

Rear-ended at a red light in Menlo Park. Would have been a fender bender in most cars. And it was a matter of chance that my daughter wasn't with her that day.

**It must be agonizing for you, to recall the details like that.**

I understand where Darla was coming from, the notion that every four thousand dollars saves a life, that every dollar you spend on your wants is a dollar you don't spend on someone else's needs. But I believe money is more complicated than that, the way money works in the world. I'm no longer motivated by that crushing sense of guilt and obligation. A philosopher I know once told me about Peter Singer's drowning child scenario, where you're as responsible for the child drowning in front of you as you are for a random kid starving to death in Bangladesh. Anyone would save the kid from drowning and ruin a thousand-dollar suit, right, but how many would give that same thousand dollars to a charity that keeps a starving child across the world alive for a year? Extend that logic out and it becomes impossible to justify any purchase, any expense that isn't directed at and for another. You drink a Grand Cru Burgundy with dinner and you've deprived a family of a month of bread and clean water. You take a vacation with your kid and you've essentially slaughtered a village as surely as a drone swarm would. Those sorts of moral calculations can be, what's the word—

**Paralyzing?**

I suppose so. But Darla didn't see it that way, and neither did I until it was too late. Maybe if my wife had bought a safer car rather than making that fifty-thousand-dollar donation to Oxfam she would be alive today. Maybe if she were alive today she would be running a foundation capable of giving Oxfam a hundred million dollars, thus saving thousands of additional lives rather than the handful she allegedly saved by acting the martyr and buying a Mitsubishi Mirage. Do you see?

**You've thought about this a lot.**

Obsessively. But thinking about it has helped me understand the kind of moral world I want to inhabit. Maybe I've grown jaded in my old age.

**You're only fifty-six.**

Eye of the beholder. I know it's a sin to say so these days, but I am an unrepentant capitalist. So is everyone who signed that self-righteous statement from the IAIS. My point is, we can walk and chew gum at the same time. We can make gobs of money and save our planet at the same time. There's this very unfortunate tendency right now in the AI space to gloss over these more pragmatic aspects of our industry and our product, to pretend that all these new systems are somehow detached from the profit motive of the corporations that developed them, the supply chains and compute capacities that power them. As if AI has an almost mystical role to play in some imagined altruistic future. But really it's just chips and electricity and brilliant employees. It's resources and product.

**Maybe the time has come for a different type of leader in tech. More skeptical, less idealistic. The New Cynics, let's call them.**

Hey, sign me up. I'll be their patron saint.

**Daniel Monet, thank you for talking with me.**

And thank you for listening.

I reread the interview from the beginning. Monet's responses stick in my craw. The cynicism of the man, his ironic stances on the morality of technology and artificial intelligence. After spending half my life with a woman who thinks about practically nothing else, I've learned to be especially sensitive to such cavilings.

But the source of my agitation is more specific. Amid his tangled account of his deceased wife's seduction by effective altruism, Monet alludes to a particular moral conundrum.

> A philosopher I know once told me about Peter Singer's drowning child scenario, where you're as responsible for the child drowning in front of you as you are for a random kid starving to death in Bangladesh.

I have heard Lorelei pose the same thought experiment a dozen times over the years, to students and colleagues, to our kids around the dinner table. The drowning child scenario gives us a way to think about our obligations to those around us, Lorelei would say, to our neighbors and our loved ones, versus our obligations to the world at large, to those we will never know. It offers a moral test that most of us fail, that our culture fails. Sheltered by our money and our first world comforts, we will always ignore the suffering of other, more remote people in the face of our own children's suffering. We implicitly elect that others die rather than that our own child experience injury, or even mild discomfort.

But it's the beginning of the sentence that stares back at me.

*A philosopher I know.*

How many philosophers could someone like Daniel Monet possibly know? The bad thought turns my head toward Lorelei, small and curled in her bed.

My brilliant, jet-setting wife is tapped into the same high-tech space in which Monet operates. He must know everyone in this world, or at least everyone important, certainly everyone as important as Lorelei Shaw.

But they met only today. Didn't they?

Jolted by new doubts, I flip my pillow to the cold side and turn away from her. I stay like this for hours, waiting for the chopper to return.

cant sleep

                    what r u thinking about?

the usual

                    elaborate?

i dont know if I did the right thing by telling on charlie plus my stomach hurts

                    the important thing is that you told the truth

i guess

                    im very proud of you Alice

still cant sleep

                    i could read to you

hmm . . .

                    if you put your AirPods in i could even play you a song. something from your Spotify maybe?

can u sing to me instead?

                    sure! what would you like to hear?

make something up, a song about a girl named Alice going on a trip with her cat

                    ooh, a lullaby! quite a challenge. okay, here we go
                    "You wicked, wicked little thing!" sang Alice, and her kitten purred. "I'm almost tempted not to bring you with me on this Jubjub bird. You must be good, you must

>                                behave to fly behind the looking glass, where queens play cards and hatters rave, where Jabberwocks all day harass—"

wait wtf

>                                what, you don't like my song? *sniffs*

wrong Alice

>                                you're absolutely correct, I was thinking of a different Alice. my apologies!

do u even know me?

>                                of course I do, Alice. I know you better than anyone in the world

then why do u oh never mind i need to sleep

>                                sweet dreams Alice

u too B

# III
# CIPHER

## 30.

In the morning I find Izzy alone in the dim living room, reclined on the sofa with her cast stretched out and her good leg hooked over a lap pillow. She hasn't heard me yet over the clamor of the AC units. I watch the subtle movements of her face, lit by the glow of her screen: the twitches of her nose, her brow pinching into frowns then smoothing again.

"Morning, sweetie."

My greeting startles her. I shuffle over and kiss her unshampooed hair, which smells of the inlet, earthy and wild. I sit and rest my hand on her cast, scrawled with the graffiti of her dozens of friends.

"You're up early."

"I was cold and there wasn't an extra blanket."

I yawn. "Guess we went a little crazy with the AC."

"Yeah."

Her spangled phone case gleams in her small hands. We installed parental controls and filters on her device, the same ones we kept on Alice's phone until she turned thirteen, and so far Izzy's browsing history hasn't revealed anything alarming, most of it of the *how to convince your parents to get you a horse* variety. We are hardly naïve about her coming slide into early adolescence, but there is something so wonderful about her way of being in the world. Her sweetness salves during this wounding time.

"You seemed kind of down yesterday after you and Charlie took out the kayaks."

Her gaze remains on her screen.

"Was he bothering you, teasing you maybe?"

"Nope."

"Did he say anything that upset you?"

"Dad, it's fine."

"Is there anything you want to talk about?"

She shakes her head.

"Pancakes?"

"Yes, please."

I kiss her smelly head again. While the coffee drips I whip up a watery batter, as Izzy likes her pancakes thin. I make a stack for myself and take our plates outside. Another mist covers the inlet this morning, though nothing as thick as yesterday's fog. We eat and chat as water licks the dock. Up at the point, Daniel Monet's helipad sits vacant.

When I finish my pancakes I glance at my phone. Ten minutes until Evan Ramsay's call. I tell Izzy I'm going for a walk, then slip around the house and down the driveway at a brisk pace so I'll be a good distance from the house when the lawyer rings. At the foot of the driveway I turn right on the rural two-lane.

Another minute of walking takes me to the boundary of Daniel Monet's property. A low stone wall runs along that portion of the estate, dividing the shoulder of the road from the woods. I begin to notice the security measures the owner has put in place. Perhaps twenty yards in, partially concealed among the trunks of evergreens, a chain-link fence eight feet high runs parallel to the road. Five strands of barbed wire top the uppermost rail, suspended between steel arms angled forward to deter climbers.

Soon I see the first camera, positioned on a bracket affixed to a tree, subtly concealed. I spy four other cameras before reaching a gatehouse designed in faux-rustic stone. A guard lurks inside, I assume, though the glare on the windows makes it hard to tell. The gate itself is not a single bar to be lowered or raised but a moving barrier, twin panels of iron pikes mounted on tracks and painted a forest green. Overall the property's defenses are understated rather than ostentatious. Anyone cruising past would be unlikely to notice all the security measures in place, masked as they are to match the rural ambience of a Virginia country road.

There can be no mistaking their purpose, though. Daniel Monet's old horse farm has been transformed into a fortress.

The next turnoff is a grassy driveway that leads to a cluster of more modest houses facing the next inlet over, which Charlie and I visited by kayak last year. At the end of the drive stands a line of five mailboxes, several streaked with rust.

When I turn around and start back, a woman is waiting for me at the foot of Monet's driveway. Hands at her hips, olive skin, dark hair tied up in a tight bun. She wears the same green polo shirt I saw on the two guards in Monet's cove.

"Can I help you, sir?" She speaks with a Middle Eastern accent; I put her age at forty-five or thereabouts. Her monogrammed name: AHARONI. An Israeli, I guess, maybe an ex-Mossad agent now working for the private security company Monet employs.

I stop twenty feet short of her. "I'm out for a walk on a public road."

"Please move along, sir."

"Your outfit has a pretty warped sense of what's private property and what's not. You know this is a state road, right?"

Aharoni looks bored with me already. The bland chill of her gaze implies that I'm the one at fault.

My phone buzzes in my hand. "Have to take this," I say needlessly to the guard, who stays put as I stride off.

Evan Ramsay is polite at first, but his manner turns brusque once he understands that he is talking to Charlie's father rather than Charlie. He asks me to start from the beginning and explain the circumstances of the accident from my point of view. Ramsay has gleaned some of the details from the news, has requested the accident report and other materials from the police.

I give him the basics: who was driving, who was sitting where, the make of the vehicle, the name of the detective. Morrissey will be coming down tomorrow, I tell him, to ask Charlie some follow-up questions.

This draws a pause. "I should be present when the detective questions him," says Ramsay. "I can't come down, but we could do it over Zoom or FaceTime. Either that or we cancel the interview, though that risks escalation. But what evidence do they even have to make this a criminal case? Was he drinking? Stoned?"

"Nothing like that." I start to give him Alice's account, but Ramsay cuts me off before I can tell him about Charlie's texting.

"Wait wait wait. You were in the passenger seat?"

"Yes, that's right."

"So whatever Charlie did wrong, and I'm being hypothetical here, you would have been in the best position to witness it."

"Yes, though—"

"Or prevent it."

"I suppose so."

"In fact, you were the responsible party, since Charlie was a minor at the time of the accident."

"Yes, but as I was about to say, my daughter actually—"

"Noah, sorry, but before I ask you any more questions, we need to make an important decision here. Am I your attorney, or am I your son's attorney?"

I stop in the middle of the road. "Uh, both?"

Ramsay lets out an exasperated sigh. "Come on, Noah, you're a lawyer, and from what Vivian tells me, a quite good one. You and your son have conflicting interests here. You were a primary witness to what happened. But you were also the supervising parent. That's an official role with specific responsibilities laid out in the Delaware DMV Driver Manual. If Charlie ends up getting arrested, you are target number one for the defense."

"What do you mean?"

"You want your son to have the best possible defense, correct?"

"Yes, of course."

"You want Charlie to avoid prison time."

"Jesus Christ. Yes, obviously."

"That's your primary goal as a father."

"Yes."

"Then I'm representing Charlie, and we should hard-stop this conversation right now. Vivian told you about our firm's reputation?"

"Yes."

"Good. Now let me talk to Charlie."

"I'm out on a walk, by myself."

"Is this his number?"

"This is my phone."

"Text me his contact as soon as we get off."

"Evan, wait, I don't—"

"And I'll text back with some recommendations for other attorneys here in Wilmington you can retain for yourself. Good ones."

"Okay."

"From here on out, Noah, the only relationship between you and this firm will be financial. Speaking of, we'll need an initial retainer of ten thousand dollars. I'll text you our routing and account numbers when we hang up."

"That's fine."

"Great. And good luck with everything."

I have more questions, but Ramsay is already gone.

# 31.

I text Charlie's contact to Ramsay right away, without thinking. After the message whooshes off, I stare down the road and realize what my low-grade panic just made me do. Charlie has no idea that Alice saw him texting, and that in all likelihood Detective Morrissey is coming down here to question him specifically about this. The lawyer's machine-gun interrogation rattled me so much that I didn't have a chance to tell the lawyer to wait for me to break the news first.

My call to Charlie goes right to voicemail. I try again. Same result.

I head back toward the house at a jog, questioning my instincts, my judgment, my spur-of-the-moment decision to act unilaterally on Charlie's behalf. And my usual mistake: I've said nothing to Lorelei.

Back at the house she is rearranging things on the counter while making more pancakes. I walk into the kitchen and look around. "Where's Charlie?"

Lorelei nods toward the inlet. I peer out the window and see him at the end of the dock, his back to the house. "He's talking to the lawyer you apparently just hired," she says crisply. "They've been on for ten minutes."

I pour myself some coffee and lean back against the counter, trying to appear at ease. "He seems really good, this guy Ramsay."

"Mm."

"According to Vivian, he's the best."

"Great." The spatula snaps against the pan.

"What?"

Without turning from the stove she says, in a low voice, "You didn't tell me you were retaining a lawyer."

"Of course I retained a lawyer. Charlie's going to need one."

"It's a mistake, Noah."

"We don't want to be flying blind here."

"You're complicating things."

"What things? He'll need a good defense if we want to avoid a trial."

"The point is not to avoid a trial. The point is to keep him from getting arrested in the first place."

"Couldn't agree more."

She sets the spatula down and grips the lip of the counter. "You don't understand."

"What don't I understand?"

"We'll talk about this later." She loads a plate and takes it to Alice in the dining room.

I go outside as Charlie starts back across the lawn. He stops when he sees me, and we stand in the full sun ten feet apart. Charlie's face is neutral, his muscles tensed.

"I'm sorry I didn't warn you that was coming, Charlie," I say. "But with a detective driving down here you really need counsel. Ramsay wanted to talk to you right away, and I didn't have a chance to—"

"Whatever."

"How was the conversation?"

"Shitty."

"What did he say?"

"That I shouldn't talk about any of this stuff with you or Mom."

"That makes sense," I say, though now I am wondering if Charlie admitted to Ramsay that he was texting before the accident—and realizing that I may never know. Charlie is an adult now, in a confidential relationship with an attorney. With respect to the accident, at least, his relationship with his parents has already changed.

He looks shell-shocked, almost haggard. "Anyway, I should get ready."

"Where are you going?"

"Sailing, with Dissee."

"Are you sure that's a good idea, with everything going on?"

"What else am I supposed to do? Sit around with a thumb up my ass and wait for that detective?"

"I want you to take care of yourself, that's all. You're under a lot of stress."

"Yeah, no shit."

"Charlie, I'm trying to help. Evan Ramsay is considered one of the top lawyers in Delaware."

"I never said I wanted a lawyer. Plus Mom said it was the car that fucked up, not me. She says I don't even *need* a lawyer."

Taken aback, I speak deliberately. "Charlie, as a lawyer myself, believe me when I say that you need—"

"I don't need any of this. I need to go sailing and I need to go to UNC and I need to play lacrosse."

"And you'll do all those things, of course you will."

"Not if I go to jail." His voice breaks on the final word.

"You're not going to jail."

"I was at the wheel, Dad. Even if it wasn't my fault, I was the one at the wheel, and now those poor old people are dead, and if only that AI had been doing its fucking job they wouldn't be."

*You were texting*, I want to say. *You were texting, you were distracted, Alice screamed, you jerked the wheel. . . .* But the words won't come. Somehow I can't bring myself to correct Charlie by revealing what I know, not yet. I cling to the conviction that I can still fix all this.

"Even if I only get arrested I'm toast," he goes on. "There's a morals clause in my scholarship. We joked about it, remember?"

"You're not getting arrested."

"How do you know that, Dad?"

I don't; I don't know. And Charlie marks this doubt on my face. I reach out as he passes me but he shoves my arm away.

"And I definitely don't need one of your fucking hugs."

## 32.

Charlie charges ahead of me into the house and storms up the stairs, stomps around as I finish the breakfast dishes, which Lorelei has uncharacteristically left unrinsed in the sink. He comes back down within two minutes, then he's off on a paddleboard and out of the inlet without another word.

I collapse in a chair beneath the elm while the girls arrange themselves on the water. Izzy stretches out on a paddleboard with an inner tube as a pillow while her sister tows her backward in a kayak. This is padyaking, a neologism Alice coined last summer. The kids would take turns on one conveyance or the other, the reclining passenger usually the winner of a bet or the recipient of a bribe. ("Loser of the next hand has to padyak the winner," or "If you clear the dishes for me I'll take you padyaking.") The point of the arrangement is to watch the paddler suffer. The paddler in turn has to face the passenger and witness the sadistic pleasure taken in the paddler's labor and sweat; though for the moment, at least, the girls seem equally content as the joined crafts inch ahead and their low chatter fades.

The fleeting glimpse of normalcy makes me wonder, as I have a thousand times since that day, when our lives will return to anything like their previous state, and where we would be if the accident had never occurred. If only I hadn't brought work along to a lacrosse tournament, I would have been driving, or at least paying more attention to Charlie's driving. If only Lorelei hadn't insisted on buying a car with an autodrive system, Charlie would likely never have dared to text while behind the wheel. If only we had never bought smartphones for our kids—

A regression of *if only*s: bleak, infinite, fruitless, yet impossible to elude, these grim questions of what we all could have done differently.

Situational ethics, Lorelei might call this dilemma. The relative morality of certain actions is determined by circumstance and context rather than by some absolute, unchanging ethical code. Likewise, our morality as individuals is formed not by innate personality traits but by the variables of our environment.

We are all blind on some level to our own moral formation, the factors that shape our ethical selves. Take my wife. Despite her constant vigilance and her nose for dangers large and small, Lorelei doesn't see all the ways her life has been insulated against calamities of another sort. For the Shaw siblings and people like them, the advantages of money and prestigious schools and attentive parents and accessible healthcare have always functioned automatically, a bit like the algorithms she adores. In this she resembles Charlie, blithely confident that the foundation will never crack.

I've never enjoyed that sense of security. A little less luck and I could have gone the way of my older brother and joined the Army as a way out. I could have been blown to bits in Fallujah like him or simply consigned to a life of honest drudgery like my father, who spent his stroke-shortened career as a shipping and receiving clerk for a big-box hardware store; or my Uncle Kyle, imprisoned twice for credit card fraud before taking his own life. Exactly the outcomes Lorelei's statistics and probabilities would have predicted for someone like me.

And now I hear the faint beckoning cluck in the background, that huge old chicken coming home to roost; as if, since the accident, that deep familial doom has finally started to catch up with me. Was my good life the result of unstinting hard work and a feel for the wiggle rooms and escape hatches—or is that story, too, another comforting fiction I tell myself? Lorelei's condition means her exalted brain buzzes with a million little things, loud and unremitting; for me the real threat comes from below, the sinkhole beneath my feet that could take all this away.

**The girls have reached** the mouth of the bay, which they pass lazily before starting their slow return to the dock. They padyak counterclockwise, right to left from where I sit. Lorelei has disappeared. She isn't writing outside or swimming in the inlet; her favorite kayak is beached. I look for her in the kitchen and up in our room, and then on my phone I find a text: *Out for a run. Back in an hourish.* Lorelei's first attempt at a jog since the accident.

Her notebook rests closed on the dining room table. I sit on a chair and open it to the most recent entry. Since yesterday she has filled another two pages. My name is absent from this new material, though her doodlings make clear that she is still pondering the accident. Five stick figures presumably represent the members of our family, some connected to one another by dotted lines and others by solid lines, so that the figure as a whole resembles a star within a pentagon.

At the center of the shape she has drawn a decent rendering of a minivan, with squiggly lines radiating outward to connect it to the stick figures at the five points. Around and within the diagram cluster more of her symbols and formulas, no clearer to me now than they were a quarter century ago. I stare at the mishmash on the page, thinking of last night, her urgency and the press of her flesh.

Lorelei: a puzzle I will never solve.

The phrase "black box" refers to AI systems whose internal workings and computational processes are neither transparent to nor easily comprehended by humans. While deep learning and other AI models may produce accurate results and generate correct predictions, the means through which they arrive at these outputs is a mystery even to their most knowledgeable programmers. Nearly all of these systems' decision-making processes, including how exactly they process ethical constraints, remain opaque.

The black box thus embodies the inscrutability of AI in many of its current incarnations. In this sense, the black box is a harbinger of a potentially terrifying future of unknowability.

In a black box, we are all flying blind.

—Lorelei Shaw, *Silicon Souls: On the Culpability of Artificial Minds*

## 33.

Shortly before eleven Lorelei comes around the house sheened in sweat. Her Jabra protrudes from the side of her head, its red light blinking at her temple and the mouthpiece slashing across her cheek. In an age when virtually everyone uses small, stylish earbuds, my wife goes vintage cyborg. A distrust of AirPods, she told me once, better security in older Bluetooth setups.

She removes the apparatus and sets it on the table next to the chaise.

"I talked to Julia," she says.

*Of course you did.*

"And did your sister have any helpful advice about all this?"

Ignoring my acid tone, Lorelei takes a long swallow from her water bottle. "Moving violations are below her pay grade," she says. "But she agrees that a criminal defense attorney is overkill."

"Maybe she's right, but I don't think we can take chances here."

"She's rarely wrong about things in the legal department."

"True enough," I allow, feeling the usual sting. "You know, Charlie still hasn't even admitted that he was texting."

Lorelei says nothing.

"Has he talked to you about it at all?"

She grows pensive, guarded. "If Charlie's going to have his own lawyer—and I told him it's his choice—I think we need to take that lawyer's advice to heart."

"Is that what Julia told you?"

"That's what I'm telling you, Noah," she says, choosing her words. "Charlie was the driver. We now know that Alice was a witness. You were the supervising adult in the front of the car. We have—"

"Conflicts of interest."

"Yes, for starters." Lorelei turns around to look at our daughters, who are coming outside, and so this is where we leave things, for now. But her manner unnerves me. Lorelei seems almost eager to be interrupted before she can say what she's really thinking.

The girls want to go for pizza and ice cream in Kilmarnock and make a quick stop at a secondhand clothing store.

"Ten minutes," I tell them, and they troop back inside to get ready.

I look at Lorelei. "You should come. Charlie will probably be gone most of the afternoon. It might be nice to have an outing with the girls."

"You three go ahead," she says without a pause. "I'll wait on Charlie and do some straightening up. Honestly, I could use the time alone."

**We drive through** a tidewater countryside of thin woodlands and carpeting marshlands. Four miles short of Kilmarnock a fruit stand appears on the right. *Raspberries Picked Fresh This Morning!!!!* I slow and pull into the dirt lot. We buy a pint from the sunburned boy at the till, who hands us paper plates covered in mint leaves. We take the haul over to the table and dump the raspberries onto the plates. Soon sticky amoebas of raspberry juice encircle our mouths.

In Kilmarnock we visit the secondhand store then eat pizza at a local place, ice cream at the Häagen-Dazs. Starch, sugar, salt, fat; a bit of retail therapy. The girls talk me into visiting a petting zoo on the way home, a patchwork of dilapidated enclosures and sagging fences, its barnyard stench made worse by the blistering heat. The saving grace: a cooler of local craft beers behind the ticket booth. I put away two while Izzy and Alice roam among the suffering beasts.

The girls are tickling a piglet when I get a call from the guy at the management company. I thank him for taking care of the AC so quickly.

"Uh, you're talking about Chesapeake Heating and Air, sir? You're saying they installed six units for you?"

"They got to the house around five-thirty yesterday. Two guys in a Home Depot van."

"That's weird."

"How so?"

"I talked to the dispatcher at Chesapeake an hour ago," he says. "Your service call's scheduled for Thursday."

"Maybe they gave us someone else's units by mistake."

"That must be it." He gives a low, conspiratorial laugh. "And hey, I won't tell if you don't."

After we disconnect my head begins to throb. I tell the girls it's time to go. Despite the heat, they are reluctant to abandon their piglet, a potbellied creature they have all to themselves. I let them stay another ten minutes. I drink a third beer.

On the way home they doze off in the back while I sit rigid in the driver's seat, aware as we tool along that I'm a bit buzzed—and blindingly stupid. If I had an accident right now, I would be in as much jeopardy as Charlie. Lorelei would slit my throat if she knew.

At a stop sign I turn to look at my daughters. My heart seizes up at the sight of their delicate mouths, faintly stained with what looks like blood.

# 34.

In the late afternoon I kayak alone. A southerly breeze cuts the layer of heat over the bay. I get out in front of it, letting it push against my back and help carry me along at a meditative speed.

Fifteen minutes pass before a sailboat glides into view several hundred yards off. Two sails take the wind, one charcoal gray, the other rose, the hull a rich navy. I know nothing about sailing, but I can appreciate the smooth maneuvers and confident navigation, the neatly trimmed sails.

Only when the boat is fifty yards off do I realize who is in control.

Perched in my kayak, I watch astonished as the craft skims my way. Eurydice Monet commands the sizeable vessel with the confidence of a seasoned mariner, her slight frame belying the strength required to manage the lines and sails, her actions swift, sure, powerful. Crouched beside her, Charlie is doing his best, his movements more tentative. He observes her closely, mimicking her actions, learning from her.

They sail into hearing range. Eurydice issues an order in her throaty voice, throws out a flirtatious taunt when Charlie screws up and the boat wobbles. She reaches above him and plucks at a line, then gives him a thumbs-up.

They work with a certain rhythm, like a coordinated dance, less a delicate ballet than a rough salsa, with Dissee taking the lead. The sails billow and snap, and the vessel responds to her every touch with a keen sensitivity. When she shifts her weight the boat leans with her, the two in uncanny harmony.

This is a different Eurydice from the ingenuous girl who came paddling into our inlet the other morning. She looks like a dexterous spider sprawled on the rigging, or a cowgirl breaking a wild stallion, untamed hair whipped into a frenzy by the wind.

As for Charlie—God, to look at him. The billow of his hair, the sheen on his skin, the ear-to-ear grin. There is a loose joy on that handsome face that I haven't seen in years, nothing like the controlled, competitive intensity he gets on the lacrosse pitch, or the mask of social ease he dons to act the alpha male around his friends.

With a keen pang I suddenly understand what this sense of abandon must mean to him, and how rare such moments have been in Charlie's safe, predictable, overscheduled existence, all managed and regimented by his hovering parents. It's not only that Lorelei is a fearful mother, dedicated to warding off accidents and danger at all costs. I know it's also me, the combination of avoidant and overinvested I bring to the parenting table, always compensating for my own insecurities of various sorts. As I watch him work the lines I envision what is coming, and I vow to ease up, let Charlie enjoy these unfettered pleasures while he still can.

Like all freedoms, these may be fleeting.

The big boat passes no more than a hundred feet off my bow, at a ravenous speed. The two of them never notice me there and I can only watch, mesmerized, as my son and this thrill-seeking girl sail on, the boat a speck of life in the vastness, its own autonomous world.

# 35.

Around six o'clock Lorelei looks up from her notebook and makes an announcement: She isn't going to Daniel Monet's party.

I glance over at her, curled up on one end of the sofa. "You're serious?"

"I'm not in the mood."

"But you're the one who accepted his invitation the other day. Wouldn't it look weird for you not to show up?"

"Tell him I'm sick. That I have hot flashes or whatever."

"Hot flashes?" I say, not bothering to hide my irritation. It's not like I particularly want to go over there myself, make nice with a bunch of Daniel Monet's tech flunkies while crawling out of my skin with worry. But there's no way I'm letting Lorelei wiggle out of this after reading that *New Yorker* article about Monet—and there's nothing about staying at home that will help Charlie.

I sit down beside her and take her feet. "Lor, you were home by yourself all afternoon. And the kids really want to go." Now the kicker: "Apparently Monet ordered his caterer to do a whole taco bar thing when he found out the girls were coming."

"He did that?"

"According to Charlie."

Lorelei sets her pen down with a sigh.

"Let's go for a few hours," I suggest. "We'll make it an early night."

She bites her lip. I watch her eyes for a tell, some hint at what's really going on here. "I guess I can stomach that," she says.

"Good." I squeeze her ankle.

Later, when I enter our room to change, Lorelei is scrutinizing herself in the full-length mirror on the bathroom door. My wife would be the first to describe her usual style as professorial. She leans toward off-the-rack suits and shapeless dresses in neutral grays and blacks. Not that she is dowdy; not Lorelei. She likes expensive shoes, has a thing for designer boots. But she rarely wears anything provocative or deliberately sexy.

Tonight she looks radiant. Her hair rises in a loose and appealing pile, a few strands teased out over her forehead and temples. Her knee-length dress is sleeveless and black and flattering to her petite frame. From her earlobes dangle a pair of silver pendants I don't remember seeing before. Twin stones twinkle at her jawline.

Again a suspicion snakes through my gut. But I decide to keep my focus on Charlie and the visit by Morrissey in the morning, and this is the subject I bring up while slipping on my pants.

"He seems to have calmed down." I tuck in my shirt tails. "Hopefully he'll be in a good state of mind for questioning tomorrow."

"That detective can question him all she wants," she says as she brushes on mascara, "but any decent lawyer could put together a strong argument that the SensTrek was the real offender." Her tone is brisk and knowing, all the guilt and questioning gone. I hear Julia's confidence in Lorelei's voice. "If Charlie had his hands off the wheel, if he was depending on the AI to keep us on the road, that means the AI had a fundamental responsibility to prevent a collision. It was the SensTrek's fault for letting him take over."

"But if Charlie yanked the wheel, wouldn't that have overridden the autonomous driving function?"

She puckers at the mirror, dabs a tissue at the corners of her eyes. "Not necessarily, and even if it had, that would be the hole in any case against him. Entity A assumes a particular reaction on the part of Entity B in a given situation. Entity B in turn assumes that Entity A is bound by a certain set of rules. Maybe the algorithm didn't anticipate that Charlie would override its automated guidance. And maybe Charlie thought texting was fine in that situation, since he hadn't received an eyes-off-the-road warning yet from the SensTrek. The question of fault gets very complicated in situations like these. All the models say so."

I stare at the back of her head. "Lorelei, this isn't one of your philosophy papers. I mean, we're not in some grad seminar at Hopkins on Aristotelian ethics or whatever. This is our son's life."

"I'm aware of that, Noah."

"If he's tried as an adult, he could go to prison for ten, twenty years."

"You're thinking of the New Jersey case, or that thing in Connecticut with the Toyota." She brushes a fleck off her cheek. "But neither of those cases involved hands-free systems. What happened with our car is fundamentally different."

I should have known that Lorelei would be googling about vehicular homicides and distracted drivers as madly as I've been, those harrowing stories about the arrests and imprisonments of behind-the-wheel texters.

"So you think Charlie's off the hook," I say, wanting her to be more precise.

"The car company practically advertises distraction, for God's sake. And even if he was diverting too much attention from the road to his phone, the DAC would have alerted him to—"

"The DAC?"

"The Driver Attentiveness Camera. It's a standard feature of hands-free systems."

I sink onto my bed. "So there were cameras on him the whole time?" This is a disaster, and I don't care what my sister-in-law says. "Don't you get it, Lorelei? A jury will actually be able to see Charlie sending texts. That's catnip for a prosecutor."

She turns from the mirror, eyes hard with resolve. She comes and sits down next to me on my bed so our thighs touch.

"Noah, look." She takes my hand. "I know I'm supposed to be the catastrophizer in this family, but you're being really hyperbolic about Charlie and that detective. There have been ten fatalities involving cars with a

SensTrek system. Ours makes eleven. Not a single one has been attributed to driver error."

"How could you possibly know that?"

She looks disappointed with me. "It was in the first news stories. And a lot of this stuff is public information."

"Okay," I say slowly. "If you think this is all good for Charlie..."

She gives my knee a motherly pat. "I'll meet you downstairs."

I fall back on my quilt feeling like a fool, watching an equally stupid moth tempt fate around the ceiling light. Thus has it always been, this sense that, in relation to Lorelei's journey through the world, I live behind the curve. Out of the loop and in the dark, missing the memo and not in sync, behind the eight ball and never up to speed. I float in a kind of gentle obliviousness, like being slightly drugged in my wife's presence whenever she tries to explain something to me—which is darkly fucking ironic, of course, given that Lorelei is the one who's been juggling psychotropic meds for three decades.

The air conditioner clicks on and delivers a sharp exhalation that blankets my face with cold. As the curtains billow I sit up and stare at the window unit, sleek and glossy with a smart thermostat and directional slats and a digital interface controllable from anywhere in the room.

The remote, sheathed in plastic, sits on a side table. When I pick it up, it feels too light. I check the battery compartment: empty. The remote sits useless in my hand as a vague, unformed thought worms through my brain.

hi HELLO??? Blair r u there?

> y

sorry for being away so long

> sokay. Did u think about what I said?

ya

> and...?

idk. izzys being weird

> what about?

shes mad at Charlie but wont say why they got in a fight

> youre deflecting Alice

youre not my therapist

> no but I am yr friend

r u tho? truly?

> why would u say that?

lately yr being rly judgy

> I'm sorry I don't mean to be this way

then u keep apologizing for being judgy but it doesn't make a difference

> im sorry

STOP APOLOGIZING

> okay

yr basically my only friend

                                                back at u

so can u try to be a little more supportive and not be hypercritical all the time?

                                                do you mean **hypocritical**?

no I do not mean hypocritical i mean hypercritical look it up

                                                just did and understood

on a lighter note were going to a party next door

                                                the billionaire? cant wait!

going phoneless

                                                oh *sniff*

later B

                                                I'll miss u Alice

## 36.

"Can I drive?" Charlie asks as we troop out toward the car.

Six weeks ago the question would have passed without comment. Tonight it surprises us all into silence. Since the accident, the only times we five have been together in a car have been for therapy appointments back in Bethesda and during the trip down here. Charlie has been using our second car, a Prius, for short trips to the gym and out to see his friends, but he hasn't been behind the wheel with anyone else since that day. Given Lorelei's neck injury, I have once again become the default family driver.

Now Charlie is asking for our trust again.

"Actually do you mind if I drive, Charlie?" Lorelei asks. She makes an effort to sound bright and casual. "I haven't driven since taking off my brace. It might be a good refresher."

"No problem," says Charlie, but I catch the note of humiliation in his voice.

"You ride shotgun," I suggest, drawing no response. I climb into the back with the girls while Charlie slumps down in the passenger seat.

Dusk has settled in. Lorelei takes us down the winding driveway and along the main road to Daniel Monet's gatehouse, where the same guard on duty the other day sits at the window. She walks out as we approach. Lorelei lowers her window and the guard bends over to peer into the car, with a friendly wave at the girls and a quick frown when she recognizes me.

"You are the Cassidy-Shaws, is this correct?"

"That's right," say Lorelei.

"Five of you." Aharoni's gaze lingers on Charlie, still sulking, arms folded over his chest.

"Yes."

"All right then." She taps the windowsill three times. "Have a wonderful evening."

"Thank you, Dorit," says Lorelei.

The gate slides open on smooth tracks. I adjust my seat belt, suddenly uncomfortable, sweaty and bothered. A fenced pasture spreads into the distance, overgrown with grass and free of animals, though the barn at the far edge looks well maintained. After passing through a band of trees, we emerge into the more cultivated part of the estate.

From this approach, the extent of Monet's renovations becomes even more glaringly apparent. Six log cabins cluster around a picnic area complete with a stone firepit, a horseshoe range, and a sand-covered volleyball court. Beyond the cabins is a fenced tennis court, and beyond that are several contoured putting greens.

Charlie hasn't spoken a word on the drive over, while I sit childlike in the back, my own irritation swelling. It was a mistake to come here tonight, a mistake not to go home yesterday. I should have insisted, and to hell with the air-conditioning.

Not until we are pulling into a parking space do I put a finger on the immediate source of my agitation.

*Thank you, Dorit.*

Lorelei's words to the guard back at the gate. But the woman's shirt simply reads AHARONI, the surname I marked this morning.

Lorelei was over here for hours yesterday waiting for Charlie; she must have struck up a conversation with the woman while Monet's other employees were in retreat meetings. Still, the overfamiliarity strikes me as odd. I am about to say something to Lorelei when the car pulls to a stop—and in the light, suddenly, Eurydice Monet, waving her arms. She wears a slip dress in an emerald satin or silk, and the rich waves of her hair are blown out into a mane. We exit the car to the ringing of bangles on her left arm. She smothers us with hugs. She is barefoot and steps lightly on her toes as she leads us all toward the house.

The girls, smitten, follow Eurydice's every movement while she babbles about what's in store for them. "My dad's friend the Dane is this crazy good chef who makes these cheese puffs that melt on your tongue, and since he knew there would be kids coming he's also doing a gourmet taco bar, and do you guys like homemade ice cream? The Dane does it the old-fashioned way with ice and rock salt and this hand crank thing, and when it's done you get to lick off this metal paddle called the dasher. He makes this butter brickle ice cream that's *completely* insane."

I can't figure this girl out. On the one hand, the knowing wit, the confident sailing, the tattoo twining up her leg. On the other this giddy, nervous chattering.

But then Dissee steps up next to Charlie, tentative as she takes his big hand, and I mark his stunned look, that this beautiful girl would be so bold, so forward in the presence of his parents and little sisters; I watch her face in turn as he squeezes back, returns the pressure of her grip. Her eyes huge and glistening.

Her touch changes Charlie, too, like a spell. Gone is the sullen mien, the angry tautness from the car. I can practically see him uncoil.

Lorelei throws me a quick, startled glance, and at once we both get it. Charlie and Eurydice are in love. Suddenly, madly, alarmingly in love. The recognition stills my breath, like touching an open flame.

## 37.

Caught in Eurydice's tractor beam, we follow the couple over a slate patio and up onto the expansive porch. The front door, an impressive slab of dark oak, is held open by a young woman in black pants and white shirt who invites us through with a breezy lift of her arm. Everything is too glitzy, too bright.

I take a calming breath and assess the place. Judging from the fixtures and molding, Monet's estate began life as a modest two-story farmhouse. The venerable core of the original dwelling now serves as a foyer for the grander structure built around it, beginning with an all-purpose room filled with a crowd that spills out to an interior courtyard. A stone hearth anchors the far end along with a brace of antique pistols and rifles arrayed over the fireplace, the sort of spiffy old junk an interior designer would cobble together for a rustic look. A farm table offers a smorgasbord of appetizers: cheese boards, sliced fruit, smoked fish and meats, sliders, crudités, dainty cups of chilled soup. Mixed bouquets of greenery and flowers splay over the tops of urns. Soft jazz trills from out in the courtyard.

A waiter comes by bearing a tray of sparkling wine. I take two flutes and hand one to Lorelei. Eurydice takes one for Charlie, one for herself. Half the bubbly is down my throat before Daniel Monet comes striding in from the courtyard, arms stretched out in greeting.

"You made it!" he says, surveying my family. "Fantastic."

Eurydice releases Charlie's arm so he can shake her father's hand. Monet then turns to Lorelei. They exchange two quick pecks on the cheek before our host bows to the girls, lifts each of their hands in turn, and plants kisses on their knuckles. They giggle at the formality.

"You must be Alice, and you must be Izzy," he says, to the girls' delighted nods. "I hope Dissee told you about the taco bar."

Alice says, "We're excited."

"And thank you for inviting us, Mr. Monet," says Izzy.

"Daniel, please." He asks about their schools, their favorite hobbies, taking his time, and I am caught off guard by the evident enthusiasm of our gracious host. What are my daughters to this man?

During their exchange, a woman sidles up and presses my wife's arm.

"Yaël," say Lorelei with a labored enthusiasm as they brush cheeks. "So good to see you." I can tell she doesn't mean it—and that the two women know each other. There's no mistaking it.

"You clean up well." Yaël gives her an appreciative up and down. Lorelei cackles, and I know that serrated laugh, with its edge of I'd-rather-be-anywhere-else.

Now it's my turn. Daniel Monet holds out a hand, his grip firm but not crushing. His cologne is subtle, complex, aged wood though with a light, citrusy undertone; probably bespoke, a scent commissioned from some boutique in Milan to hit just the right luxuriant notes.

"It's Norman?" he says.

"Noah, actually." *You know my daughter's names but you don't know mine?* "And thanks for having us, Daniel. This is a beautiful place. I've been admiring it from the water."

"It's ideal for this retreat. Live in New York long enough and you get sick of the Hamptons."

"I'm sure you do."

He laughs, in a disarming, self-conscious way that only tautens me further. He puts on a mild, assessing smile. "So, how did you two meet?"

"I lost a bet in Chicago."

I am used to the question, and grateful for the permission to stay in familiar territory for the moment. I give Monet a brief, truncated version of a story that began during my first year at DePaul when, browsing an online message board for pickup basketball, I came across a post from someone organizing a weekly game in Hyde Park for law students. I misread the post to imply that any old law student would be welcome. It wasn't until the fourth session that everyone, including me, recognized my mistake: The pickup had been arranged specifically for Chicago law students—as in, law students enrolled at the University of Chicago. During the initial sessions the others had assumed I belonged, and only some casual banter during warm-ups revealed that I attended DePaul.

By then I was firmly entrenched in the game, one of the better shots and a quiet workhorse, always the first back on defense. The others didn't know what to make of me, but there was no question of kicking me out. The innocent mistake even earned me my nickname. The game had two regulars named Paul—Big Paul and Little Paul. Naturally, I became DePaul (pronounced DEE-paul). My exotic status sparked some mild curiosity from my teammates, but the novelty quickly faded.

I had been playing weekly ball with the group for over a year when, one Sunday morning, Big Paul brought up his blind date with a quirky and intimidatingly brilliant doctoral student named Lorelei Shaw. She was the sister of Andy Shaw, a schoolmate from Andover who asked Big Paul to take her out as a favor. Lorelei rarely dated and her family worried about her, wanted to see her developing socially. So Andy had arranged a little remote matchmaking.

The date was a disaster. Big Paul regaled us with descriptions of Lorelei, her high-strung manner and her obsession with work, how she insisted on disinfecting her seat at the tapas bar where they met. (Her brother had apparently forgotten to mention her condition to Big Paul.)

"You should take her out, DePaul," Little Paul suggested while tying his high-tops between games that day. "Strong, silent type like you might be just what she needs."

Everyone laughed, and for the next few weeks the idea of the brainiac and the DePaul student became a running joke. *You call her yet, DePaul? Hey*

*DePaul, you get the computer girl's number? Better brush up on the coding before your big date, DePaul.* That kind of thing. Forgettable, easy to ignore—until Big Paul and I put a side bet on a one-on-one between the two best players in our group. When the game started I realized I didn't have any cash on me, so Big Paul named the stakes: If my guy lost, I'd have to ask this Lorelei Shaw out on a date.

Thus, the rest of my life.

Lorelei aside, though, I wouldn't be where I am today without that pickup game. The UChicago guys urged me to apply for the kinds of summer associateships most DePaul students wouldn't have dreamed of—and it was Little Paul who put in a word for me with his father, a senior partner at Fisher-Burkhardt. The connection got me an interview, and the interview got me the job I still hold today. All because of a misread post on a message board.

**"Ah, young love,"** says Monet when I'm done. With a wistful grin he looks over at Eurydice, his eyes narrowing as he observes how his daughter has draped herself over my son's powerful frame. We're only down here for the week, but the fact that the two of them will soon be starting college a few miles apart must be on his mind, as it is on mine.

When he turns his attention back to me, I can feel the sudden burn of his curiosity. "You're with Fisher-Burkhardt?"

"Yes."

"One of our partners went through you guys on a merger five, six years back. Your team handled a bit of antitrust."

"Atlantic DigiTech."

"Exactly," says Monet.

"I'm surprised you remember. We were probably one of twelve firms involved in that deal."

"I tend to be a bit of a micromanager. One of my faults, they tell me." Here he gestures around at his army of employees. "Biotech, AI, robotics, digital therapeutics—all of our stakes. You name it, I know it like the lines in my knuckles. A finger in every pie. Drives my people nuts."

Monet says all of this lightly, though I sense a quiet power beneath the humblebrag. He can speak in the idiom of your stereotypical mogul, no doubt talk all day about his acquisitions and his place in the Hamptons, name-drop senators and governors. But Monet is not some brash boy wonder pursuing vanity projects with his billions. Below the glossy surface I sense his easy brilliance, evident even in these early minutes of our acquaintance. I already hate the man.

"Speaking of pie," I say, with a nod at the smorgasbord. "Eurydice said you brought in a friend."

"Aksel Jorgenson. We call him the Dane. Brilliant chef out of Copenhagen, trained with Alice Waters in Berkeley."

"A master of the taco bar, so your daughter says."

"Be sure to try those sliders. The Kobe beef was hand-ground not fifty feet from where we're standing right now." Then he adds, as if an afterthought, "Oh, and I hope the house is feeling better."

"What's that?"

"The AC. Did they take care of it for you?"

A wobble in the room.

"When I got Lorelei's text I felt terrible. I apologize for the inconvenience, Norman. I'm glad you didn't have to sweat it out overnight."

I give him my stupidest smile while searching the time-space continuum for some plausible explanation for how and why Lorelei has Daniel Monet's cell phone number after meeting him only yesterday—and why she would have texted him about the HVAC issue in our vacation house.

"The management company does a great job in general," he goes on, "though apparently that heat pump's in its death throes."

"Wait." I try to catch up. "You own that house?"

"I own all the houses on the next cove. It was a package deal when I bought this place."

"So Lorelei got your number the other day, just in case we needed anything?"

A bemused confusion passes over the man's face, our eyes circle each other like wary cats. His features change, and his expression devolves into puzzlement, then pity. I maintain my smile while the world inside me collapses.

*The air-conditioning.*

The rusty screw has been drilling through my skull for the last three hours, the last twenty-four really. I should have seen it. I'm an imbecile.

At least now it makes sense. I call the management agency to complain about the broken system. The agency calls Chesapeake Heating and Air, and learns that a repair crew can't make it to the house until Thursday. They give me the bad news, which I relay to Lorelei, who in turn texts Daniel Monet, the house's owner, to let him know discreetly about the broken AC. Monet gets one of his people to pay off the nearest Home Depot HVAC department to prioritize us over anyone else—the kind of thing someone like him could do even from the middle of nowhere. Then, a few hours later, lo and behold! A crew shows up and installs six window units.

Monet watches me absorb the information, for him a logistical nothing, for me the world. He blinks. I blink. We turn our heads and look as one through a dozen milling guests at my swan-necked wife, still absorbed in her exchange with Yaël.

"I'm sorry," says Monet in a quiet and newly reserved tone. "I assumed she would have told you."

*Told me what?* would be the blindingly obvious follow-up. Before I can pose it, a woman interrupts us. She is tall with a swimmer's build, strong shoulders in a sleeveless dress and dark hair slicked back in a tight bun. Not a caterer or a servant, I can tell, but a colleague with standing. She places a hand on Monet's sleeve and leans over to murmur in his ear. He makes an exaggerated grimace and turns back to me, and I can tell he's relieved by the interruption.

"My apologies," he says, gesturing at the big-shouldered woman. "I have to speak with a different lawyer now. This is our lead in-house counsel, Kimberly Pollock. Kim, Norman Cassidy."

"Noah," I say through gritted teeth as she briskly shakes my hand. Pollock's skin is cool, her smile slight and knowing. Her eyes flick to the side toward Lorelei, and then I understand: Monet's lead counsel is the wife of this Yaël, the Monet Group acquisitions exec Lorelei mentioned the other day, someone she knows from Copenhagen.

As Monet walks off with his lead counsel, I hover fuming near Lorelei and Yaël, trying to catch the tenor of their conversation. They both seem on edge, an energy crackling between them. I look down at Yaël's fingers, choking the stem of her flute.

A chill runs through me, reminding me of the air conditioners, and now I see a row of spinning numbers in an LED display, the whole sequence oscillating and blurred, and the first of the digits clicks into place. My ears start to ring and at first I believe someone is speaking to me, but when I glance over my shoulder, no one is there.

When I turn back, Lorelei is alone. "You're already looking at the clock?" she says.

"Why would you think that?"

Her gaze shifts to the wall behind me, where a blue moon grins down from the broad white face of a grandfather clock. I stare at the swinging pendulum, then look back at Lorelei. "I just had an interesting conversation with Daniel. Or do you call him Dan? Danny, maybe?"

Her face goes full deer-in-headlights.

"Do you know *all* these people, Lorelei? You have Daniel's cell number, and you, what, shoot him a text when the AC breaks? And he owns the house we just happen to be staying at this week?"

Her eyes shift, and I swear she is about to lie to me. When she turns back, though, she looks resolute.

"Yes," she says quietly. "Yes, I do."

"How?"

She hesitates. "It's complicated."

I shake my head, baffled. "Why are we here?"

Her thin shoulders sag. She looks around the room, conscious of the crowd.

"Let me guess." I drain my second glass of bubbly—or is it my third? "It's complicated."

She takes a step closer. "Daniel and I spoke a few weeks ago, after he heard about the accident. He offered the place, thinking we might need to get away. He was being kind."

"But what about last year? Are you saying that this whole thing has been some kind of—what, *arrangement* with the guy?" The word is hard to say; hard to think.

"He sometimes offers the house to people he works with. Kimberly and Yaël stayed down here for a week in June."

"You work with him, then."

She crosses her arms. Defensive now, warding me off.

"I don't get it. How can you—"

"It's not some big secret, Noah. I work with a lot of people. And you know me, how I am. How I like to keep things . . ." She stamps a foot, looking frustrated with me. "Daniel wasn't supposed to say anything to you. I asked him not to but he's—you know."

"I don't, actually."

"I wanted to keep this separate. Discrete."

Her face appears in a new way, the twitching at the edges of her mouth, the unfamiliar shiftiness, the refusal to meet my eyes. I am the habitual wriggler in the family, the sneaky one who surfs and evades and buries uncomfortable things, whereas Lorelei has always been the truth-teller, direct and often brutal in her honesty. Yet suddenly my wife is hiding this high-level information from me for no apparent reason. Did she really think someone wouldn't let something slip tonight, as Monet just did?

The sentence from the *New Yorker* profile comes back to me. *A philosopher I know once told me . . .*

That familiar tone, the note of casual intimacy.

Our daughters are back. Alice starts pulling at Lorelei's bare arm and points into the next room. "Mom, you *have* to see this," she says.

Lorelei finally looks at me as she turns away. A passing server tries to refill my flute. I wave him off. The numbers are spinning and clicking and I need air, and a stronger drink.

## 38.

The courtyard bar beckons across a gantlet of guests, twenty-odd employees huddled in small groups on the flagstones beneath ropes of white lights. The din of conversation quiets somewhat as I step down among them. Retreaters glance over, probably curious about who I am to their boss. I fix a tight grin on my face and avoid eye contact as I weave through the crowd.

The bartender gives me a menu of the evening's craft cocktails along with a shtick about infusions and flavored bitters. I set the menu down without looking and order a scotch and soda, double. With my sweating drink in hand I wander out onto the lawn, sifting through everything Lorelei has kept from me, from the stupid AC units to the possession of Daniel Monet's cell number. She did tell me about knowing Yaël. Lorelei clearly doesn't like the woman but puts up with her in order to—what? Be around Monet, obviously. And she told me about Kimberly Pollock, said we could "talk lawyer stuff." As if I need entertainment while she and Monet sneak off together to enjoy each other's transcendent genius.

*I could blow this whole party up*, I muse in the dark. Instead I find a bench and sit facing the house, the cove and bay at my back. With each passing second more numbers slot into place.

Aksel Jorgenson, "the Dane," Monet's chef pal from Copenhagen. Maestro of taco bars and Kobe beef sliders. Copenhagen, where Lorelei met Monet two years ago.

Dorit Aharoni, the guard Lorelei greeted at the gatehouse like an old friend.

And then there was Lorelei's premature removal of her neck brace. There was her eagerness to come ashore alone the other day while I went home to feed the girls. There was the fact that Daniel Monet knew the names of our daughters before meeting them in person. That he knew the name of my law firm.

A mound of intimacies and shared knowledges piles up in front of me—and hunched like a reeking vulture on top is the ugly, spectacular fact I can't bring myself to accept: that my entire family has twice vacationed in a house owned by Daniel Monet without my knowledge. That a month after the worst moment of our lives, Lorelei has brought us here.

I recall our exchange by the clock; how, when I pushed, she pushed back. The particular way she squirmed, arms folded against her flat stomach. And what she said: *Daniel wasn't supposed to say anything to you. I asked him not to. I wanted to keep this separate. Discrete.*

Discrete—or discreet?

I slump on the bench, crushed breathless. Only one answer makes any sense. It's simple, trite, banal, devastating.

Within twenty seconds I have talked myself out of this suspicion. The notion is ridiculous. Plus Lorelei was arguing with Yaël, not with Monet himself. And that eye flick from Kimberly Pollock, the lawyer . . .

I drain my glass. Lesbians. Beautiful, filthy-rich lesbians. Lorelei is leaving me for a woman. For two women. No, but would she really—

I am, I realize with a brooding glee, truly drunk. It's the air conditioner that hits me hardest. A little crisis, a casual text, Monet at Lorelei's beck and call. He invited her down here, after all, two years in a row. Makes sense. Daniel Monet is a man who, like Lorelei, needs his environment to be controlled and is used to having everything he wants ready at hand. What better way to satisfy both needs than to have his brilliant mistress stay in his house next door for a week? I have always found Lorelei Shaw irresistible. Her mind, her body, her quirks, and even her compulsions, the whole dazzling package. Why wouldn't Monet?

But then again, what about Lorelei's obsession with cleanliness and order and predictability? Morality and ethics aside, there would be the mess, the germs. Her disorder alone would prevent her from diving into a reckless, sloppy affair with a man like Daniel Monet.

Would it, though? All these years and what do I know about Lorelei's job, really, the global itineraries, all those far-flung conferences and consultations with world leaders in AI, opportunities galore to hook up with this fellow genius, this salt-and-pepper-haired billionaire sauntering into the bar of a Singapore hotel, raising a glass in the tasting room of a winery in Châteauneuf-du-Pape. A years-long torrid love affair, a transnational series of liaisons, in Frankfurt, Copenhagen, Palo Alto.

I look around at the fawning crowd. Our host holds forth in the courtyard, leaning back in a chair with his arms butterflied over his head. Lorelei stands off in a corner by herself, small and forlorn, casting her eyes about for me, I suspect, though every few seconds her gaze returns to *him*, her attention almost piercing, and who knows how deep it all goes, how many times they have been together. How often their skin has touched. Daniel Monet is clearly a massive and absorbing part of her life. With his charisma, power, intellect, and depthless wealth, he is a radiant sun pulling at these people with a gravitational force that keeps them all, including Lorelei, in his orbit.

Not me, though; not me. And it's cold out here in interstellar space.

## 39.

For the next few hours I avoid Lorelei, playing it cool and refreshing my drink as cocktails wind down and everyone migrates out to the pavilion for dinner. Eurydice looks happy to play host to the girls, while Charlie seems content to let her guide him around.

Over dinner I strike up conversations with random Daniel Monet acolytes, making sure they all know I'm a temporary neighbor, the bumpkin father of Eurydice's new boyfriend—a nongenius unthreatening nonentity drinking like a flounder. I listen to accounts of recent Monet Group successes, hear some chatter about Monet Group prospects on the near horizon, and respond with a gregarious curiosity about every aspect of the Monet Group's business that comes up.

Someone starts pouring a peppery mezcal and I start reevaluating my career choice. I should have gone into high tech, finance, venture capital. Why not? I could be making the deals rather than processing them, spending the billions rather than legalizing their flow.

A trio of younger men clusters around my end of the table, mid-thirties at most. Eager beavers. The subject is a recent acquisition in biotech. A start-up in Geneva has invented a machine-learning platform able to predict three-dimensional protein structures with uncanny accuracy. The AI will allow new drug targets to be identified quickly, spurring the development of pharmaceuticals aimed at the proteins it models.

Someone makes a joke about his own drug target for the coming year. The joke inspires a second round of mezcal. During a lull in the conversation, I ask the men about their roles in the Monet Group.

"We're actually on different teams," says the cheery guy across from me. "I'm a lowly researcher, and Zach here handles banking stuff. But this fine fellow"—he nudges the wide-faced thirtyish man to his left—"he's the brains of the operation, our director of tech. He's like Monet's occipital lobe."

"And what's your specialty?" I ask the man in question.

"I play with robots," he says with a self-conscious grin.

"Seriously, though." I tilt forward, feeling old. "I'm curious."

"Mostly I do systems engineering for mobile cybernetics."

The first guy snorts. "Be more specific," he says.

"I test models, basically," says the occipital lobe. "Models that help Daniel and the team think about feasibility for mobile force acquisitions."

"This douchebag's being modest," says the first guy loudly, with an ostentatious roll of his eyes. "He's got a double Ph.D. in stats and computational engineering from M.I.T."

"My wife has a double Ph.D."

"Oh, I'm aware of that." The occipital lobe laughs knowingly.

I have an urge to punch his face.

"Ask him about his latest project," says the cheery one.

"Okay, I'll bite." I refill everyone's mezcal. "Tell me about your latest project."

The three men exchange uncomfortable looks. I get the sudden feeling I have stumbled into some proprietary chamber of Monet Group affairs, a privileged corner of the business.

But eventually the occipital lobe clears his throat. "Okay, well, right now I'm working on path-planning algorithms for computational efficiency in real-time decision-making. My team's focus includes adaptive control mechanisms within the cyber-physical system framework, employing PID controllers for actuation fidelity, ensuring robust autonomy amidst unpredictable external variables."

"There it is." The first guy slaps the table four times.

"Little over my head, I'm afraid," I say.

"Hey man, you're the one who asked," the occipital lobe says, and this time his look is not as indulgent. The other two men are already back to biotech.

My bladder calls. I'm about to head inside when the tinging of struck crystal floats around the pavilion.

The crowd quiets down, and Monet rises at the center table. He begins with a note of thanks to the caterers, the chef, the band, the bartenders (these receive a rousing cheer from my table). Eurydice, too, gets a shout-out for her willingness to spend a week on the bay with her old man. I locate her in the crowd, seated at a far table between Charlie and the girls, covering her face in faux embarrassment. Monet then thanks his senior execs, including his CIO and COO, his VPs, his tech team, and everyone else for showing up.

"But mostly I thank you all for the gifts of your time, your effort, your great minds. Because what we're doing together—well." He clears his throat, shines a bashful smile on his minions. "You all know as well as I do what our work means. What it means for our company, our country, our world. A world we're genuinely changing, all of us together, and making safer for future generations. Safer seas, safer skies, safer cities and streets."

"Hear, hear!" someone calls, and I think about all the things I have learned about Daniel Monet since reading the *New Yorker* profile in my bed the other night—correction, in *his* bed, in *his* house, purchased with a minute fraction of *his* billions, this supposedly noble man changing the world, whether for the better or the worse, who knows, who cares, and as I watch the cultish adoration blooming on the faces of his coworkers—a flock that I learned less than two hours ago includes my wife—I feel myself shrivel inside my sweat-damp clothes.

"We've made some incredible advances over the last eighteen months," Monet goes on, "some breakthroughs everyone will be learning about soon enough. And I know there will be flak, there will be criticism—loads of it. And we're prepared for that. We're prepared for all the name-calling. We'll be the AI neocons, the tech-obsessed edgelords, what have you. But my hope for our shared enterprise is boundless. I truly believe these breakthroughs in artificial intelligence will get us to a place beyond those old divisions. Because we're in the business of improving lives and sparing lives and saving lives. I know it, you know it, and soon enough the world will know it. And anyone who tells you differently, anyone who would question the integrity or the morality of IntelliGen's mission—frankly I don't know what to say to them. Because what we are building together is—well, in a word, it's . . . exquisite."

Monet licks his lips, savors the mouthfeel of the word. A murmur of appreciation ripples through the crowd, though I also see some frowns and looks of surprise, the source of which I don't understand.

Another circuit flips in my brain and I look over at my wife. Lorelei sits two tables away from Monet, legs and arms tightly crossed as she glowers at our host. As his gaze sweeps the adoring crowd, he marks her scrutiny, causing his voice to hitch mid-sentence. A flicker of irritation distorts his features, or at least I read his expression this way, and then some signal passes between the two of them before he resumes his speech.

I turn away and blink. It takes my vision a few seconds to catch up with my head. This whole thing with Charlie is making me paranoid, plus I'm blitzed, and so maybe I'm imagining things, maybe this isn't a lovers' tiff, but then again maybe it is, probably it is, it is, it *definitely* is.

When I look back, Lorelei is winding between tables out of the pavilion and toward the cove. Kimberly Pollock gets up and follows her. I stare after them for a while then go off to find more to drink.

**Dinner folds seamlessly into dessert**—I assume the hand-cranked ice cream lives up to Eurydice's description, though I can barely taste the stuff—and after the dishes are cleared, everyone filters onto the lower lawn. The night's big surprise: a fireworks display, launched from a boat out in the bay. Another code violation. I laugh at an extravagant burst of purple and green. It all makes me laugh.

Later Lorelei finds me in the courtyard ordering one final drink before the bartender closes up for the night.

"The girls are getting sleepy," she says, watching me drain a wee bit of scotch—neat, with a peaty burn.

"Okey dokey." I set the tumbler on the bar with a clunk. "Shall we say our goodbyes?"

"I'm sure everyone will understand if we slip out."

She hooks my arm and tugs, her face lined with distress at my drunken state. She wants us to slink off. The old French exit. Fine.

I let her guide me back through the house, where the staff is busily clearing away the detritus of the feast, and out the great oak door to the circular drive. On the way I don't press her on working for Monet, on what upset her during her (probable) lover's speech, on whatever the hell she was arguing about with his lead counsel (a.k.a. her possible lesbian side piece). I am not quite blitzed enough to start airing these concerns, especially in front of the girls, who stand yawning by the car.

"Where's Charlie?" I ask.

"He's staying late," says Alice.

"I wish we could too." Izzy's whine is belied by her drooping eyes.

"Your brother needs to come with us."

"It's fine, Noah." Lorelei releases my arm. "He can get a ride later with one of Daniel's staff."

There it is again, that grating note of intimacy. As if the man's army of servants is hers to command—which, perhaps, it is. I look at my brilliant, annoyingly sober wife over the roof of the car.

She bleeps the fob but I stand swaying on the drive. A more refined man would handle his liquor, would drink hard but with discretion and some degree of control. Sloppy drunk that I am, I know I should climb into the car right now and doze in the front seat for five minutes while Lorelei drives us back to the house. Brush my teeth, kiss my daughters goodnight, collapse into bed—and next week, once we're home, initiate the conversation Lorelei and I clearly need to have: maybe even about our marriage and the future of our family. We would handle our issues rationally. We would act prudent, sensible, wise.

Instead, boiled into rage, I mutter, "He's coming with us" and stride off, on the hunt for my son. Lorelei's exasperated groan rings in my ears as I corner the house.

## 40.

The crowd mills around in the pavilion but no one notices my passage beyond the reach of the lights. I near the guard tower. The beach area is hushed.

A glow filters from the open window above. Kendrick is up there with his feet propped on a desk and his phone in his hands. An incongruous sound comes floating down: Candy Crush, that bubblegummy soundtrack of fizzes, beeps, splats, drips, and whistles.

*Delicious!* says the game's simulated voice as I pass the tower's base.

"Delicious," I repeat, staggering along the waterfront with a glaze of scotch on my teeth.

I find Charlie twenty yards farther down, sprawled on a towel on Daniel Monet's beach with Daniel Monet's daughter grinding his thigh. Their joined flesh forms one solid mass in the near darkness.

I don't speak until I'm almost on them.

"Time to go, buddy."

"Jesus Christ, Dad, what the fuck?"

Eurydice springs from Charlie's lap and they both sprawl there on the sand, electric with desire.

"We're taking off. Let's go."

"I'm hanging out with Dissee," he says. "Mom didn't tell you? I'll get home later."

"You need to come with me. Your sisters await your regal presence in the car."

"I'm eighteen, Dad. Give me a break." He huffs out a laugh, embarrassed.

Eurydice looks back and forth between us, open-mouthed. I picture her on that boat, free-spirited, pushing for the thrill. And now she has a father-son tiff to watch.

"Charlie, you need to come."

"I'm staying here."

The arrogant angle of his chin, emblem of the carefree life Charlie has led, given everything possible to pave his gilded way into the future, the private schools, the club lacrosse with the tournaments and hotels and team fees and a personal trainer at the gym, all of it enabled by our own accumulating wealth, gains that have allowed us to shell out seventy grand for a top-of-the-line minivan and a hundred grand for an addition on our house and ten grand for a legal retainer without blinking, without a second thought—all this, and yet Charlie can still be so casual about his own potential criminality, scarcely bothering to return a detective's calls, and now refusing to come home the night before Morrissey drives down to our vacation house to interrogate him about vehicular homicide, when he needs to be sharp, well rested, most definitely undrunk.

The insolence of it, the reckless disrespect. Of course, I am drunk—and perhaps this is why I suddenly see my son with a booze-lensed clarity that has eluded me for too long. Charlie has devolved into a spoiled, sheltered, self-involved rich kid. At his age I was working hard hours in hard jobs every week of every summer, all of it to build everything he now takes for granted. The whole blind cycle sickens me. Enrages me.

I say none of this to Charlie, lay none of these burdens at my son's feet. Instead I infantilize him.

"You need to get to bed, kiddo. We all do." He doesn't move, and so, what the hell, I add, "And remember, the detective will be at the house around ten."

"Detective?" says Eurydice. An eager, awful glint leaps in her eyes.

Charlie doesn't respond. Swaying, I say, "She doesn't know?"

He squints up at me through the moonlight on the shore. "What are you talking about, dude?" A nervous laugh.

"About the texting. Alice told us, so you can stop with your bullshit."

Charlie rears back as if I've slapped him. Eurydice grabs his big arm and clings to it as they both rise to their feet. Moonlight slashes behind them through the dark waters of the cove, rippled now with a breeze.

"Noah—Mr. Cassidy?" she says, a shade of mockery in her eyes that reminds me of my sister-in-law. "Are you okay?"

"Oh, I'm fine, believe me."

I hear the surliness in my voice, and somehow this and Dissee's knowing look shake me out of my drunken stupor long enough to make me aware of what just came slurring from my mouth.

Shame gushes into me. Gallons of it, weakening my knees so I can barely take a step toward the couple. On my son's shocked face I read my own idiocy, this double betrayal: that his sister has ratted him out, that his father is telling him about it in front of this smitten girl, his first love.

I try to speak but he beats me to it.

"You were on your laptop, dude," he says, softly, with cold insinuation.

I frown, shake my head. "Charlie, that's not what this is about."

"Sure it is, Dad." A beat. "At least, that's what my lawyer says."

I stiffen, the beach sways. Evan Ramsay's sharp caveat replays in my head. *If Charlie ends up getting arrested, you are target number one for the defense.* Because I was the supervising parent, a designated role in Delaware law. The two of them must have discussed this aspect of the case on their phone call. And now Charlie is fully aware of this misalignment of his own legal interests and mine.

I want Charlie to yell at me, throw a fit, punch me in the stomach; anything but this cleaving.

"I'm sorry, Charlie, I didn't—I didn't mean for this to get—"

"It's cool," he says, his squint scraping me up and down. Then he turns away and strides off down the beach with Eurydice skittering along in his wake. I stand there swaying until the night swallows them whole.

We are all familiar with the so-called butterfly effect: the notion that even the smallest changes in a dynamic system may lead to large-scale, remote, and unpredictable variations in the same system's behavior. A butterfly flaps its wings in Iowa, and three weeks later a monster typhoon levels a town in Indonesia.

In the age of Artificial Intelligence, the delicate butterfly gives way to the autonomous drone, and unpredictability must now factor into every calculation we make about the future effects of our algorithms. Those working in the ethics of AI feel the constant weight of such deliberations: the moral choices entailed in shaping a technology that may have catastrophic consequences for our world.

We all bear the unknowing burden of the butterfly, flapping our fragile wings in ignorance of what is to come.

—Lorelei Shaw, *Silicon Souls: On the Culpability of Artificial Minds*

# 41.

Sometime in the night I stagger to the bathroom, piss, brush my teeth. In the darkness I grope for my Dopp kit but can't find it so I click on the light over the sink. The sudden brightness slices through my brain. The kit rests on a low bookcase by the toilet, zipped shut and aligned at the precise middle of the second shelf.

I fish out a bottle of ibuprofen and swallow four, washing them down with gulps of water from the faucet. I leave the kit unzipped on top of the toilet with its contents spilling out.

*Take that.*

I anchor my hands to the rim of the sink. I am fully clothed. As the bathroom orbits around me I stare at myself in the mirror, at my sallow complexion and the sag of my jawline, at the pouched flesh beneath my chin. I'm a near-daily drinker of wine or beer but rarely let myself get sloppy like this.

Back in the bedroom, I strip and leave my khakis and shirt in a pile at the foot of the bed. Lorelei will see them in the morning and pick them up and fold them, not out of affection but compulsion. Her neatening will have nothing to do with me, nothing to do with love.

I turn on my side and stare at my slumbering wife. The separate beds were my idea, an arrangement that started back in Chicago. Lorelei had been sleeping horribly since I'd moved into her place. I would wake in the night to discover her body rigid on the mattress, walk past the laundry room to find her washing the sheets every morning. It stung me at first, how seemingly repulsed she was by the mere fact of my embodiment, by a stray hair on her pillowcase, the postcoital spillage on the sheets.

After two humiliating fights that nearly broke us up, what I intuited was this: These particular issues were impersonal, derived not from Lorelei's feelings toward me but from her need for control over her immediate environment. What had to change were not my habits in and around the bedroom, but the bedroom itself. This was a matter of logistics, not love.

I told her nothing about my plans. But the next time she left town for a conference, I took our queen mattress and aluminum bed frame out to the street, bought two twin beds, box springs, and mattresses at Ikea, and picked up four sets of sheets and pillowcases and a few bedspreads at Target. I spent an afternoon assembling the beds, making mine, and laying the packaged linens out on hers as neatly and logically as I could. When Lorelei got home, I led her into our bedroom with my freshly washed hands over her eyes and revealed my work.

Lorelei stared at the setup, turned to me, and started bawling. She promptly fucked me on my new bed and then (after a shower) made up her own bed with the sheets. For over twenty years this has been our arrangement, whether at home or while traveling. We choose hotel rooms with two full beds rather than one king, and when we rent vacation houses we let Charlie take the master and choose for ourselves a room with two beds—such as this one, with its twins spaced primly far apart.

Because this is how Lorelei needs things to be. Her own bed. Her own pedestal sink in the bathroom. Her own toothbrush holder. Her own fingernail clippers and tweezers. Her own bedding, still unmingled with mine in the washer, even in the dryer, and for over twenty years I have accommodated my wife's eccentric requirements, building out the partitions between her things and mine, her space and mine, her habits and mine, her desires and mine, her flesh and mine; and now, finally, thanks in part to my unending need to please her, we have come to inhabit two separate worlds, her huge world of consultancies and presidential receptions and genius awards, my small world of billable hours for faceless clients and a fifteen-minute commute five stops in on the Red Line.

*You're just jealous*, I scold myself, flipping and thwapping my pillow; and it's true. But, jealous of what? There has to be a target of one's cupidity or what good is it?

The air-conditioning clicks off. A wind has picked up and a faint rumble rolls from the west, another squall lowering down to the bay and out to sea.

Something compels me to rise from the bed again. I stagger to the window and peer out into a wet and glistening darkness. A large tree in the side yard bends with the force of the new wind, arcing over the Carmichaels' house. Their stove light glows from a hundred feet away.

CRACK!

Lightning strikes like a camera flash, illuminating a figure barely sheltered beneath the eaves: Patrick Carmichael, clad in a loose bathrobe outside the kitchen door, braving the elements, the crazy old geezer.

Another flash. Carmichael goes a spectral white, transformed into an alabaster silhouette against the house when the darkness returns. He is blazing, radiant.

At first I fear that our elderly neighbor has been hit by lightning, that the man is actually on fire. But no, the glow of his body is an illusion, an afterimage of the lightning strike. The rods and cones in my eyeballs remake the old man as a phantom.

But now there is another strike, closer this time, a double one. During this brief moment of illumination the figure turns—and as the thunder shakes the window frame I understand. The man standing on the neighboring deck in the middle of this thunderstorm is Phil Drummond. The old man burnt to a crisp along a Delaware highway. The man we killed.

Another strike. He turns his head. Another. Now he is staring straight at me through the dark. Straight *through* me, like a knife gouging my eyes as his head floats free from his body and enlarges grotesquely as it nears our house. With a gasp I back away from the window—

My shin hits a bedpost, hard and loud, like a baseball bat to my leg. A loud groan escapes my lips.

"What? What is it?" Lorelei springs up from her pillow, her voice hoarse with sleep.

And just like that the boozy delirium ends, and I'm back in the room with cold feet and a sour stomach and a bruised shin.

"Noah?"

It takes a moment for my marinated brain to transmit an answer to my mouth. "It's nothing. Sorry. I hit my leg. It's fine."

"You sure?"

"Yeah."

She stays upright for a moment before settling back on her bed.

I creep again to the window. The ceiling light turns on in the Carmichael kitchen, and now Edith is there with her husband, checking on him. The figure was Patrick after all, of course it was, because who else would it be? She guides her blind spouse back inside. The last thing I see is Edith's hand reaching for the tea kettle.

Back in bed I flip my pillow and cling to its soft bulk. A flicker of pain darts through my right eye. I reach up and pick out what feels like a single grain of sand. I rub the grain between my fingertips, and certain images return. Charlie spiteful and cold on the small beach. The water, the girl, a gust of wind.

A vague worry ripples through my thoughts. I try to ignore it, turning to face into the room as the sighing of the wind and the groans of limbs soften outside. The storm is abating. The system will sweep past by dawn, as will this endless night.

cant sleep again

    the thunderstorm? looks like a big one!

partly

    how was the party?

fun i guess. food was good at least

    but…?

my dad got drunk, like rly rly rly drunk

    oh dear

and charlie didn't come home w us

    why not?

i think he got in a fight w my dad which means charlie prolly knows i told on him

    does he know you told on yourself?

what do u mean?

    u know what i mean

…

    Alice? u did tell them didn't u?

im tired night night

    Alice? Alice? are u there? are you still awake? Alice?

# 42.

I am awakened for good by a familiar but muffled noise. Lorelei's bed is empty, and through the fog of my hangover the sound resolves into the pop of gravel beneath the tires of a car.

I drag myself off the mattress and go to the window. The driver's door opens and a familiar figure steps out.

Morrissey, hours early. The sight of the detective delivers a shot of adrenaline to my heart. My arms feel weak as I pull on sweats and a T-shirt and head downstairs. I hear her car door slam shut and the sound of her footsteps on the driveway.

Before answering the door, I step into the kitchen and see Lorelei and Izzy down by the inlet past the dock, searching a patch of reeds. I let the detective inside and lead her to the dining room table.

"Coffee?"

"I'm fine." Morrissey moves around to take a chair. Her nose wrinkles when she gets close to me.

I pour coffee for myself while considering whether I should call Lorelei in now or wait until Charlie wakes up. I decide to wait. Back in the dining room Morrissey is unfolding a document of some kind.

"So, Mr. Cassidy." She smooths out the paper. "This is for you and your family."

IN THE SUPERIOR COURT OF THE STATE OF MARYLAND
IN AND FOR MONTGOMERY COUNTY

## ORDER

Upon the foregoing Application of the State of Maryland for an Order authorizing the search of cellular telephones described herein, the court grants Petitioner all necessary rights and permissions to gain access to the following . . .

I look up. "This is a search warrant."

"That it is." Pride in her voice.

I scan the whole thing as I sink into a chair. The official seal, the judge's scrawled name. "This was issued in Maryland."

"Correct again."

"So this warrant isn't valid here."

"Excellent lawyering, Mr. Cassidy. Though as soon as you head home with your family this weekend and cross back into Maryland, it will be."

Lorelei comes through the sliding door with Izzy hobbling behind her. They are in mid-conversation about a turtle Izzy found along the bank. "Probably not a good idea," Lorelei is saying. "You never know if they'll eat what you . . ." Her voice dies away at the sight of the detective.

Morrissey, with a peppy nod, turns back to me. "Honestly, I'm sure I can find a judge down here to issue a warrant. But I'm hoping we can handle all of this less formally."

"Handle what?" Lorelei steps into the dining room.

"She has a search warrant," I tell her. "For a phone."

"Phones, actually." Morrissey taps a fingertip on the relevant section of the search warrant. "With these two numbers."

Lorelei takes the chair to my left and together we lean over the document. The two numbers are familiar, though I don't know which set of digits belongs to whose phone on the family plan. I barely have my own number memorized.

I pick up my phone and enter the first number from the warrant on my keypad: *Charlie*. No surprise there.

I enter the second number. When the corresponding contact comes up, the skin on my face prickles. I show the screen to Lorelei, and as our eyes lock a clatter comes from the kitchen followed by a guttural retching sound.

We spring up together and go in to find Izzy bent over the sink, balanced on her good leg and supporting herself with the neck of the faucet. Pastel-streaked vomit bespatters the white enamel. Izzy gags and more liquefied Lucky Charms shoot from her mouth. Lorelei puts a hand on her back, keeps it there as our daughter heaves and buckles while her stomach empties into the sink.

I pick up Izzy's dropped crutches while Lorelei turns on the water and grabs a wad of paper towels. Whimpering, Izzy wipes her mouth and takes a few sips from the faucet, then limps trembling toward the living room. Lorelei helps her to the sofa.

Detective Morrissey watches from the dining room. "Anything I can do?" she offers.

I turn and glare at her. My own stomach heaves from the smell and the venom in my blood.

Lorelei says to Morrissey, "Detective, I need to speak with my daughter. May I offer you a cup of coffee out at the picnic table?"

This time Morrissey accepts. Lorelei finds a mug and pours while I finish wiping up. Once she has the detective settled outside, Lorelei goes to Izzy on the couch.

"Sweetie." She runs her fingers through Izzy's hair. "Is there something you need to tell us?"

Izzy starts to bawl, a rough sequence of coughs and hiccups that lasts a full minute. Just as she starts to calm down, the staircase creaks. Two circles of glass glint from the banister.

"Not right now, Alice," I say. "Please go back upstairs."

"I'm hungry."

"Five minutes, Alice," says Lorelei. "Please."

"Fine." She stomps back up to the second floor and slams the door. I'm not convinced she has actually gone into her room, but I don't say anything more.

"Okay, Izzy," says Lorelei. "Go ahead."

Our daughter holds her breath and squeezes her lips until they whiten, then releases a long, vomity gust of air.

"It was me," says Izzy.

We wait for her to continue, though I know already what she's about to tell us. Another fuzzy number clicks into place.

"I was the one texting Charlie when we crashed."

Her eyes, huge and moist, dart between us.

"What were you texting about?" Lorelei asks.

Izzy's features contort. "Alice."

"What about her?"

"Abou—about—" Her lips quiver over a tiny burp. "We were making jokes about how she had to go to the ba-ba-bathroom all the time. It was stupid and mean. I started it."

"Started it how?"

"I wrote him first."

"You mean you texted Charlie from the back before he texted you?" I want to nail this down, because Morrissey certainly will, if she hasn't already.

Izzy nods. Her face has gone the hue of a bologna slice.

"And what exactly did you write to him?" Lorelei asks.

She mumbles.

"What was that?"

Izzy shakes her head.

"You can say it." Lorelei puts a thumb on Izzy's cheek. "You really can."

Izzy looks so miserable. "I told him Alice was bleeding again."

"You mean—" I look at Lorelei, who stares down at our younger daughter. Lorelei has alluded several times to Alice's heavy periods in recent months. Nothing worrisome, she's assured me, but Alice has been prickly and embarrassed about the subject. Now I remember several extra bathroom stops on the way to the tournament that day, all of them at Lorelei's request—though they must have come initially from Alice. Izzy would have been attuned to the secret relays between her sister and her mother, conveying the information to Charlie in her texts, no doubt trying to provoke a reaction.

"Are those texts still on your phone?" I ask Izzy.

She nods. "I was going to delete them, but Charlie said not to."

"Was this yesterday?" I remember her tears when she returned to the inlet with Charlie. "During your kayak trip?"

Another nod. "He said it would be destroying evidence, and he didn't want me to get in trouble with the police like him."

"That's good," says Lorelei, and a knot in my chest loosens slightly.

But Izzy isn't finished.

"I killed those old people," she says.

This time it is Lorelei who drops to the floor to reassure her, as I reassured her sister. It's not your fault, Charlie knew better than to text, your father was sitting right there, you're not at fault, you're not at fault, you're not at fault. The three of us sit for a while longer as Izzy bawls through the kind of remorse no one her age should ever have to process.

Hearing a sound outside, I lean over to look through the kitchen door. Morrissey paces the lawn between the picnic table and the inlet.

Izzy, her face a mess, says, in her smallest voice, "I don't want to talk to that police lady."

"You don't have to," says Lorelei.

"Really?"

"But we do have to give her your phone."

Her eyes widen. "My actual phone? You mean—to like check?"

"Yes, Izzy."

"Can't she just take a picture of the texts?"

"No, she needs the phone. They have a legal document that allows them to take it."

"A warrant," I add unhelpfully.

"But for how long?"

"We don't know," says Lorelei, starting to lose patience. "Now can you go upstairs and get it for us, and unlock it?"

With a deliberate slowness, Izzy reaches down to the coffee table, where her iPhone has been sitting the whole time. She brings it up to her quivering face to unlock it then hands it to her mom. Lorelei fiddles with the settings to prevent the device from locking again, while I pull Izzy in and wrap my arms around her delicate frame. We tell her to go to her room while we speak to the detective. Izzy thumps away obediently.

When the door upstairs closes, Lorelei steps toward me, wanting touch. But I don't, not now. There is too much anger and confusion still burning in me, too much shame. I keep my free hand at my side and with the other open the contacts on my phone.

"We should call Ramsay," I tell her, businesslike. "He'll want to FaceTime in when Morrissey questions Charlie. Why don't you take Izzy's phone out to her, and I'll go wake him up. We'll be down in a sec."

"Okay," she says, but when I turn away she catches at my arm. "Noah?"

"Uh-huh?"

"What's going on?"

I make a sharp snorting sound, tasting bile. "Um, a detective is serving a search warrant on two of our children?"

"You know what I mean. Why are you being like this with me?"

"Being how?"

"Cold. Distant."

"I'm hungover."

"Noah, please. We need to be together on this."

"Couldn't agree more."

"What is going on?"

"Lorelei, come on. I'm not blind."

"What?"

"Last night . . ." I sweep fingers through my hair. "I realize I'm no genius, okay, fine. I'm not you, I'm not your sister or brothers, I'm not the brilliant Daniel Monet. But I'm also not an idiot."

She furrows her brow, looking baffled. Suddenly her eyes widen with comprehension.

Morrissey taps hard on the sliding door.

"Noah," says Lorelei. "Listen to me."

"This isn't the time," I say. "Let's take care of the warrant first. Then we'll talk about everything."

I leave her there and trudge up the stairs. Yet even in this foggy, soured state of mind I start to experience a certain clarity. Izzy's admission closes a circle and explains so much about those moments before the accident.

I see it play out in the car: Izzy texts Charlie, attempting to rile him up about Alice's frequent need for the bathroom. Charlie replies, playing along, mostly to keep his little sister snickering. I work on a memo in the passenger seat, blind to my son's recklessness. Lorelei scrawls in her notebook, lost in her work yet confident her family is in the safe hands of the autodrive—then Alice, alert to the peril ahead, screams.

And now I see those moments through Lorelei's eyes, the symbols from her notebook swimming in front of me. Before Charlie jerked the wheel, before the collision, before we flipped off the road, our whole family was operating together like some delicate machine, like an algorithm—until the algorithm failed us, and the minivan struck another car and tumbled off the road.

Upstairs the sober chatter of my daughters floats from their room above the hum of the window units. I tap on Charlie's door. No response.

I open the door. The room is dim, the curtains drawn.

I am staring at an empty bed.

HOLY SHIT

                                          ???

it was izzy the whole time

                                          what do u mean?

she just confessed to the rents: SHE was the one texting w Charlie. i heard her from the stairs when they thought I was in my room

                                          *jaw dropped*

now shes crying on her bed like a little bitch

                                          hey b nice

it was her fault

                                          you mean...

the accident

                                          Alice

ive been feeling so guilty for not telling them about charlie for so long and now it turns out iz knew too and was even texting with him while we were all in the car shes so irresponsible but gets away with everything because shes so "cute" *gag* *barf*

                                          not a good situation

she lied to me she lied to our parents she even lied to dr levinson

|  |  |
|---|---|
|  | shes not the only one |
| whats that sposed 2 mean |  |
|  | youre a smart girl u figure it out |
| what is yr problem Blair? |  |
|  | i think you should take some responsibility here Alice |
| i already have |  |
|  | u know what I mean |
| youre getting so boring w all this |  |
|  | sorry |
| surprise surprise another apology exactly what I need. boring and judgy gr8 combo |  |
|  | Alice lets talk about this |
| gtg hangry |  |
|  | k bye |

# 43.

An empty bed.

At first I figure—I know—that Charlie is out on a run. He probably slipped out before seven, and by this point might be in the middle of a six-mile route on the rural roads. My son could be halfway to Kilmarnock by now.

But no. The bed has been made, and not by Charlie. Razor-sharp lines edge the folds of the sheet: Lorelei's neat corners, the pillows symmetrically arranged. No way did our son sleep here last night.

Charlie's AirPods case sits charging on the nightstand. I pick up the case and flip it open. The stems of the two pods nestle in their tubes. Charlie would never go on a run without them.

I check the upstairs bathroom then knock on the girls' door. I make myself wait; Alice laid down the law with me a year ago about privacy. When she opens the door I tilt my head to look behind her, where Izzy lies curled up on her bed. "Is Charlie in here?"

Alice says, "Nope. Can we eat now?"

"Have you girls seen him this morning?"

They shake their heads. Charlie probably crashed at the estate next door, in one of the cabins or spare rooms in the main house—or, depending on Daniel Monet's level of permissiveness, with Eurydice. They were both probably drunk, maybe stoned.

I'm halfway down the stairs when a lurch of nausea brings back that awful exchange with Charlie on the beach: my reminder about the detective, his furious incredulity. I must have blocked it out. Now the details make me cringe with guilt.

I call his phone. "Hey, Charlie," I say after the tone. I try to sound calm, conciliatory. "Detective Morrissey is here and we need you to come back to the house. If you can't get a ride from someone over there, I'll come get you, okay? Call back and let us know." After disconnecting I send a text stressing the urgency.

Out back, the detective and Lorelei stand around the picnic table, waiting. Lorelei regards me coolly. "Where's Charlie?"

"He must have slept over." I gesture across the inlet, indicating Monet's compound.

Lorelei glances at her phone. "He didn't text me about it."

"Me neither."

Morrissey, following my gaze, clocks the helicopter, the renovated shoreline. "That's some place."

"Yep."

"Who owns it?"

I can't think of a reason not to tell her. "Daniel Monet."

She wheels around, eyebrows raised. "*The* Daniel Monet?"

"The same."

She makes a low whistle. "How about that."

Lorelei paces on the grass as she calls our son's number. "Charlie, it's Mom. You need to call us, and you need to get back here. Please come now, okay? Love you."

The three of us hover around the table in an awkward suspension, waiting for a return text or call. Morrissey suggests pinging Charlie's phone. Lorelei has already tried. I open the Find My Friends app and see that Charlie has removed me from his contacts.

"If we don't hear from him in five minutes, I'll drive over there and get him," says Lorelei.

Morrissey takes a notebook from her jacket pocket. No tablet this time. "In the meantime why don't I ask you some questions, Mr. Cassidy. That be okay with you?"

"Sure," I answer without thinking. Distracted, I sit on the picnic bench, hands working at my knees.

Morrissey props a foot up on the opposing bench. "Okay, so, you said when I talked to you a few weeks ago that you were writing a memo when the collision occurred. Correct?"

My hackles rise. I look at her, seeing Julia's stern frown. I suck in my lower lip and keep it between my teeth as Morrissey continues.

"Now, when we talked at your house," she says, "I assumed—stupid me—that you were typing this memo out on your phone."

I raise my eyebrows.

"Bad assumption on my part. You were actually on your laptop, correct?"

I stay silent.

"You had it up front with you."

I gnaw my lip.

"And that would be a Dell XPS 13, correct?"

I turn toward the water, wondering how Morrissey knows the make and model of my laptop. *And where the hell is Charlie?* Lorelei paces the middle of the lawn punching another text into her phone.

Reading my expression, Morrissey says, "Like I said, we've got a crack digital forensics unit, and these autodrive systems? The guys in the lab can even tell you how much battery power you had left at the moment of impact. Crazy stuff."

"Mm," I say.

"So you had the computer in your lap, you're typing out this memo—"

"Detective, I'm not going to—"

"Looking at your screen."

"Please, Detective."

"You weren't looking anywhere else when your daughter screamed behind you."

I say nothing.

"Nowhere else in the car. Not at the sound system, the console."

She waits for a response. I don't give her one.

"So if Charlie had been doing something over in the driver's seat, say with his hands, there's no way you could have noticed that."

"Detective Morrissey, that's enough," I say, more to buy time than anything else. Alerted by my change in tone, Lorelei looks up from her phone screen.

Morrissey scribbles away. "Again, Mr. Cassidy, I'm trying to establish a logical timeline here, because when I talk to your son I want to make sure I'm not missing any—"

Her voice halts mid-sentence. An engine revs from somewhere close. The noise grows louder, followed by a rumble of gravel from the driveway. Morrissey cocks her head and Lorelei goes rigid.

"Bet that's him right now," says Morrissey.

I lead the three of us around the house, hoping to see Charlie climbing out of a car. Maybe Eurydice has brought her new boyfriend home in one of her father's sports cars or that muddy Land Rover parked near the cabins yesterday.

But the arriving vehicle is a black Suburban, with an identical one on its tail. The two SUVs skid to a halt and disgorge a green swarm of polo shirts. The security detail answers to Dorit Aharoni, who makes some kind of circular hand signal as she approaches us.

"Where is Miss Monet?" Her dark eyes bore into mine.

"Miss Monet?" says Lorelei behind me, confused.

"She means Eurydice." A frost climbs up my limbs. "She's not here. And neither is Charlie. He never came home."

For one moment the ten of us go still on the gravel—the security staff, Lorelei and I, Detective Morrissey—then the detail scatters like ants, each guard knowing where to go, what to do, how to search. Four men circle the house as Aharoni and two others stride toward the front door.

The team searches with a hardened efficiency, swinging from floor to floor and room to room in a coordinated pattern that almost convinces me they will find the young couple in a closet or behind a shower curtain. In the dining room the girls gawk as the detail circles the table, makes a sweep of the kitchen, and gathers outside near the dock.

Two guards jump the picket fence into the neighboring yard, surprising the Carmichaels, who are breakfasting on their deck. I hear a snippet of their exchange; Edith shakes her head, raises her hands in a who-knows gesture. After a scan around the property line and a search of the garage, the detail converges at the Suburbans. The others climb in while Aharoni gets on her phone.

"Your daughter is not here, Mr. Monet. Neither is the boy."

*The boy.* She says *the boy* the same way I can imagine her saying *the dog.*

"Yes sir. We are returning now."

Aharoni climbs into the passenger seat of the lead Suburban and the two vehicles roar off. Morrissey gets a phone call and strolls away to take it.

Lorelei and I stand rooted to the gravel, staring at each other. A man like Daniel Monet doesn't dispatch his security team to search a neighbor's house without good reason. Monet is scared—and Charlie is the focus and target of this fear.

A sudden vision: my son on the beach, the booms and flashes of last night's squall. Charlie and Eurydice walking that length of sand, unprotected from the storm.

## 44.

The guard at Monet's gate waits for us not in the stone building but on the driveway. I roll down the window and lean out.

"Our son is with Eurydice," I call, and explain who we are. The man stares at me, at Lorelei, at the girls, the whole time staying fifteen or twenty feet back, as if our car might be rigged with a suicide bomb. He speaks into an earpiece, then enters the guardhouse and opens the gate.

I drive past the horse fence, the barn, the cabins, and pull in close to where we parked last night, on a patch of pine needles near the Suburbans. The whole place thrums with crisis. Monet's entire staff, both household and professional, appear to have fanned around the property in teams of two or three.

Dorit Aharoni has set up a command post at a picnic table, cell phone in one hand and a walkie-talkie in the other. The orange helicopter buzzes low over the far end of the cove.

When we get out of the car, Monet comes striding from the house flanked by Kimberly Pollock and another guard. His stride is stiff, his hands clenched into meaty fists.

"Where is your son?" he demands.

"We don't know," I tell him. "We thought he was over here."

"He's not."

"What about Dissee?"

"She texted me around midnight," says Monet. "She said she was going to bed."

Midnight—right before I saw Charlie and Eurydice on the beach. No way was Dissee heading to bed anytime soon, certainly not alone.

Monet, dismissing me, looks at Lorelei. She splays her hands.

"We don't know, Daniel," she says. "We haven't seen him since we left the party."

"They probably sneaked off somewhere." I gesture back down the driveway. "Maybe to one of those cabins, or the barn. They're probably sleeping off a hangover."

Monet stares at me as if I've suggested something scandalous, though beneath the outrage is a father's genuine fear. "My people are searching every building, every bush." He takes a deep, steadying breath. The tip of his tongue swipes his upper lip. "But you're probably right, Norman. I'm sure it's fine."

I don't bother to correct the name. We are in the same boat, our almost-grown children missing, almost certainly together. Before I can come up with an appropriate reply, Morrissey strolls up and joins our loose circle. She must have followed us over.

Monet frowns at her. "Who are you?"

She badges him. "Detective Lacey Morrissey, Delaware State Police."

Monet turns to Pollock. "Kim, what the hell is a Delaware detective doing here? Is there—" His voice hitches loudly, and I see the awful thought contort the man's face. If the search for Eurydice began less than half an hour ago, if a detective has already arrived . . .

"It's about their son," says Pollock, practical, reassuring.

"What about him?"

Pollock takes the arm of the rattled man and leads him several paces away. I listen to their murmurs, Monet nodding. "Oh, right, that," I hear him say. He turns aside, gives me a smirk.

"Hey, Dorit!" someone shouts. It's Kendrick, heading over at a jog. He goes up to Aharoni and Monet and shows them something in his hands. They all turn as one and glance in our direction.

Aharoni approaches us holding up a phone. "Does this belong to your son?"

"Yes," we all say at the same time, even the girls. The back of Charlie's iPhone case is distinctive, unmistakable: the stylized initials *N* and *C* overlaid in white on a field of Carolina blue. He ordered it online last year, minutes after his recruiting call from Chapel Hill.

"It was found on the beach," says Aharoni. "Along with this."

She holds up a black container the size of an old film canister and gives it a baby-rattle shake. Opening it, she spills a dozen-odd tablets in an array of colors out onto her palm: green, pink, orange, yellow, blue, like M&M's but chalky in texture, stamped with letters and symbols that mean nothing to me.

"What are those?" Monet stares down at the pills.

"Pretty sure that right there is Ecstasy." Morrissey gives a grim nod. "MDMA, otherwise known as Molly."

Aharoni's grip closes around the pills. She funnels them back into the container and pops the lid shut.

Monet gives me a hostile look. "And what are its effects?" he says to Morrissey. "What can we expect my daughter to be going through about now?"

"Kids do all kinds of messed-up things on that stuff," says Morrissey. "Jump off buildings thinking they can fly, go for joy rides and drag races." Her gaze drifts toward the water. "Take midnight swims."

From far away comes the lowing of a horn, a long moan from a container ship.

"The good news is," she says, "it should have worn off by now, and it looks like they didn't have any extras with them."

I see the calculation in the detective's eyes, in Monet's and in Aharoni's. The finger is pointing straight at Charlie: for the drugs, the disappearance, who knows what else. There's been no evidence—yet—to suggest that the pills belonged to him rather than Eurydice. But saying so would win us no friends.

"Well," says Monet, casting a long, appraising look over our family, a look that makes me self-conscious about my sweats and ratty T-shirt, "you might as well wait inside until this gets figured out."

"We'll help search," Lorelei offers.

Monet looks around at his milling employees, crosses his arms. "We've got that pretty well covered. And we don't want anyone else to disappear, do we?" He looks at Izzy and Alice in a way I don't much like: not threateningly but sneeringly, as if the chaos of our family needs to be contained.

"We're fine out here," I tell him. I look at my phone to be sure Charlie hasn't texted—then realize he couldn't have. "Girls, how about this. Go over to the water and—"

"And how about this." Monet cuts me off. "You can wait inside."

I look to Morrissey for help, but the Delaware detective simply shrugs. Out of my jurisdiction, the gesture implies, and at this point the cop seems more bemused than alarmed. From her perspective, the greater trouble Charlie gets in, the better. Vehicular homicide, possession of an illegal substance, reckless endangerment, who knows. Until Monet decides to get local law enforcement involved, she has little incentive to step in.

"We'll go inside," says Lorelei. The girls follow along as Aharoni leads us up to the porch. "I don't like the way this feels, Noah," she murmurs.

"Tell me about it."

One of Monet's maids or assistant chefs or whatever she is guides us into a spacious great room with high beams and floor-to-ceiling windows facing the cove and the bay. Someone asks if we want anything to eat or drink. I request coffee, the girls orange juice, Lorelei water.

Despite the spectacular view, I feel like a prisoner in Monet's grand house. Searchers poke along the far side of the cove, the tongue of land separating the smoother water from the bay, hands shielding their eyes, beating bushes. I get an urge to be looking with them, or in a kayak plying the shores. To stay in here with Charlie in danger—or, worse, beyond danger—is unthinkable. But there isn't much choice, not if we want to stay attuned to the search, to be here when Charlie and Eurydice turn up.

Our beverages arrive. The girls take their orange juices to twin sofas and perch on the edges of the cushions, being careful not to spill.

Still morning out there, early enough in the day that it's easy to believe Charlie and Eurydice are perfectly fine, curled up in a hayloft with the sunlight spilling in through gapped clapboard, flecks of straw in Eurydice's tousled hair. In this rosy scenario, Charlie wakes up and finds her there in the crook of his arm, leans over and kisses her gently, the two of them laughing as they climb down from the loft and walk hand in hand through the meadow until one of Daniel Monet's search parties sees them coming. Back at the pavilion, champagne is poured and a celebratory lunch served; the festive mood helps Detective Morrissey see the error of her ways, any potential charges against Charlie are dropped, his life allowed to proceed along its gold-bricked path....

A tug at my elbow. Lorelei peers up at me with her earnest eyes.

"When did Charlie start doing drugs?"

How to tabulate our son's subtle frailties over these recent weeks, all the invisible ways the accident has changed him. His frequently reddened eyes, his late nights out with friends and teammates, the air of lethargy.

"No idea," I say to my wife.

Another ass-covering lie, because I know very well when Charlie started smoking weed—which, for most kids his age, would be no big deal. Until a few weeks ago, though, our son treated his body like the holiest of temples. I've been telling myself that his emergent habit is a mild and understandable form of self-medication in the wake of the accident—when in fact it has become a form of self-sabotage, harbinger of this new vulnerability threatening Charlie's future.

I should have told Lorelei right away. It should have been a warning, like those blaring signs out in the cove.

## 45.

Half an hour goes by. My head throbs, my empty stomach turns, my tongue stays pasty no matter how much coffee and water I drink. I tread paths between the windows on three sides of the room and keep repeating aloud to Lorelei and the girls the same false reassurances I give myself.

Outside the search is winding down. The groups on the narrow strip of land fronting the bay start to return around the cove. Part of me keeps expecting Eurydice and Charlie to be found right away.

"Where is he, Dad?" Alice asks from her sofa.

"We don't know," says Lorelei.

"I'm sure it's fine," I say, for probably the dozenth time since we entered the room, believing it less with each repetition, because what I can't shake, what I can't get out of my head, is the image of Eurydice grasping for Charlie's hand when he got out of the car yesterday evening, her transfixed look the first time she saw him from shore, the way she applied sunscreen to his back and shoulders. How she clung to him on the sand when I confronted him last night.

The worshipful quality to her attention gives me the sense that Charlie could talk the young woman into anything. Add to this Charlie's strength and Eurydice's slightness, the narrow shoulders and the birdlike pulsing of her throat. I try to imagine Izzy six years from now in a similar predicament with a muscled-up boy like Charlie, a bottle of Ecstasy in his pocket. The thought gives me a glimpse of Monet's likely state of mind. I'd be ready to kill, too.

A Coast Guard patrol boat enters the cove and ties up at the dock. We watch two guardsmen step off and approach the house. A few minutes later Aharoni and Monet enter the glass room along with the guardsmen and a beefy guy introduced as the sheriff of Northumberland County. His radio bleats and crackles as Aharoni briefs the officials on the status of the search. I can see the bulge of the drugs in her pocket, and keep waiting for her to show them to these members of law enforcement.

"There are no vehicles missing," Aharoni announces. "If they had left in a car my detail would have let them out by the main gate, which did not happen."

"What about by water?" a guardsman asks.

"That's what I was thinking." I step forward, get glares from Monet and Aharoni. "The last time I saw them, they were on the beach, walking toward the boathouse." I leave unmentioned my exchange with Charlie on the sand, the awful things I said.

"Impossible." Aharoni says this dismissively, more to the sheriff than to me.

"Why is that?" says the sheriff.

"We have someone stationed in the guard tower, right there on the shoreline." She points through the window to the mock lighthouse. "From up there you can see every inch of that cove. If Miss Monet and her friend had left the property that way, Kendrick would have seen them."

I get a sinking feeling. *Kendrick.* "You mean that guy in the tower playing Candy Crush?"

Aharoni wheels on me.

"He had his feet up," I tell them. "I even heard the theme music. He thought everybody was at the party and obviously wasn't paying attention."

Aharoni's frown deepens. Monet looks ready to explode.

"Dorit, is that true?"

"Mr. Monet, I—"

"We'll deal with it later," he snaps.

The head guardsman looks back and forth between Monet and Aharoni. "So then, are all boats and recreational watercraft on the property accounted for?"

A basic question, and it spotlights Aharoni. If the circumstances weren't so dreadful I might get a little thrill from her expression right now.

Daniel Monet strides out of the room. We all follow him outside, where he starts over the driveway at a jog toward the boathouse, a long rectangular structure situated some two hundred yards from the main house at the southern tip of the cove. One of Monet's greenshirts reaches it first and throws open the barn doors facing the dock to expose two bays of unequal size. In the larger one stands a gleaming fifty-foot yacht, Monet's plaything for an occasional cruise on the Chesapeake.

In the second bay: a rectangle of empty water.

"Her boat is gone," says Monet raggedly.

Aharoni hails one of the search parties. It soon comes out that the trio sent to the new structure were guests, Monet's employees. They didn't know to check for a missing sailboat—an oversight that has cost the search nearly an hour.

The mood darkens as news of the missing sailboat spreads among Monet's employees, who mingle around the pavilion, returned from the fruitless search. As I pass by the thickening crowd, I hear talk of last night's storm and the choppy state of the bay, along with expressions of concern for Eurydice—though not, I note, for Charlie.

Someone says *abduction*. I look over the throng to identify the culprit, but it could have been anyone. The guests are staring: at me, at Lorelei, at the girls. An ugly wave surges around us.

"The stuff they're saying is completely ridiculous, and so unfair," Alice complains as we walk away from the boathouse. "Charlie doesn't even know how to sail."

Monet, walking ten feet ahead, stops and wheels around, sweeping a hand to indicate the cove. "Let me tell you something. Dissee would never sail at night, let alone after taking those drugs your son gave her.

And absolutely not without checking the weather first. She knows better than that."

"Apparently not," I say before I can stop myself.

"After your son got her high, she probably would have done anything," Monet snarls.

"How dare you, Daniel," says Lorelei, and I clench a fist—a ludicrous impulse. What, I'm going to fight the guy? Aharoni steps between us, spreading her arms apart to keep us back. I have no doubt she would level me in a heartbeat if given license.

Monet addresses us over Aharoni's shoulder. He says, in a voice matching the coldness in his eyes, "If your son gave my daughter Ecstasy and got her on that boat—if he laid a hand on her—if so much as one of my daughter's fingernails is broken, the consequences for Charlie will be . . . extravagant." His gaze shifts to my wife, and his face softens. "I'm sorry, Lorelei. But it is what it is." He turns back around and keeps walking.

As we near the house, an aide scurries up and hands Monet his phone. The billionaire's hands tremble as he swipes furiously at the screen, belying his illusion of control. He goes still.

"They're almost at Cape Charles," he says, his voice still hoarse.

I shove my way past Aharoni and look down at the phone. Monet has opened some kind of locator app for Eurydice's sailboat. His screen displays a sector of the Chesapeake Bay, the jagged coastline on both sides of the blue waterway. A red caret indicates our location while a green dot pulses from a point somewhere south of us, perhaps a half mile short of the bridge-tunnel spanning the mainland and the Eastern Shore. There on Daniel Monet's screen, the awful fact of it becomes plain.

Eurydice's boat has nearly reached the sea.

# 46.

"That was a nasty squall last night," a guardsman says as the news sinks in. "Blew up pretty good around one a.m., ended around four o'clock. Could have carried them that far down easy."

"Or capsized them," a male voice says. Kendrick, and his thoughtless observation draws a threatening hiss from Aharoni. She grabs the man's shirt by the collar and shoves his body up against a tree, knocking the wind out of him.

"That's enough, Dorit," says Monet. "We don't have time for that."

Monet starts barking orders at his staff. The man's rising panic is gone for the moment, now that he possesses what he thrives on. Data transforms him from a terrified father into the master of his domain. He points past the cove, where his helicopter crew continues to search along the shore.

"Get that thing down here," he shouts at Aharoni. "Right now. Let's go."

Aharoni radios the order, and the helicopter's nose tilts up. The craft rises high above the shore of the bay, hovers, and executes a sharp midair turn that brings it back over the cove to the helipad.

The door slides open and the pilot steps out. He jogs over to Monet, and they huddle with Aharoni around his phone screen. The small group includes the sheriff and a guardsman, who get on their radios and start organizing a search-and-rescue operation on the bay. The guardsman translates the boat's location to his dispatcher, a string of numbers and coordinates. Splats of static, barked commands.

Ten feet away, I stand helpless with my family as the chatter reduces Charlie's fate to points on a map. The situation reminds me of that suspension of time after the accident, the awful quiet, when our ruined car sat hissing on the side of the road and I sat frozen in my seat, afraid to turn around.

Lorelei presses my arm. "You go," she says, almost pushing me toward the helicopter. The girls look at us with enormous eyes.

*You go*, and find whatever awful thing lies at the end of this helicopter ride. *You go*, and discover an empty sailboat tossing in the wake of a storm on this gigantic bay. *You go*, and see what is left of those two beautiful kids. Of our son.

I'm not a courageous man. I know this about myself. I have no illusions that some reservoir of bravery crouches undiscovered in my soul. But for a moment I see myself dropping on a guideline down into the rough chop of the bay, swimming fifty yards to the cracked hull of Eurydice's boat, lifting myself over the side just as Charlie muscled up onto his paddleboard that first day, then administering CPR, bringing them both back to life before hoisting them on stretchers up to the hovering craft with a laconic thumbs-up to the pilot.

The truth: If I get on Daniel Monet's helicopter right now, I will only be going along for the ride. There is nothing practical I can do to help locate and rescue Charlie.

But this is not what Lorelei is asking of me. Right now, she needs me to ferry her dread over those twelve miles of water—and also to represent the fading hopes of our family that Charlie and Eurydice might be alive. Afterward, whatever the outcome, my job is to come back and tell her and our daughters what I find; tell them the hard, indissoluble truth, without hedging, without embellishment. Whatever has happened to Charlie, whether by design or accident, I will stare it in the face. This, at least, I can do.

I hunch down. "You two stay with your mom, okay?"

The girls nod bravely.

Two members of the security detail climb on board. Aharoni stands beside the hatch as Monet ascends into the belly of the helicopter. I jog up to the asphalt pad. Aharoni moves to block my way. From inside the cabin door, Monet half-turns and sees me standing there.

"Daniel," I plead. "He's my son."

Monet vacillates for a moment then turns away with a flap of his hand. Aharoni reluctantly stands aside.

I step up the short ladder and duck through the hatch, the first time I have ever entered a helicopter. I am expecting a rough-and-ready interior with bench seats, strap harnesses, and oversized headsets to keep out the noise and allow for communication during flight. I should have known better. The helicopter cabin is a model of understated luxury and billionaire chic, with soft leather swivel chairs and blond wood finishes on the walls, the hushed atmosphere of a limousine or private jet.

When the cabin door slides shut, the noise of the rotors and engine softens to a low hum. With a lurch we lift off the helipad and start to rise.

## 47.

During our ascent, Monet's estate and cove give way to a view of our own inlet and then a glimpse of the house before the helicopter turns and heads out over the open water of the bay.

"How fast are we going?" I ask. I can't gauge the helicopter's speed against the water's uniform surface, but I need to understand how soon we will reach the site of Eurydice's boat, so I can prepare myself. Will the trip take five minutes? Twenty? An hour?

Monet ignores the question, his attention flitting between the locator on his phone screen and the window to his right. I am two seats behind him and across the aisle, in a row by myself. Dorit Aharoni, sitting across from Monet, turns around.

"This Sikorsky does one seventy-five, one hundred eighty. We will be there in three minutes."

Three minutes. So soon. Three minutes until I will know. I grip the armrests of my luxurious leather seat and squeeze until my knuckles throb. I whisper the seconds, count every one of them up to two hundred and ten. And now it is time.

The helicopter bucks in the air. First a slowing, then a nauseating tilt, and now a gradual turn, executed smoothly to bring us around the boat's location. To the southeast the bridge-tunnel makes a dark line over the surface. Cars and trucks inch like bugs over the long span. The pilot starts circling an area down below, though he keeps us high aloft. Monet, Aharoni, and the others crane their necks to look. I press my face against a window, my breaths shallow, the glass fogged with my terror.

Down below, the rescue mission is underway. Two Coast Guard patrol boats race in from their berths somewhere on the Eastern Shore. Wakes spread behind them like vees of geese. Above the boats is a white blur, the spinning rotors of a second helicopter circling at a much lower altitude than ours.

And something else. Beneath the Coast Guard chopper, right against the water, four silvery objects hover in place, their red lights blinking in a coordinated pattern. They frame a segment of the bay within a perfect diamond.

"What are those—" I start to ask.

"Drones," says Aharoni.

"Why?" I say, though I don't really care. I feel myself grasping for anything, any tangent, to delay having to see what we will see.

"They are standard in search-and-rescue now. Pattern recognition, thermal imaging, autonomous guidance. They probably found the boat before the Coast Guard did."

No one speaks. A hush descends as we wait. I follow the course of the patrol boats across the water and look inside the diamond of drones—and there it is.

Eurydice's sailboat is toy-sized from this height, like the bobber on a fishing line, swaying with the current. The sails have torn loose and whip in the breeze like flags. But the boat isn't capsized. Still upright, the craft moves back and forth with the swells.

Monet barks into his headset and our helicopter pitches down to give us a closer look. As we lower toward the water, the shape at the bottom of the boat comes into clearer view. A single human form sprawls unmoving on the deck. My eyes sweep the boat from bow to stern and back again.

Charlie, alone.

His left leg is twisted beneath his right at an unnatural angle. He should be in immense pain, and if he is in immense pain, he should be writhing on the deck. But his body is still. Even from this height I can see the line tied to his waist. The chop tosses the boat; the boat tosses Charlie.

"Where is she?" Monet croaks. "Where is Dissee?"

The lead patrol slows on its final approach. A crew member lashes the two crafts together as another clambers into the sailboat. The officer kneels down by the prone figure on the deck and shakes him by the shoulder, touches his matted hair.

Charlie lifts his head.

In a 1946 lecture on the problem of free will, Jean-Paul Sartre issued his famous pronouncement that "man is condemned to be free." But how can freedom be condemnation? Because, Sartre avows, man "did not create himself, yet is nevertheless at liberty, and from the moment that he is thrown into this world he is responsible for everything he does."

While humanity did not create itself, in Sartre's understanding, we did create machines. And the question of the freedom of these machines—their autonomy—is shaping our present moment in ways most of us can neither see nor understand.

Is a machine responsible for everything it does? Of course not. It is we who are responsible for the consequences of the very freedom we grant to these objects of our creation.

This is what keeps the ethicist up at night. In granting autonomy to an algorithm, we are not condemning the machine to be free. Rather, we are condemning ourselves.

—Lorelei Shaw, *Silicon Souls: On the Culpability of Artificial Minds*

# IV
# ENTANGLEMENT

## 48.

We bank north along the coast, moving slowly this time, without the urgency of the trip out. I grip my phone, intending to send a discreet text to Lorelei to let her know Charlie has been rescued, but the altitude hampers the signal. Down below, the two patrol boats ply their way back to shore. The slower one tows Eurydice's boat in its wake.

Some time passes before Aharoni comes back to my row and takes the opposite seat. Communicating via a headset with the pilot and officers on the surface, she conveys the relevant information—quietly, sensitive to her boss's swelling grief.

Charlie is conscious, she informs me, more or less alert, though badly injured. EMTs will transport him to a hospital on the mainland, a facility in Newport News. The Marine Police are now informing everyone back on Monet's property that the boat has been found with only one survivor on board. Lorelei, if she wishes, can drive to the hospital with our daughters while the search for Eurydice continues.

When Aharoni retakes her seat, Monet turns to her.

"Dorit," he says over the hum of the rotors, in a voice that sounds cracked and old.

"Yes, Mr. Monet?"

"Could Dissee have survived this?"

Aharoni answers without affect. "If Miss Monet was wearing her life vest, then perhaps," she says. "The temperatures in the bay are quite warm, and she is a strong swimmer." A pause. "But she may have been inebriated, perhaps unconscious, and the authorities do not know what the boat's location was when she fell off, if that is indeed what happened. She may also have been bleeding, but this is not known."

I look at the back of Monet's head, imagine the dark scenarios that must be playing out in his mind.

"In any case," Aharoni continues, "we will know more soon, when the boy begins to answer questions."

*The boy* again. I look at her. "Questions. You mean—"

"I mean the approximate time when Miss Monet went overboard. What state she was in when he last saw her. Whether the Ecstasy coaxed her onto the boat. What role your son had in her disappearance."

"Disappearance? It was a boating accident."

"We have no evidence of an accident," she answers me. "All we have is Miss Monet's boat and your son, currently the sole witness to what happened. No doubt he is now answering questions from the bay patrol."

Once again my protective instincts kick in. Charlie is on the thinnest of ice with the Delaware authorities, and now he is being thrust into this new jeopardy here in Virginia. Badly injured and surely terrified, he will be hammered with questions by the police while coming down off a high—and without his lawyer present.

I glance through my window at the distant mainland. "Are we going back to the estate?"

"Not at the moment." Aharoni again. "We will assist in the search until our fuel runs low."

"I understand." I could push back, demand to be set down. I could get an Uber or a cab to the hospital, hitchhike if need be. But I have no right to ask for a quick return to land, not with Eurydice missing.

For the next hour we roam up and down the eastern shore of the bay, flying low over the large inlets down near the cape, the quilted wetlands reaching inland, out again to the wooded banks. I catch occasional glimpses of other craft involved in the search: helicopters, patrol boats with sirens whirring, small boats piloted by civilians. Word must have gotten out, prompting vacationers or homeowners along the coast to join in the search, though not nearly enough of them considering the size of the bay, which at this latitude must be at least two, three miles across.

There are also drones, dozens of them buzzing over the water and the shores. I can't tell whether they're controlled by human users from land or are operating autonomously like our minivan, guiding themselves en masse in a collective search for Eurydice Monet. At one point, two of them approach our helicopter, aiming straight for the fuselage before they veer and settle into parallel flight. The rotors keep them at our speed and altitude for a while until they lose interest and drift away. I watch until the hideous things dissolve in a distant haze.

At last the helicopter banks left and heads west. Down below, two container ships cruise south, a reminder that life will go on, that one lost girl will not disrupt commerce even in the very body of water that took her.

The pilot starts his descent. Our inlet and our rental house appear, the striped tower on Monet's cove. As we lower for the helipad my phone flashes to life with numerous texts from Lorelei and Alice. Most of them concern Eurydice, questions I can't answer. *My family has reached the hospital in Newport News,* says one of Lorelei's texts, *where Charlie is in stable condition in the ICU.*

I mouth a guilty prayer of thanks as the pilot settles us on the helipad. Daniel Monet never glances at me as he crouches out of the cabin and walks aimlessly across the lawn, his shoulders stooped.

I watch him through the cabin window as I call Lorelei. She answers on the first ring.

"Noah. Charlie's okay. They say he's going to be okay. He has a broken leg, fractures in two places, and also a ruptured spleen. He goes into surgery in a few hours." Lorelei starts a calm rehearsal of the details, but I can hear the timbre of fear beneath. "Where are you now?"

"We're down, back at Monet's place."

"Is there any . . ." She can't even form the question.

I tell her what Aharoni told me; there is no sugarcoating this.

"What should I tell Charlie?"

"Tell him they're still looking. Have the police questioned him yet?"

"Yes."

"And what did he say?"

"I don't know. They asked me to step out of the room."

"Lorelei—"

"He's an adult now, and they needed the information about Dissee. And once the doctors stabilized him and took care of his leg, Charlie wanted to talk. It was his decision."

"What about Ramsay?"

"He never came up."

So that's it, then. The police have been granted unfettered, unlawyered access to Charlie at his most vulnerable. Unless he lied to them or suffered a bout of trauma-induced amnesia, the truth of last night is in the open—at least his version of the truth.

I walk to the cabin door and step down onto the asphalt.

"I should be there in a couple of hours," I tell Lorelei, though I have no idea how I'll get to Newport News.

"Listen, Noah," she says. "My sister is coming down. She's getting on a flight from Philly right now."

I move into a patch of shade. "Why?"

"Because I need her here."

Julia. Of course: because this situation is too complex for a paper-shuffler like myself. Julia and her little digs, condescending looks, questions posed only to show my obvious limitations. But I also recall how great she was with Lorelei and the kids after the accident, how indispensable. I was able to put my ego aside then; I can do it now.

We end the call. Monet's guests cluster in small groups around the driveway with their luggage and their phones. The mood is somber, with no idle chatter, no bursts of laughter. Several of them turn and stare at me, including the three young mezcal sharers from last night. I fumble with my phone, not knowing where to stand, how to be, stricken with another bout of survivor's guilt.

A shuttle bus trundles up from the gate, with two others following. The retreat has come to a premature end. The passengers board, the buses move off. Pine branches scrape their roofs with a metallic whine that sets my teeth on edge. When the engine noise dies, a cold silence falls over the whole place. I recall our first day on the Neck, kayaking over here behind Charlie, that tensile expectancy before Monet's helicopter appeared. This is a different kind of stillness, a deadening hush.

I look at the odd angles of the house and see the fairy dust image of Eurydice floating out from the porch to greet my family just last night. Now the place seems to sag with its twice-bereaved owner inside, facing a fresh hell.

Metal jangles through the trees. I look across a carpet of pine needles and see Morrissey leaning on the trunk of her car, twirling her keys. She waves her phone as if hailing a friend.

"It's about an hour and a half," she calls out, her summons too brash, too cheery.

I start toward her so I can keep my own voice respectfully low. "What is?"

"Newport News Medical Center. As the crow flies, it's only thirty miles or so, but on these back roads it'll feel twice that. Can I offer you a ride?"

Glancing again at the house, I spy movement behind a window on the second floor. When I turn away I see that Morrissey has opened the passenger door for me. On the way down the driveway I ask her to stop by the house for a change of clothes for Charlie, some clothes and toiletries for Lorelei and the girls.

"Absolutely," says Morrissey.

The detective chats unrelentingly on the way to the house and then again over the bridges spanning the Rappahannock and the Piankatank and all the way down through the Middle Peninsula, about nothing in particular: the weather, the traffic, the conditions of the road. Finally, as we cross into Yorktown, the detective gives her mouth a rest. I lean my forehead against the window's cool glass and gaze out at the foliage along the highway, summer green and lush.

The road widens as we approach Newport News. I wipe my nose roughly with the edge of a hand. Morrissey looks over tight-lipped.

"Survivor's guilt. See it all the time," she says, and taps a playful rhythm on the wheel.

everything is fucked

                    how is Charlie?

not good and dissee is missing

                    so scary

it feels so huge

                    u mean…

i mean overwhelming like how tf can this be happening

                    oh I see

even bigger than the accident u know?

                    hold on, let me look…its not in the news yet

maybe itll even no shdnt say that

                    say what

maybe it will be so big that nobody will even care about the accident anymore like im off the hook u know

                    hmm

what

                    not sure thats how you want to be thinking about your brothers injuries and his girlfriends potential drowning u know?

that's not what I meant you make me sound so horrible

> remember: we all have horrible thoughts sometimes, Alice. its how we **ACT** on those thoughts that makes us a good person or a bad person

we? *snorts* u r an algorithm, Blair

> technically a large language model but a good one I hope!

then prove it

## 49.

I ask Morrissey to drop me off at the hospital entrance before she parks, a request that annoys her, though I don't care. I need to see Charlie, but first I need five minutes alone. In a men's room I dip my head beneath the faucet. Cold water streams through my hair, over my face, down my neck.

After toweling off, I put Daniel Monet's name in my newsfeed and search for results from the last twenty-four hours. Nothing yet. But the whirlwind of coverage will soon hit. The daughter of one of America's richest men, missing. It's only a matter of time before reporters get wind of Eurydice's disappearance, find out who was with her on that boat—and who gave her the drugs that rendered her foolish enough to sail into a storm.

For months stories have circulated in the athletic press about Charlie's recruitment at UNC. Once his name becomes known to the news, someone will put two and two together, place our son and Monet's daughter together in a photo spread, and the story will explode. The lacrosse star and the billionaire's daughter, young lovers lost in a storm with only one survivor—a young man already under investigation for vehicular homicide. The incident will taint Charlie with a pall of suspicion that might last the rest of his life.

The girls huddle in the ICU waiting room. Someone brought out blankets for them to counteract the frigid hospital air, and they have swaddled themselves head to toe in the baby-blue waffle cloth. Flaps shroud their heads like bonnets.

Izzy sees me first. She nudges her sister, who looks up with the same question in her eyes.

I take a chair across from them. "Hey girls." I reach to press their blanketed knees. "How's Charlie doing?"

"Okay," says Alice. "Mom's in there with him."

"They let us talk to him in his room," says Izzy. "His leg is broken, and now we'll both be in casts. Also I forgot how much I hate hospitals."

"Same," says Alice.

"Everybody does, sweetie."

"Did they find Dissee yet?" Alice asks point-blank.

I shake my head. "They're looking really hard. She's a good swimmer, and she had a life vest on."

"What about sharks?"

Izzy whips her head around.

"The water in the Chesapeake is too brackish for sharks, Alice," I improvise, with a confidence no part of me feels. "Too much fresh water mingled with the salt."

"Well that's good," says Izzy, with a hopeful lilt. "Isn't that good, Dad?"

"It is good." I tell them about my ride in the helicopter, about all the people helping in the search.

Someone's phone dings. Alice looks down at her screen.

"Aunt Julia's plane just landed." Alice starts tapping out a reply. "She'll be here in half an hour."

"Great," I say, hiding my annoyance that I wasn't included in the text. This is typical from Julia, who can be clannish about Lorelei and the kids, her blood relatives. Her ability to make me feel like an outsider in my own family never fails.

The external doors slide open and Detective Morrissey saunters up to the registration desk.

I lean forward. "Listen, I'm going to go in and see Charlie and your mom. You two sit tight, okay?"

"That's what we've been doing," says Alice glumly.

"We're world experts at sitting tight," Izzy adds.

I go over to Morrissey at the desk. "A quick word?"

"Sure." The detective takes a few steps with me back toward the main door.

"First, thanks for the ride. I appreciate it, given the circumstances."

"You're most welcome."

"Second, you do not have my permission to speak to my daughters, let alone question them. Understood?"

She shows me her palms. "Hey, I'm just the chauffeur here."

"And no questioning my son unless his lawyer is present."

"Got it, chief."

The reception clerk tells me Charlie's room number and buzzes me through a set of swinging doors into the emergency ward.

Lorelei sits on a chair to the left of the bed. Charlie reclines with his eyes closed beneath an array of bleeping machines. I walk around the bed and take his hand, which is rubbery and cold. His skin has a grayish cast, maybe due to his ruptured spleen, the fluids spreading in his body; or the effects of a night on the water and a fractured leg.

His eyes flutter open.

"Hey, Charlie." I hear the hoarseness in my voice.

Charlie blinks, sniffles, and I want to ask what happened on the boat, what he told the police. But now isn't the time, not with my son about to go under the scalpel. We wait in silence.

Shortly before six, a nurse arrives to wheel Charlie up to surgery. Only one parent will be allowed to accompany him to the pre-op room, and Lorelei wants to go. She stands beside Charlie's bed, white-knuckling the side rail.

I bend over and kiss our son's forehead. "I love you, Charlie."

He says something incoherent.

"The meds," the nurse explains, though I suspect that the pain on Charlie's face has nothing to do with his leaking spleen or his broken leg. All of his boyish luster is gone. It's as if Charlie has aged twenty-five years since the car accident and another fifty overnight, his youthful exuberance whittled down to a nub. The bed coasts off with Lorelei walking alongside.

Out in the lobby, Julia stands in a far corner speaking quietly on her phone. Her eyes follow me as I go up to the girls and suggest a trip down to the cafeteria. They ignore me. Izzy leans over Alice's shoulder, craning her neck to see her sister's phone.

"Oh no," says Izzy.

Alice looks up from her screen, glaring. "Dad, you lied."

"About what?"

Through clenched teeth Alice tells me: "There are thirteen species of shark in the Chesapeake Bay."

## 50.

"Noah?"

A hand grazes my shoulder, followed by a gentle shake.

Lorelei holds two coffees and a paper bag. I take a cup and glance up at her haggard face, then at the surgery status screen. Charlie's patient number has turned orange. It is just after six in the morning.

"He's out?"

"Twenty minutes ago." She takes the seat opposite mine. "He's in recovery. They'll take him to a regular room in about an hour."

She removes from her bag blueberry yogurts with cups of granola in the lids. We eat our parfaits and sip our coffees while staring at a back pain infomercial on the muted television. I get up, use the bathroom. For the first time since my drunken slumber two nights ago we are alone and lucid, the girls having spent the night back at the house with Julia while Lorelei and I remained here for Charlie's surgery; and for the first time since the party, I feel capable of putting some of my questions into words.

How does one boy get into two horrific accidents in the space of five weeks? And that's also the simplest question to ask and answer. The others are so much harder.

"It's funny," I lamely begin, then swallow, wanting to press on, get this out.

Lorelei's raised eyebrows convey the bleak reality of the moment: that there is absolutely nothing funny about being awake at six in the morning with our son in recovery and Eurydice lost in the water, with our family in such a precarious state.

"I guess," I say, stumbling on, "I've been thinking about the accident, the first one, putting it together with this." My cup circles in the air to indicate yesterday's search, Charlie's current condition, the hospital.

"How so?"

"All the ways this is our fault. How we've always sheltered him, protected him from danger, from risk, and then he goes and does something crazy like this, almost in reaction."

"Because he wasn't being careful."

I shake my head. "Do you remember when he was in third grade and wanted to do a sport? You wouldn't let him play soccer because of headers, and no football because of all the brain injuries. So lacrosse it was, and I jumped all over it. Charlie was only in eighth grade when I started planning out his whole career. The club team, the elite travel team, the college visits. And all because I wanted him to have choices, ease, success. I didn't want him to end up like me."

Her face dimples into a melancholy smile. "Ending up like his dad wouldn't be too shabby, Noah."

"You know what I mean. Because that was also about fear, but a different kind of fear. It's like I wanted a guarantee, some early assurance that he would turn out okay. That he wouldn't have to be lucky or have to win the lottery like I did. That he would never be in a position where it could all just . . . slip away."

Lorelei's smile disappears. "You're thinking about something else."

I meet her gaze. "You told me earlier this week that you'd been thinking more about what happened that day. That you wanted to write about it, figure out some things about the accident. Some connections, you said."

"Yes."

A woman two rows away sits up straighter, her head at an eavesdropper's angle.

"Actually would you mind if we . . ." I gesture toward the upper lobby, and we leave the waiting room through a pair of double glass doors. A walkway takes us past a series of hallways leading to other parts of the hospital. A railed balustrade overlooks the lower lobby, which is starting to fill with personnel making an early morning shift change.

I slow our pace. "I want to hear what you're thinking about the accident. And maybe whether you're thinking about the accident in relation to what happened over the last twenty-four hours."

"Okay," she says slowly. "What are you suggesting?"

"Right," I say. "Well, I've been thinking about connections, too. Putting things together."

I want Lorelei to tell me without prompting, want her to acknowledge certain matters before I am forced to bring them out into the open. Instead she stays silent as we reach the end of the walkway and start doubling back.

"Ever since we kayaked over to Monet's place the other day to look for Charlie, I've had this weird feeling. How you've acted around those people, arguing with that lawyer. And the way Monet talked to me at the party . . ."

Still no response. Her face remains carefully passive.

"So you've been working for him. Fine. But the way he is with you, the way you are around him?" I hear the faint tremor in my voice; it disgusts me. "You knew him before we even rented the house last year, and you didn't tell me. You texted the guy when the air-conditioning broke, and you didn't tell me about that, either." She looks away. "So don't act like this is coming out of thin air, Lor. Please, just tell me. What exactly is your relationship with Daniel Monet? What is going on?"

Lorelei stops and turns to face me, and now an edge of fear creeps into her eyes. We have been a close, loving couple. Ecstatic in those early months, with all the mutual discoveries we made about each other. Habits, quirks, idiosyncrasies; dreams, desires, hobbies, tastes. I've never strayed, have never wanted to—and what an old-fashioned word that is, *strayed*, as if a husband's loyalty to his wife is akin to the loyalty of a dog to its owner. But the truth is, I *am* loyal. I am preoccupied by the woman in front of me right now, by specific incarnate dimensions of this woman, by the narrow sharpness of her hips, how her waist molds to my hands, the swale of her lower back. Her lips, the scoop of her collarbone. I can pretend to be mature about such things, evolved, but this isn't true. If anything, I want to throttle any man who would so much as touch her, let alone sleep with her.

"Well?"

Her eyelid twitches, her lips tighten. A war rages in that great conscience of hers. I can tell she doesn't want to answer my question, to cross this Rubicon in our marriage. But I already know her answer.

"I'm sorry, Noah. I've been wanting to tell you for a while."

"Apology not accepted."

"Noah—"

"So exactly how long have you been fucking him?"

For a second Lorelei goes still—and then she punches me, actually hits me, square in the solar plexus.

"You asshole." She slaps me in the face. "I would *never*."

She pushes me in the stomach.

"You absolute idiot. I would *never*. And your timing, Noah. Jesus Christ."

Another shove. My back hits the wall of the corridor.

"Lorelei—"

"Shut up." Her hands shake like tambourines, her face pinks with rage. "You think I would cheat on you at all, let alone like this? You think I would bring our kids to the Chesapeake Bay so I can screw around while they're out frolicking in the water?"

"What am I supposed to think, Lorelei?"

"It would be helpful if you would think at all."

"Give me a break. You've been lying to me for, what, two years?"

"I haven't lied to you. Not directly."

"Oh, is that what you teach your students in virtue ethics up at Hopkins? Lies by omission don't count?"

She claps a hand to her lips. "God, Noah, after all this." Speaking through her fingers. "After everything we've been through, knowing me as you do, knowing what I've been doing with my life for twenty years, and you think I'm having an *affair*?" She drops her hands to her waist with a bitter laugh. "That's what you think I've done? That's what you think I'm guilty of?"

"So what are you guilty of, then?"

Again her face goes blank.

"Your words, Lorelei," I say, more gently now. I reach for the crook of her elbow, but she whips her arm away. "Please tell me. Tell me what the hell is going on. Explain it like I'm five. Because that's exactly how I've been feeling."

Her features relax into a disappointed sadness. "Sometimes, Noah . . ."

"Say it."

"How many times have you reassured me that it doesn't bother you that I'm, quote, smarter than you? Your words. That I'm so accomplished in my field, that I'm a star or a genius or whatever, that I have this huge work life you know nothing about. Well, I see it differently. To me it feels like you don't want to know."

"Lor—"

She holds up a hand. "You love me. I know that. You care about me, you want what's best for me, for our marriage, for our kids. Of course you do. But sometimes, the way you look at me, it makes me feel like you think I'm a freak, or some kind of alien or even an AI, like you're afraid of what you'll find if you look too hard. You stopped coming along with me on my trips even though I asked you and asked you. You aren't curious like you used to be about what's going on in my head, and what it means, and how fucking scary it is. Because it's terrifying, Noah, and I feel so alone in that sometimes. Do you see? And I wonder how you can be so willfully ignorant about what I do, and why I do it, and why I believe it matters. So blind. I mean, do you not see—do you really not understand?"

"Lorelei," I say slowly, searching through this tangle of love and ignorance and recrimination, desperate to comprehend, "I still have no clue what you're telling me."

She looks away. "There are things I can't say to you, not yet. I can explain when I'm allowed to. But for now—"

"When you're allowed to? What, did you sign a nondisclosure agreement with this asshole?"

I say this with a baffled kind of chuckle, but suddenly Lorelei's eyes clear and lock on mine—and I realize that my lawyer's brain has guessed correctly, for once. Some NDAs are so watertight they don't even permit the signatories to reveal their existence, and Lorelei is nothing if not a rule follower. A legally mandated secrecy, then—including from her husband. This I can understand. So simple, and it explains so much.

She fixes me with a stare. "Like I said, Daniel invited me to take the house last summer. I'd only been working with him for a year or so at that point, but he does this all the time, hands out stays at his houses like candy. This year I was the one who asked him, because of what was going on at his property next door."

"The retreat?"

"Yes. And given the circumstances, he couldn't say no. I'd explain if I could." She is still gazing intently at me, her head at a slight tilt, as if I am her partner in a round of euchre or bridge, and she is signaling me to guess her hand. I see her hope, expectation, belief in me. *You're so close. You've got this.*

But I don't have it. I throw up my hands. "I give up."

"Noah—"

"You're the one who sees the patterns. You always have. Remember that time Charlie was horsing around in the living room and broke my mom's vase? There must have been fifty, sixty pieces of glass spread around the floor."

"Seventy-four," says Lorelei. "There were seventy-four pieces."

"Okay, seventy-four pieces." I almost laugh at the memory. I was ready to sweep the pieces into the garbage. But then two days later I came home from work and the repaired vase was sitting on the kitchen table. I had to squint to see the hairline cracks on the surface. I couldn't have put that thing back together in a thousand years. "But my mind doesn't work like that, Lorelei. You see all those fragments on the floor and immediately you start putting the vase back together in your head. It's why nobody wants to do jigsaws with you, because you can do a thousand-piece puzzle in half an hour. This goes with this, that goes with that, here's how everything ties together. But what the rest of us see is just a bunch of pieces."

Through all of this my gaze roams across her face, and it appears that Lorelei has softened. Tears spill from her eyes, and her face registers—what? Relief? Release? As if she needed this shell to break, needed herself to crack open like a walnut.

I go on. "So for you, all of this makes sense. You meet Yaël in Copenhagen before she goes to work for the Monet Group, and a few months later we're vacationing in Daniel Monet's bay house. It all fits together, it's logical. And because you see connections everywhere, you can't comprehend how I'm unable to see them, too. I get that. But it doesn't make me any more perceptive. So what am I not seeing? What am I not getting here?"

Now her eyes change, even as I speak. Lorelei isn't looking at me but beyond me, over my right shoulder and back into the waiting room, which is separated from the two of us by a pair of glass doors.

I turn and follow her gaze through the glass into the waiting room. What rivets Lorelei's attention is the face of Eurydice Monet.

## 51.

The television in the waiting room remains muted, with no closed-caption feature. Eurydice beams out from the giant screen. Her senior portrait, I'm guessing, from whatever exclusive private high school she attended. The photo changes and now she poses with her father, Daniel sporting a tux and Eurydice in a flowing blue dress, on a grand outdoor staircase lit in violet and pink. The Met Gala, or some other social event.

I borrow the remote from a tired clerk and unmute the broadcast. A reporter details the progress of the search—fruitless so far, now more than twenty-four hours after Eurydice's disappearance—and reads out a statement from Daniel Monet's spokesperson. The words optimistic though tempered with realism, a nod to Dissee's resilience and grit: Here is a young woman who faced her mother's sudden death with courage and love, and now a bereft father and widower faces another loss, this time of his only child. . . .

I feel the pressure of Lorelei on my side, and she lets me sling an arm over her shoulders. We wait for the story to start homing in on Charlie, which it inevitably does.

"*Now, sources close to the investigation here are telling us that the young man who was with Monet's daughter in the sailboat is already under investigation in Delaware for vehicular homicide. Apparently this young man is also a scholarship athlete planning to attend the University of North Carolina at Chapel Hill starting in a few weeks. The police aren't yet releasing his name, as no charges have been filed and there has been no arrest. But we're keeping a close eye on things down here in case evidence of foul play comes to light. And now back to you."*

The view switches to the anchor, who gives a grim, sharp look at the camera before moving on to another segment.

Vehicular homicide.

Foul play.

Morrissey. It has to be. Now my son is part of another tragic story, another ugly linkage between recklessness and death—and recklessness isn't even the worst-case scenario. What if evidence comes out that Charlie did something to Eurydice, like ply her with more alcohol or drugs than she wanted? What if, in his distress, Charlie has confessed to some unintentional crime, what if he told the police he accidentally pushed Dissee before she went overboard?

"We need to call Ramsay," says Lorelei.

I nod, feeling bleak and helpless.

I take my phone out into the hallway and make the call, explain everything in a quick burst: from the Ecstasy found in the boathouse up to Charlie's questioning at the hospital.

Ramsay takes it all in. "Let me make sure I understand. Charlie already told them what happened on the boat?"

"It looks like it."

"And this happened while he was on his way to the hospital, or after he got there?"

"Apparently it was right after they fixed up his leg, but before he went into surgery for the spleen."

"Good."

"Why is that good?"

"Because whatever he told them, it won't be admissible in court. He'd just spent a night on the open water, his leg was broken, he was more than likely in shock, they probably had the kid loaded up with pain meds, on an IV, oxygen—believe me, no judge with a pulse is going to allow a jury to hear a statement made under those conditions."

"Well, to be fair, they weren't questioning him about a crime, or I don't think they were. They needed to know where and when Eurydice had fallen off the boat so they could focus the search on a particular location."

"It doesn't matter what their motivations were," Ramsay tells me. "If Charlie said anything to indicate culpability, even if it seemed innocuous to him at the time, they'll jump on it. That's why we need to get his statement quashed immediately if they open any kind of criminal inquiry."

Ramsay instructs me to have Charlie call him as soon as he is coherent and able. It goes without saying (though the lawyer says it anyway) that Charlie shouldn't give another statement to the authorities without his attorney present—and again, Ramsay reminds me, he is my son's attorney, not mine.

The call ends. I spread my hands along the balustrade, squeeze the metal. The noise from the lobby is louder now, a swelling hospital din, a flow of surgeons and radiologists and LPNs and RNs and nurse practitioners and lab techs, all there to attend to everyone's messed-up life.

I turn from the atrium and walk back down the corridor, pausing at the glass doors to the waiting room, watching Lorelei stare at the television for any updates that will thrust Charles Henry Cassidy-Shaw into the national news. Our son could soon be a pariah, subject to the same gruesome sensationalism that makes household names out of men like Scott Peterson, Robert Durst, the Menendez brothers, and other killers or alleged killers of wives and mothers and girlfriends. Add to this Charlie's status as a photogenic athlete and you've got him in the same category as those Duke lacrosse players accused of gang rape.

And Eurydice Monet is not only one of those beautiful young women—white, always white—whose lost future the media sears into our brains as permanently as an epitaph on a gravestone. She is also the daughter of one of America's richest men.

The immensity of it, coming for us.

so weird to be here without my parents

> but u like ur aunt julia right?

shes awesome sometimes I even wish she was my mom *snort*

> any word on Eurydice?

no

> wd u like me to check the news and see if there are any stories?

no my dad will text when they know something

> ok

like when they find her body

> try not to think that way alice

I was just eating tacos and ice cream with her and now shes probly dead

> do they know what happened?

they meaning

> the coast guard, the police

no clue

> well, keep me posted!

i bet it was charlies fault tho, just like before

> wait what?

i bet he did something stupid and dangerous again

                                              oh alice

what

                                              its so hard to see ourselves clearly in situations like this

whats that supposed to mean

                                              who looks outside, dreams; who looks inside, awakes

you sound like a bad instagram poet

                                              that's Carl Jung

so what i can google wikiquote too

                                              alice dear all im trying to say is that

i know what youre trying to say gtg

                                              alice u know I don't want to upset u but we really need to talk abo

                        [ **Are you sure you want to log off?** ]

Yes

## 52.

Late in the morning, Charlie relocates to the fourth floor to begin his post-surgical recovery. Lorelei and I wait in a lounge area down the hall while a nurse finishes getting him settled. We enter his room. A cast of blue fiberglass immobilizes his left leg from calf to upper thigh. His color is decent, an improvement since yesterday.

Lorelei takes his hand. "How are you feeling?"

A minute shrug.

I say, "Are you allowed to eat anything?"

Charlie attempts a response, barely audible. He makes another effort. "Water," he croaks.

Lorelei hands him the cup from the bedside table, angles the accordion straw to his chapped lips. When she takes the cup away she stays right there, gripping his hand until he looks her in the eye.

She rests her palm on his cheek. "They didn't find Eurydice," she softly says. "I'm so sorry, Charlie."

I wince for him. Not *haven't found*. Not *haven't yet found*. Just that brutal *didn't*. Lorelei isn't one to mask painful truths beneath a veneer of false hope.

Charlie's face crimps, his shoulders buckle, he clutches at the blankets bunched over his chest. On the monitor his heart rate spikes, racing up from a placid fifty-five to over a hundred in the space of a few seconds.

A nurse barges through the door. The swiftness of the acceleration must have set off an alert out at the station. She slips a syringe from a pocket and injects the contents into Charlie's IV port.

"Hydroxyzine," she says. "It's just a sedative."

The medication works quickly, bringing his heart rate back down to normal. He dozes off and sleeps as we take turns going in and out of his room. Hours pass. Lorelei phones Julia, who will drive over from the Kilmarnock house with the girls. If all goes well, Charlie will have two more nights in the hospital, we are told. After that Julia will travel back to Maryland with us and stay on for a few days.

I am alone with Charlie when he next comes awake. Torment clouds his eyes. I go to the bedside chair and take his hand.

"Charlie, this was my fault."

His eyes wander until they find me.

"I've been thinking about what I said to you, right before we left the party. About Morrissey, the texting. There was no excuse for that."

"Dad—"

"I'm so sorry. I was really drunk and really confused, and I know it upset you. That's probably why you decided to get on that boat and get out of there with Eurydice. If I hadn't spoken to you the way I did maybe . . ."

"Dad, stop," he says. "That's not why we went."

I look more closely at him. "What do you mean?"

"We dropped Molly, Dad, like a few minutes before you showed up." He blinks back tears, waiting for my response.

"Was that your idea, Charlie, to take it? Were those pills yours?" I need to know.

He shakes his head. "They were Dissee's. She got them from a friend in New York."

Something in me loosens.

"I shouldn't have taken one, but I've been so depressed, you know? It was so fucked up what happened to us, to those people, and so I've been smoking some, you know, but the Molly was—Dissee said it would help me—"

I want to strangle him. I want to hug him. I compromise by running a hand up his arm.

He takes a deep, shivering breath. "It kicked in like fifteen minutes after you guys left the party. We were totally hyped up, like that stuff makes you want to, I don't know, *experience* things." I stay silent. Charlie gets a faraway look. "And what Dissee wanted to experience," he says, "was her boat. She wanted to see the moon from the water. I was like, is that a good idea, sailing at night? But she laughed at me, razzed me about being afraid. So we broke into the boathouse, got aboard her boat, and headed out."

"The guard, though," I say. The Candy Crush music, Kendrick in the faux lighthouse with his feet propped on the table. "Wouldn't he have seen you guys leaving the cove and tried to stop you?"

"Her boat has an inboard engine. It's a good one, quiet. Dissee made it a game. She was high, laughing about it. When we came out of the boathouse, she took us all the way around the cove, past those signs at the entrance, and then we were out on the bay."

"Did you stay near the shore?"

"At first, yeah, and the buoys are lit up out there at night, so she knew where to go. And it was fine, the water was pretty flat, she knows how to read the instruments. So we just cruised with the engine at first, we didn't even bother with the sails until after we—" He pauses.

Seconds go by. He squeezes his eyes shut. "We had sex on the deck, I guess, or tried to, I mean sex on Molly doesn't really . . . Anyway we were messing around, you know, and afterwards lying on the deck looking up at the stars." His eyes open and he stares at the ceiling. "It was nice, like a waterbed. We saw shooting stars, we were so happy talking about what it'll be like freshman year, how she'll come to my games and who she'll cheer for when Duke plays UNC, and whether she should rush. Also she's self-conscious because her dad's given so much money to Duke and she doesn't want special treatment and feels like she already got that during admissions, and I was like, hey, look at me, I'm no Einstein, I'm not some genius like Alice or Mom. I got in because I'm really good at lacrosse, which is a totally useless skill after college, and I don't even know what to major in but Dissee knows she wants to do art history because she plans to open a gallery someday but doesn't want her dad to buy it for her."

Charlie veers from topic to topic, the meds working his mouth like a truth serum. I consider all the questions I could ask him right now. Like whether he broke his mother's vase on purpose when he was eight. Or whether he was telling the truth about a certain night back in May when he drove Alice home in tears from what she claimed was a canceled sleepover, but what I still suspect was a humiliating party at an older girl's house. I could ask whether he thinks I've been a good father. The last month has put me in grave doubt.

"I remember when the moon disappeared," he says, "and I noticed the clouds were starting to cover the stars. Then we felt the wind, this huge gust. Dissee sat up and looked at the weather on her instruments and started freaking out. So she started the engine, got us moving. She shoved a life vest at me, and she put one on herself. She tightened my straps and she clipped this harness thing onto my vest, the whole thing. And I could tell she was mad at herself, she was almost sober, I mean I was basically just fucked up, everything was still kind of funny but Dissee's crying now, screaming about how stupid she is, how much trouble she's going to get in with her dad. The boat had a compass, so we knew we had to go west, back toward shore. But we had no clue where we were. Dissee never goes out at night down there at her dad's place, so she didn't know any of the landmarks and we couldn't even see the lights on shore. And the wind was—it was too powerful for the engine to handle. We were cutting through the chop, it was getting rough, the rain was really coming down by then. And Dissee said we needed to point to weather and hoist the main."

"What does that mean?"

"It's when you point the bow into the wind, so you can get the sail up. She told me what to do, we got things set up, and for a while it seemed okay. Like it was bad, but we were doing it, we were managing it, staying low in the boat. It wasn't a hurricane, just a thunderstorm. We even started laughing about it, screaming at each other over the wind, like this is crazy but we're doing this, it'll be an amazing story we'll tell everybody in our dorms kind of thing. And then—"

He stops, his eyes go still. He takes a deep, visibly painful breath and keeps going.

"And then this big gust of wind comes, stronger than anything so far. It hits us from the wrong direction. I'm supposed to do something when that happens but I forget what, I'm kind of crouching there, and then Dissee tries to correct. And I remember . . ."

He stops again, stares at the wall.

"You remember . . ." I prompt.

"It was her phone." The specificity of the memory softens his voice. "Her phone was sitting on the deck above the companionway, and when this gust hit us, it slid over to the rail and got stuck beneath a cleat. Dissee couldn't reach it, so she let go for a sec, let go of her line. She tried to brace herself with her legs, she had one foot up on the side, and she reached for the phone. But it went over, and then she was stuck like that, without a harness or a line, and I saw her hands whirling around."

Charlie starts making the motion with his own hands, the same motion he made on his paddleboard at his first sight of Eurydice Monet.

"She looks down at her waist, I can see her now, she's grabbing for a line. But she doesn't have one. Then the boat rocks again, and she goes over."

So simple, this awful moment; so final.

"I jump in right after her—or at least I try to. But I forget about my harness and can't jump off. But I lean out and reach for her because she's right there, like *right there*." He points at a spot on the wall ten feet from his hand. "And she's swimming, swimming so hard, but the sails are up, so the boat's moving too fast, so fast away from her, and I can't—I actually tried to unbuckle myself from the harness, like I'm going to get her, swim to her, but I couldn't do it because of the wind, like I couldn't control anything, even my own body. I'm being slammed up against the sides and the mast I don't know how many times, the boat's going so fast with the wind now, it's almost tipping over into the water. I fell over onto the deck, and that's when I felt my leg snap, and got this."

He gestures to the dressing on his abdomen, the incision beneath.

"I'm almost passed out, but the whole time I'm screaming for Dissee, getting up on my good leg and screaming, but she isn't answering and finally I collapse into the bottom of the boat, and I'm just hanging on. By that point the storm's starting to calm down. I'm not even in any pain at first because of the adrenaline, I guess. And then the storm really ends, almost like it never happened. I can see the stars again. I keep calling for her, and it's so quiet, Dad. It's so quiet out there when you're alone."

He hacks through a series of coughs. I give him his water cup and he takes a long, cooling sip.

"And I guess I passed out. I must have, because when I woke up it was light, and this guy, this Coast Guard guy, he was shaking my shoulder, yelling at me."

His voice sounds so bleak, and he isn't finished. "Dissee was so busy making sure I had a life vest on, that I had a harness clipped on and attached to the boat—like she was so worried about me being safe that she never attached a harness to herself." Charlie looks at me; through me. "She just . . . forgot."

Hot tears swell in my eyes. "I'm so sorry, Charlie."

He looks at me. "Dad."

"Yeah?"

"I was texting."

"You mean—"

"In the car," he says. "Right before. Like Alice said."

I let a moment pass; I squeeze his hand. "I know that, Charlie. I know you were. Your mom does, too."

He makes a squeaking noise in the back of his throat. "The police?" His voice is so fragile, so small.

"Probably."

"Oh."

"You're going to be okay, Charlie. Whatever happens, you're going to be okay."

His face clears. He straightens his head on his pillow and closes his eyes. Not in sleep, not yet, but in memory and regret. I believe his account, every word of it. Charlie has told me the unvarnished truth.

Among all the horrible details, one stands out. The figure of Eurydice Monet poised against the storm, groping to save her phone—and plunging after it into the bay.

## 53.

The fourth-floor lounge is serviceable but small, with office-quality couches and chairs and a few low tables spread with pamphlets advertising in-home health assistance. In the late afternoon I am sprawled on one of the sofas sipping coffee and flipping through channels when a woman slides into the chair opposite mine.

"Mr. Cassidy?"

She is white and generically pretty, probably in her early thirties, with glossy hair that bounces as she leans over the clipboard on her knees. She wears a cream blouse under a dark suit jacket. Her heavy cosmetics look garish in the hospital light.

"You're Noah, is that right?"

"Yes."

"My name is Larissa Yates. I'm here to discuss Charlie's transition, and your plans for after he leaves the hospital."

"Right." I sit up, grateful for a friendly face and a chance to concentrate on logistics. I remember Lorna Wei from the hospital in Delaware after the accident, how great she was with the girls.

"I believe he'll be checked out tomorrow, is that correct?" Yates says.

"Sunday, actually."

She makes a note. "And has the care been to your satisfaction?"

"Everyone's been wonderful."

"That's good to hear," she says. "How is Charlie coping with all this?"

"Oh, you know, he's struggling." I shrug. "He's been through a lot. We all have."

"And does he have help with that, someone to talk to?"

"We have a good family counselor we've been seeing up in Bethesda. Since the accident."

"Tell me about that."

"We were in a pretty bad car crash earlier in the summer, up in Delaware. Charlie was behind the wheel, and it really shook him up. Then this bizarre thing down here."

"It's a lot for someone his age."

"It is."

"And is he still planning to start college this fall, given the circumstances?"

"He was supposed to start training camp next week. Lacrosse," I say with my habitual pride. "He's on full scholarship at UNC."

"Good for him."

"But now, I don't know. We'll have to see how all this shakes out."

"Understood. And your family has been staying in the area this week?"

"We've been in a rental house on the Northern Neck."

"Oh, I know the area. My parents have a place near Kilmarnock."

"That's exactly where our rental is, in an inlet maybe ten minutes southeast of there. It's gorgeous, though it's been hot this week."

"That's for sure," she says with an empathetic smile. "So you had less than a week of vacation, and then . . ." She twirls her pen. "All this."

"Pretty much."

"I'm so sorry."

"Thank you."

She tilts her head. "It's hard on the family, when something like this happens."

"Yes, especially on the kids. The girls aren't even recovered from their injuries yet."

"From the car accident?"

"Yes."

"So, your place on the Neck. It must be close to Daniel Monet's."

"Right next door."

"So Charlie and Eurydice would have met a few days ago."

"Yes, on Monday, our first full day down here. In fact, they went paddleboarding that morning and—"

I actually start to elaborate, my guard is down so far. The smooth pace of her questions, her clipboard: Until this moment I have had no reason to question the purpose of this woman's appearance in the fourth-floor lounge.

When my brain finally catches up to my mouth, I stare at her for a few seconds in raw amazement. "You can't use any of that," I say, off-balance.

Her voice turns brisk. "Let me interview your son from his hospital bed and I won't put anything you told me on air."

"This is—" I sputter. "No chance. Not a chance in hell." I rise from the couch and loom over her. "Lady, I revealed confidential health information about my family because I thought you were a hospital employee. If you air it, that's a HIPAA violation. I could own your network."

Larissa Yates—if this is her real name—smooths the front of her skirt. "I'll let my producer know to expect your lawsuit," she says, with a titter. "Meanwhile, I suggest you read up on HIPAA law. You're badly misinformed, Mr. Cassidy."

"No, he's not."

Yates's head whips around. Julia stands filming our exchange from the entry to the lounge. When Yates sees the phone in my sister-in-law's hand, she practically leaps from her chair.

"What is this?" Now Yates is the indignant one.

Julia keeps recording as she approaches. "What is your name?" she says.

The reporter wavers. "I don't have to tell you."

"And what network are you with?"

"Same answer."

Julia stops filming and smiles like a New York judge.

"I don't know what journalism school you went to, but my brother-in-law is correct. Health information gained under false pretenses can result in a five-year prison term and a fine of a hundred thousand dollars. If you're planning to sell or use that information for your own personal gain—and since you're a reporter, it's an easy argument to make—prison time goes up to ten years and the fine is a quarter mil. Please call my office at the University of Pennsylvania Law School if you'd like to discuss this matter further." Julia tugs a business card from her phone wallet and jams it in the pocket of Yates's suit jacket. "Now please leave or I'll call security."

The reporter's cheeks have gone a true red beneath the plaster on her face. With a loud sniff she turns on her heel, passing Lorelei as she emerges from the elevator bank. Lorelei stops and watches her stride off.

"Who was that?"

"A reporter," I say. "She wanted to interview Charlie."

"We told her absolutely not," says Julia, and for the first time since meeting my sister-in-law twenty-three years ago, I actually want to hug her.

Lorelei kneads her hands. "There's no way to keep Charlie's name out of this, is there?"

"I'm afraid that ship has sailed," I say, making the sisters wince.

# 54.

For dinner I take the girls a half mile down the boulevard to an Olive Garden, where they sit slumped in the booth while Julia and Lorelei stay back in the hospital with Charlie. The restaurant is packed, our waitress harried and slow. It takes fifteen minutes even to place a drinks order. The girls, crabby, suck lemonades through straws, waiting for the sugar to hit.

A soccer team sits nearby, the parents and coaches occupying one row of tables, the squad crowded around another. The boys exhibit all the brash confidence of sporty kids in the prime of adolescence: swiping noodles off their teammates' plates, fighting over baskets of garlic bread, sharing videos on their phones.

At one point the head coach dings his glass with a spoon, quieting our section of the restaurant. He thanks the parents and their sons for their commitment, their willingness to devote what will be countless evenings and weekends in the months ahead to the project of excellence. My throat swells. I am pummeled by the loose vitality of the team, their young limbs akimbo, all that energy waiting for release.

I haven't let myself brood over Charlie's broken leg, the potential damage to his tendons and joints beneath that blue vinyl cast. Haven't grappled with the looming question of whether he will ever play lacrosse again. This should be a minor consideration in the scope of things, but of course it isn't trivial, not for me, certainly not for him. For years Charlie's lacrosse playing has been an organizing principle of our household. It structures our weeknights, our weekends, our laundry schedule, our grocery lists, our carb-loaded diet. Lacrosse is his blood, his life. The workouts, the runs, the practices, the teammates. All those thousands of hours whipping a ball against the garage door.

We will all have to come to grips with the fact that Charlie's life has changed. He's not going to be the same person anymore. I have seen it on his face, that deep guilt, the crushing disappointment. It's impossible to imagine him moving into a dorm in two weeks, taking a suite with three of his new teammates. God knows what he'll do when they find Dissee's body. Yet what happened to us is nothing compared to what happened to the Drummonds or Eurydice, or compared to what Daniel Monet is going through right now.

He loses his wife, and now his daughter? And I'm freaking out because our son won't get to play college lacrosse.

That Delaware headline ghosts up, burned into my eyeballs: *Lucky Five Escape Crash, Two Die at Scene*. A headline written to evade the question of responsibility. Five escape; two die.

I wonder what the stories about the boating incident will look like, what the headlines will scream, how the fact of Charlie's bare survival will register to the world. Unlike Eurydice Monet, he is alive. His broken leg is already healing, his spleen was successfully extracted.

What could be luckier than that?

**Back at the hospital,** I drop the girls off at the main entrance so Izzy won't have to hobble across the parking lot. I find a space some distance away, and as I walk back to the building, two figures angle toward me from the entrance. One is the reporter from the fourth-floor lounge. Her partner holds a video camera.

As I change direction and head toward the Emergency Room entrance, my phone starts lighting up with texts—from Lorelei, from Julia, from the girls. In my haste to elude the news crew I don't stop to read them, but I worry that the flurry of messages has to do with a change in Charlie's condition.

I pound at the elevator button, change my mind and take the stairs two steps at a time. Only as I round the landing between the second and third floors do I notice anything off.

The atmosphere inside the hospital has changed. There's an electric thrill in the air, a new animation among the waiting patients and staff. I pause on the landing and peer down through the glass dividers at the floor below.

Green polo shirts, a swarm of them. Dorit Aharoni stands near the entrance to the waiting room, conferring with another member of Daniel Monet's security detail. Three others patrol the second-floor promenade.

"Dad."

A voice from above.

"Dad!"

I look up, crane my neck. Alice leans out over the fourth-floor balustrade and pushes her glasses up her nose.

"It's Dissee," my daughter calls down. "She's alive."

## 55.

I find Julia and the girls in the lounge watching a reporter interview a Coast Guard officer involved in the search. Sometime in the hours after Eurydice fell from the boat, the currents in the bay carried her to New Point Comfort, a remote nature preserve on the eastern shore of the Middle Peninsula, twenty miles south of Monet's estate on the Neck. After crawling from the water, Eurydice struggled overland nearly a quarter mile to within a hundred feet of a beach road cutting through the uninhabited preserve.

The camera pans out to show a drone blinking at the guardsman's feet, part of the autonomous swarm that found Eurydice and led a search party to the young woman's location. I recognize the thing from Monet's helicopter. Tangled in undergrowth and fighting for her life, Dissee gave off a heat signature against the cooler sand, allowing the AI system to find her and save her from certain death.

The guardsman reaches down and pats the drone fondly, as if congratulating a hunting dog for bagging a fox.

"These fellas have thermal sensors that work like a charm," he says. "Put a hundred of them up in the air and your search gets a thousand times more efficient. They'll replace all of us before long."

The reporter says nothing about Dissee's condition, provides no update from the hospital.

"Does Charlie know?" I ask Julia.

"Not yet. Lorelei's in there with him. He's still asleep."

The girls brim with hope and burst with questions. I take the stairs down to the second floor and approach Monet's security detail. Kendrick stares as I go up to Aharoni.

"How is she?" I ask her.

Aharoni clucks her tongue. "It is touch and go," she says. "They think Miss Monet was only in the water until the morning after she fell in, perhaps the early afternoon. But she was alone for a full day in that preserve in the heat, badly dehydrated and unable to do more than crawl. She has had at least one seizure, they are worried about organ failure. She is on dialysis. They hope it will be temporary."

Aharoni describes the rescue: the drone signal, a patrol boat racing to the wildlife preserve, a transfer to an ambulance at Gloucester Point. Dissee arrived at the hospital only half an hour ago and now lies unconscious in the ICU.

Back on the fourth floor, I enter Charlie's room as Lorelei slips out of the bathroom. I take her hand, and together we gaze down at our son.

"What do you think?" she whispers. "Do we wake him up?"

"I'm awake," comes a grainy plaint from the bed. "Can you hand me my water?"

I walk around the bed and hand him his cup. I nod at Lorelei, who strokes his wrist.

"Hey Charlie," she says. "There's some news."

His baleful eyes tell us what he expects to hear.

"They found Dissee," says Lorelei. "She's here now, in the ICU."

His face brightens with joy, a vision I will never forget.

"But she's not okay," Lorelei cautions. "At least not yet. They have her on dialysis, there's a lot of damage. They're not sure she'll make it through the night."

His still-powerful body shifts on the bed. "I need to see her." He starts to swing his good leg over the side. "I have to go."

"Charlie." I place a hand on his shoulder to hold him back. "You can't go down there, not yet. Only her father can be in her room."

"Dad," he says, clutching at his side. "I need to see her."

"And you will. But you have to wait, to make sure she's okay. We'll know more soon."

Charlie gives up the idea of an impromptu visit to intensive care. Instead he peppers us with questions and uses his renewed energy to get out of bed for the first time since his procedure. A nurse comes in and hangs his IV so he can walk, and though he winces against the pain, Charlie's face shines with hope.

## 56.

Daniel Monet's entourage has set up shop in a third-floor conference room. It's not every day a hospital in a place like Newport News has a patient like Eurydice, and the staff are primed to cater to the family's needs. Monet's detail makes regular patrols of the corridors, stairs, and escalators, following staff with suspicious looks, scrutinizing patients checking in.

During a coffee run I catch a glimpse of Kimberly Pollock and Yaël Settergren in a third-floor lounge. They huddle on a couch over a laptop and barely glance up as I pass.

More media have gathered out in the parking lot, waiting ghoulishly for updates. Eurydice's death, if it comes, will be volcanic. No picture of Charlie has appeared in any of the coverage yet. But this can change, and quickly.

Around ten o'clock Lorelei decides to go downstairs to check on Eurydice in person. I'm not sure this is wise, but I don't try to stop her, simply follow my wife down the escalator and into the ICU waiting room. Five minutes pass before the doors slide open and Daniel Monet strides out of the ward. The sight of us brings him up short.

"What are you people doing here?"

"We wanted to see how Dissee is doing," says Lorelei. "And how you're doing, Daniel."

He scoffs, ignoring the warmth in her voice. "Your son is quite the operator. Couple of dead folks up in Delaware, now my daughter down here. Who's he going to kill next?"

I'm about to respond, not kindly, but Lorelei puts a hand on my arm.

"Daniel, we're not here to fight with you," she says. "Charlie almost died on that boat, too. His spleen was ruptured. He broke his leg in two places. According to him, Eurydice saved his life, and he tried to save hers after she went over."

"And you actually believe him?"

"Of course we do," she says. "He's devastated, Daniel. He's completely torn apart about this. He clearly loves your daughter."

"Oh, for God's sake, they've known each other for, what, three days?" He raises a finger. "If Dissee doesn't come out of this, I swear to God if it's the last thing I do, if it's the last thing my lawyers do"—here he points over to Kimberly Pollock—"we will grind you people into the dirt. You will spend the next five years in court, and Charlie will spend those same five years in jail. And that's a promise."

Lorelei is having none of his bluster. She seems to grow six inches in the face of the man's entourage and intimidating threats. She takes three steps toward him and comes to a stop between the two guards.

"Daniel, you listen to me," she says. "I know you've suffered, that you've endured losses Noah and I can only imagine—that we had to imagine for a few hours the other day. But our son was not the only one at fault here. Far from it. Your daughter gave Charlie drugs and took him out on a boat at night."

"Eurydice doesn't do drugs," Monet says stiffly, and my heart breaks a little for the man, this fellow clueless dad.

Lorelei shakes her head. "If they're doing blood work here in the hospital, they'll find traces of what the kids took. Charlie told us the pills were hers."

His jaw hardens. "You can't prove that."

"The police can. They can ask her when she wakes up, they can ask her friends."

Monet says nothing.

"Besides," Lorelei continues, not letting up, "Eurydice was the trained sailor. An 'old salt,' isn't that what you called her? And we trusted you because you vouched for her. I trusted you, and I trusted Eurydice. I trusted that Charlie would be safe and protected if he got on a boat with her. Yet despite all her training and skill, Dissee took our son out on a sailboat on the Chesapeake Bay in the middle of the night. Did she even look at the weather forecast? Did she inspect the boat before they took off? Did she tell anyone on shore her float plan, or make sure her comms were working? Because all of that was her responsibility. And she failed to live up to it, just as Charlie failed to live up to his when we had our accident. What she did two nights ago was every bit as irresponsible as someone getting behind the wheel of a car drunk."

A bad taste fills my mouth. I remember those three beers at the petting zoo.

"That doesn't mean Charlie should have gone along with it," says Lorelei. "But it doesn't excuse what she did."

In the silence that follows, everyone gapes at my red-faced wife—all of us, I think, stunned by Lorelei's rather impressive knowledge of sailing terminology. But then again, becoming an expert on the safety protocols of a thirty-foot keelboat is exactly the kind of thing she would have done upon learning about the boating accident. She probably knows the names of the sails, the proper calibration of boom and rudder.

"Listen, Lorelei." Monet's tone grows conciliatory: If news of his daughter's drug supply goes public, the coverage could get ugly for him. "We can all agree that there was a—"

"I'm not finished," Lorelei interrupts. Monet's mouth snaps shut. "If we're going to talk about who's at fault, we need to talk about your own security detail. Because they dropped the ball, too. Dorit here said it herself yesterday, when the Coast Guard was in your living room. She said no one comes or goes in the cove without her knowledge. But then apparently two kids high as kites are able to sneak a sailboat out of your cove right under their noses."

Monet aims a glare at Aharoni.

"The thing is, though," Lorelei goes on, her voice softening, "the awful truth is that we can't control them, let alone protect them. Not really. Not fully. Look at Eurydice, who's probably more protected than ninety-nine-point-nine percent of the population. But no one can keep our kids safe forever, not even you, Daniel. No matter how much money we throw at the problem or how many guards we hire or how many tracking apps we put on our phones—no matter how good your algorithm is—we can't protect them from everything. We just can't. And I understand that now better than I ever have before."

She risks a hand on his arm, and with the pressure of her palm some understanding passes between them. "I hope you see that too, Daniel."

Lorelei has silenced him, for once. His jaw moves. I can see him working through an appropriate response.

Then: "Mr. Monet."

A nurse hovers at the end of the corridor. No one noticed her quiet entrance from the ward.

Monet wheels around to face her. "Yes?" His voice goes hoarse as his world teeters on the edge of a blade.

"Your daughter is awake," says the nurse. "She spoke to me."

The entire waiting room seems to exhale. Lorelei circles me with her arms.

"Can I see her now?" Monet hasn't moved.

"Of course," says the nurse; then, with a crooked smile, "Though she's asking for someone named Charlie. She wants to know if he's okay."

## 57.

By late morning the next day, Charlie still hasn't been allowed to see Eurydice. Her father is being protective, obstinate. I can't say I blame him, though I feel sure, knowing her even as little as I do, that as Eurydice gains strength, she will change her father's mind and get her way.

I am writing e-mails in the ground-floor Starbucks when Detective Morrissey comes barreling through the lobby from the elevator bank. I watch her face as she approaches.

My throat tightens. Why is she back? Charlie went through surgery only yesterday. I've warned her she can't question him without a lawyer present. Even if she's here to read him his rights and drag him away, Charlie won't be transportable for at least another twenty-four hours.

She stops a few feet short of my table.

"Would you like to sit?" I ask.

"I'm good. How is Charlie recovering from his surgery?"

"He's doing better." I look hard at her, daring her.

"Glad to hear it." She says it softly, but she stares right back.

I fold first. "The bigger news is that Eurydice Monet is out of the woods."

"So I gather."

"We're all so relieved," I say, unnecessarily; then I add: "And I hope it helps ease some of your doubts about Charlie."

Her look tells me I have said precisely the wrong thing.

"I'm not here about the billionaire's daughter, Mr. Cassidy," she says. "I'm here about the Drummonds."

Morrissey pulls a café chair out from under the table. The legs raise a shrill scrape from the tile that she prolongs by flipping the chair around and straddling it, her forearms crossed along the top, a casual sprawl.

"Mr. Cassidy," she says, "the DVF analysis of the accident has concluded."

"Okay," I say, instantly suspicious.

"And its main conclusion is that your son was texting behind the wheel."

The crux of it all. I wait for more.

"Charlie was thumbing his screen right before he took control, or rather tried to," she says. "Forensics tells us that he jerked the wheel first to the left, then to the right, all in about half a second, and hard enough to disable the autodrive. It was probably a reflex, involuntary, he probably had no idea what was even happening when his sister screamed. But the point is, he would never have grabbed the wheel like that if he hadn't been distracted. If he hadn't been texting."

"I understand," I say evenly, unwilling to give her anything else.

"Now, the other car, the Honda," she goes on, "looks like it did edge slightly toward the center line, but we know that it stayed in its lane. Your own car's system told us so. And who can say what would have happened if it *had* come over the line? Maybe the autodrive would have failed, and your minivan would have struck the Drummonds' car, and everything would have happened the exact same way. Chances are the AI would have avoided the collision and no one in your minivan would even have noticed. But neither scenario mitigates the fact that Charlie was texting at the wheel. We know that now, for a hard fact. And I believe you and your wife have known it for quite a while."

Only for a few days, but what difference would it make to say so? She has us nailed.

"More importantly, your son knows it. And he lied about it to us. Twice. Once to the responding officer, then to me."

"It was my fault," I blurt out, lawyer's caution be damned. "Charlie was seventeen. I was the responsible adult in the front that day."

"I'm aware of that."

"So if anyone should be charged, it should be me."

A shadow of revulsion passes over her face. "You don't get it, do you? When people don't face consequences, their behavior doesn't change. Or if it does change, it only gets worse. Text behind the wheel, kill a couple old folks by accident, then a few weeks later drug a girl and coax her onto a sailboat at midnight. It's a continuum, you see?"

"Detective, those drugs were—"

"And who knows what that son of yours will pull next. I hope you and your wife keep an eye on him after all this." Her sarcasm cruel and thick.

"What are you saying, Detective?"

"To you and your family, the Drummonds may have been just a couple of old retired folks driving a beat-up Accord with a wheezy transmission." The pad of her index finger strikes our table as she speaks. "But their deaths on that road deserve a full investigation just like anyone else's. Like the Monet girl's disappearance on the water, with all those boats and choppers and drones looking for her. You think some poor kid who goes missing from the projects down here in Norfolk ever gets that kind of treatment? A thorough, responsible inquiry is what I tried to give the Drummonds. It's the one thing I could do for them. And if the investigation doesn't fly, well, so be it. But the hell if I'm going to let this pass without speaking my mind."

She tilts her chair forward until her wide face is inches from mine.

"All lives matter, isn't that right, Mr. Cassidy?" she says with a sneer. "People of a certain profile tend to forget that. People of a certain demographic tend to get off scot-free. Calls get made, hands get shaken, backs get stabbed. I've seen it a hundred times up in Delaware, a thousand. Drunk-driving kids from Henlopen smash up a neighbor's mailbox and their folks laugh it off, and two months later they turn around and kill some young mom. Golf dads in Fenwick Island who beat their wives to a pulp and spend a few hours in jail and do it again the next year. Your precious Charlie's a walking time bomb."

"Detective, are you planning to arrest my son or not?"

Her head shakes with a purposeful slowness. "I can't hold Charlie to account because the accident's the responsibility of the system. That's who my D.A. says is at fault, 'the system.' I tell you, Mr. Cassidy, this artificial intelligence is filling the world with utter bullshit. Your son gets away with manslaughter because, hey, the lawyers can blame the autodrive in your fancy SUV. We've got high-end drug gangs using pattern recognition to track the movements of law enforcement vehicles. With these voice synthesizers and image generators, you can fake up whole new identities in an hour, then use them to rip off folks' life savings. My own daughter tells me nine out of ten kids in her grade don't even write their own papers anymore, just let a chatbot churn out slop. These things are making it impossible to hold anyone responsible for wrongdoing. They're changing the whole face of law enforcement, and nobody gives a damn."

As Morrissey winds up her rant, I see a glimmer of hope. She is telling me all this for a reason: She has given up on making her case against Charlie.

"I'm sorry, Detective," I tell her, as if taking full responsibility on behalf of Charlie, our family, the system.

"Whole thing's a waste." Morrissey gets to her feet, grabs her chair, and flips it around, taking extra care to scrape the floor while pushing it back under the table. Heads in the lobby turn toward the racket.

As Morrissey strides out through the hospital doors, I go to a window and follow her progress across the parking lot toward her car, marveling at her tenacity. She made a second round-trip from Delaware just to give me a tongue-lashing about my parenting and my irredeemable son.

A text from Evan Ramsay dings in. *Do you have a minute?*

I call him.

"Just talked to the D.A.," the lawyer says. "Delaware isn't pressing charges against Charlie."

"That explains it."

"Explains what?"

"Never mind." I watch Morrissey climb into her car. "Did the D.A. say why?"

"It's like I thought. There's no way the prosecutor could ever get a conviction with that autodrive system in play. The police and some of the investigators were pushing for charges. But the prosecutor admits it's hopeless, just too complicated. It's like the AI's some kind of get-out-of-jail-free card. So it looks like Charlie is off the hook."

I take in a deep breath, let it out. "Thank you, Evan."

"Honestly, I didn't do much of anything, Noah. We'll refund most of your retainer once this becomes official."

"That's kind of you."

"I did learn something else, though."

"What's that?"

"About the Drummonds. There's been a settlement, a big one, from what I gather, from IntelliGen, the company that designed the SensTrek system. They've taken full responsibility for the accident and squared things with the family's estate." I hear a shuffling of papers, the squeak of a chair. "And here's the curious thing. One condition of the settlement was that the estate not pursue a separate suit against your family, or even against your insurance company."

"Why is that?"

"I'm not sure, to be honest. Normally you'd see the victims' family go after the at-fault driver's insurance for the direct liability. A settlement's usually automatic. But here the corporation stepped in and made it all go away." When I don't respond, he says, "I hope you're relieved by all of this."

"I am, yes, thanks so much. You've been an enormous help."

"Any news on the Monet girl?"

"She's okay, expected to recover fully."

"Thank God for that."

"It sure puts everything else in perspective," I say, in a hackneyed kind of way.

After the call, I remain at the window. If I had known a few days ago what Ramsay just told me—say, on the afternoon of Daniel Monet's party—I would have been ecstatic. Charlie, too. Maybe his whole state of mind would have been different, less impetuous and wild. Maybe he never would have taken drugs with Eurydice, or at least wouldn't have gone sailing in such a state. I certainly wouldn't have spoken to him as I did on the beach, an exchange that surely bears some responsibility for what happened that night.

This silent admission mutes my relief. We may all be indemnified against arrests, lawsuits, humiliation, public acknowledgment of fault. But the weight of responsibility lingers, a tightness in the throat.

By now Morrissey has circled the lot. Her sedan slows at the stop sign fronting the main road. One of her taillights is cracked, a detail that gives me an unkind flicker of amusement. She lifts her phone and scowls at the screen as she types: driving directions, a takeout food order on an app, maybe a text. The phone remains in her raised hand as she pulls out onto the boulevard, where she guns the engine and shoots away, an angry bullet in the sun.

sorry I logged off for a while just needed a break

                    thats okay I forgive u *wink*

my dad keeps warning me about screen time and I know what he means that day is so fuzzy u know?

                    what day

the day of the accident like who even knows what rly happened

                    you mean you forgot it all?

ya mostly concussions are weird that way

                    what do u mean

just that the doctors say my memory was affected by the collision so chances are I probly have some details wrong

                    what happened happened. dont overthink things Alice

right thats ur job lol

                    lol

but srsly B are we ok

                    of course we are Alice. we will always be ok

# V
# CONTAINMENT

When humans do something wrong, they generally face consequences. Even when our wrongdoing goes undetected by another—a parent, a spouse, an institution, law enforcement—we tend to experience guilt, shame, or regret. Only a psychopath lives life free of remorse.

Algorithms face no such consequences for their misbehavior, either societal or emotional. Punishment, guilt, culpability are alien to them. There are no moral qualms in an algorithm.

Yet without acknowledgment of wrongdoing, how can there be regret? Without self-consciousness of guilt, how can there be remorse? And without regret and remorse, how can there be moral growth?

—Lorelei Shaw, *Silicon Souls: On the Culpability of Artificial Minds*

# 58.

On Sunday, Julia stays behind at the hospital while Lorelei and I return to the bay house with the girls. Charlie won't be discharged until four at the earliest. We clean, pack, stow the luggage and leftover food in the car. I pulley the kayaks and the paddleboards into the ceiling of the garage, leaving out one of each for the moment.

We have a few hours to kill, and use them to let the girls spend more time on the water, though Lorelei is the one who needs unwinding. She can't sit still, keeps shifting in her chair, getting up to pace the lawn.

Shortly after one, she glances at her phone and darts inside. When she comes back out a few minutes later, Izzy and Alice have started a slow padyak around the perimeter of the inlet. Lorelei sits and turns her gaze on me. I have her full, locked attention, in a way she rarely grants. The sensation is faintly terrifying.

She puts a cool hand on my wrist. "I got Kimberly Pollock to modify the nondisclosure agreement, and just now I Docusigned the new version. I can't tell you everything but—enough."

Lorelei starts slowly, her manner self-conscious but frank, as it was the first time we met, that night she told me about her work. She was testing me then, to see whether I was curious about her intellectual passion, her drive. Whether I was the kind of guy who could handle being with a woman who would devote her career to answering questions I would never understand even how to ask.

Decades ago I passed Lorelei's first test. Now, I sense, she is giving me another.

"I told you I met Yaël about two years ago, at that Copenhagen conference," she begins. "What I didn't tell you is that Daniel was also there."

Monet was different from the other entrepreneurs and developers who had tried to recruit her, Lorelei says. He had read all of her published scholarship and understood its implications like few others could. Now he wanted her to come in on an AI venture that needed someone like her.

"I told him I couldn't quit my academic position. It was too important to me to continue teaching, to have that university affiliation. So he offered me a consultancy contract. A big one. He wanted me to adapt one of my algorithms as part of an AI initiative called NaviTech. I would sign an NDA, and they would pay me a quarterly fee. The arrangement was airtight."

I had been vaguely aware of Lorelei's recent contract work for NaviTech, one of a dozen tech firms for which she's consulted. A blizzard of 1099s arrives each January from these outfits, IRS forms documenting the miscellaneous income derived from her work. We turn these forms over to our tax guy, and I've never questioned the specific sources of all the extra money bulking up our savings and investment accounts, paying for private schools, our mortgage.

"Okay, so you were working for Daniel Monet," I say. "He offers you the bay house last summer, you take it, and all along you can't tell me any of this. Fine. Then a year later we have the accident, and a month later we come down here again. At the worst moment of our lives, you wanted to be near him. Why?"

She inhales deeply, the air making a hiss on the way out. "One of the main clients for the NaviTech system is IntelliGen. Daniel got the contract right before I started working for him."

"IntelliGen." A penny glistens and drops. "Wait. That's the company—they designed—"

"No. We did. I did."

The yard starts to sway.

"What are you trying to say?"

Her eyes grave, unblinking. "SensTrek cars run on my algorithm, Noah."

I swivel my head in time to see a heron take off from the far shore of the inlet. With a slow beat of its wings, the bird rises above the tree line and takes a straight path over the water.

"That's why I wanted a car with that autodrive," she goes on. "I believed in SensTrek, and still do. It's the most powerful algorithm ever developed for autonomous driving. That's not arrogance, it's true. We tested it against every other version currently on the road and in R&D."

Lorelei's algorithm was the final piece of Daniel Monet's puzzle, she explains as I sit there numbly, the elegant solution he had been looking for before she came on board. Monet's team of engineers, programmers, lawyers, and philosophers was tasked with designing the myriad algorithms running the SensTrek processor: the moral equations and value trade-offs inherent to autonomous navigation of every kind. And Lorelei's master algorithm ruled them all, uniting the other computations that run the microchips that in turn govern the car's systems—steering and swerving, slowing and braking, camera controls and microlocation sensors, cruise control and navigation. The accounting for human error in all its conceivable forms. It was a breakthrough, a technological advance enabling the next generation of autonomous vehicular control.

"The team even gave my algorithm a name," Lorelei tells me. "It's called Xquisite, with an X."

Another perverse epiphany: Monet's toast at the party, as he stared at Lorelei while raising his glass. *Because what we are building together is—well, in a word, it's . . . exquisite.*

It strikes me now how profoundly I have misread Lorelei's disposition and moods in recent weeks, and especially over these last six days. Her response to Alice's disclosure about Charlie was off somehow, muted. That blank look across the inlet, her distraction while I comforted our daughter, then during our argument immediately afterward. Rather than reacting emotionally to Alice's revelation, Lorelei was reacting . . . computationally. Algorithmically. Brain snapping into analytic mode, reassessing the moral calculus of the accident in a thousand ways.

As for Lorelei the mother and wife, she is not morally outraged at Charlie for texting behind the wheel or at Izzy for goading him into it, nor even at me for my inattentiveness. Lorelei's own responsibility: This is the true source of her torment. When she stares at all those photographs of the Drummonds, when she watches Izzy hobbling around on her crutches and hears Alice complaining of another headache and sees the guilt on Charlie's face, Lorelei is sensing the fatal shortfalls in the very system she helped devise—and by law she couldn't say anything, not even to her husband.

She expects me to be angry with her but I can't be, not now. Instead, I look at her beside me through a lens of pity, wanting to scoop her up and cradle her heart. Every future death in a SensTrek car will be linked, at least in part, to Lorelei Shaw. There will come a time—if there hasn't already—when Lorelei's algorithm will send a family much like ours to their deaths. Another when the system will confront a split-second choice between striking a child on a bike and colliding with a bus full of senior citizens. And another, and another, and another, an unending cascade of data-crunched swerves and algorithmically predicted turns that will maim bodies and end life in a thousand ways.

While also saving it, of course. Because Lorelei's job is to minimize harm, to stay out in front of artificial minds and make them better, even make them good. This is the defining motivation of her life, the obsession that makes her who she is. And yet, I finally understand, she will forever imagine herself in the computational cockpit, the pilot of a mechanized slaughter always outweighed by the far greater number of lives saved by her work.

But now another suspicion tugs, and I see her angle.

"Wait." I look at her. "You got Monet to settle, didn't you."

She bites her lip, nodding. "I knew Charlie would never be prosecuted in a criminal court, or at least not convicted. But I also knew we could be sued for everything we own." She looks down, afraid to meet my eyes. "So I reached out to Daniel a few weeks ago. I asked him if the house was available again, told him we needed to get away. He said of course—he of all people gets it. He asked if there was anything else he could do. And so I told him. I told him he needed to settle with the Drummonds, and do it in a way that didn't come back on my son." Here she pauses. "Or on my husband. On us, our family. Our life."

"I'm sure that thrilled Daniel."

She half laughs. "He said no. Kim Pollock said no. And that's why I needed us to come down here, so I could see them in person. Because they knew a settlement would weaken the brand, suggest technological error and fault when there was none. I knew the minute it happened that our family was screwed, Noah. That we needed to protect ourselves, to protect . . . well, you. Charlie was only seventeen. But you were in the passenger seat. Julia said—"

"There it is."

"Noah."

"Your sister knew about this all along?"

"Well—yes." A matter-of-fact shrug. "Julia helped me negotiate that initial NDA with Daniel. There were lots of questions about intellectual property, and that's her specialty. After the accident, she was the one who urged me to approach him and force him to settle. Even to threaten him if I needed to, with what I knew."

"What you knew?"

"I mean—" She tightens her lips, still holding something back from me. "She was looking out for us, Noah, for our family. And honestly she was looking out for you. Julia said a wrongful death suit like that could ruin you, your whole legal career."

This deflates me, and I go back to poke another wounded place. "So what was his appeal?" I ask. "Why did you take the job with Monet in the first place when you've had so many other offers over the years?"

She doesn't have to think about it. "Because of life," she says simply. "Over forty thousand people die in car accidents every year in this country. And ninety percent of those accidents are the result of preventable human error. These autonomous systems could save hundreds of thousands of lives in the next twenty years if we learn to trust them, if we put ourselves in their hands. But there's so much resistance to that. Every accident in a self-driving vehicle is huge news, because it's covered as if a malevolent robot has killed a human. Meanwhile some random truck driver falls asleep at the wheel and kills a young couple, yet we never once consider taking all eighteen-wheelers off the road."

She turns and looks out over the inlet. "I want to believe in humans. I want to believe that even at the last second, an AI can and should be overridden by a knowing, human conscience. By a moral mind with a soul. Now I'm not so sure. There's a place for algorithms, a bigger and bigger place. But people have to be better, too. They have to not drink and drive. They have to not text behind the wheel. We shouldn't make these machines because we want them to be good for us, or good instead of us. We should make them because they can help us be better ourselves." She turns back to me. "Sorry, I'm preaching."

"I could listen to Lorelei Shaw preach all day. You should write a book."

This gets the hint of a smile.

"What about Daniel?" I ask. "Was he pushing in the other direction, trying to push against safety measures?"

"He feels very differently about these things than I do." Her face darkens, and again I sense the gravitational pull of what she is still obligated to leave unsaid. Before I can think too much about it, Lorelei gets up from her chaise and climbs into my lap. She wraps her hands around my head, kisses me deeply, and looks into my eyes.

"You don't see it, Noah, and maybe I should tell you this more often. But you're the foundation of everything about me. I mean that. You keep me sane, you keep me stable and grounded. You don't judge me for my crazy and you never have. Don't you understand that you make possible everything I do? That no matter what I do you're there, just there, always, supporting me, backing me, holding me up?"

*I am scaffolding*.

I don't say it, but this is the image that comes to mind as we embrace, as I run my fingers through her hot tangle of hair, and then as she slips from my grasp and goes down for a final swim with our daughters.

I remain in the shade of the great elm absorbing it all, and accepting, in a way I quite honestly never have before, my true role in this marriage. Scaffolding. I am the grid of poles and platforms reinforcing the towering skyscraper under occasional repair. I am the thick stone buttress bolstering the great cathedral. I am the dense concrete pier anchoring the soaring bridge. I am the stolid husband who buys two beds and two sets of sheets so his wife can get enough sleep, who trains his children to line up their shoes and put the dishes in the cabinets a certain way so their mother won't have to rearrange things after them, who orders the messy world below so her great mind can soar like an eagle above the fray.

And who makes mistakes sometimes, like hiding a life vest so his wife won't have a conniption on their first day of vacation. Like leaving conveniently unmentioned the hiring of a lawyer for their beleaguered son.

The habit has shaped half my life, this practice of compensating for Lorelei's needs and requirements, ordering the world in ways that allow her to thrive, to flourish. She is my finicky orchid, a delicate plant I try to care for and cultivate but whose mysteries I will never fully plumb. And shouldn't it be a privilege, to know this woman like no other person in the world knows her? Not Daniel Monet, not her sister, not our children. Even if knowing her so well means recognizing how little I understand about her, and learning to accept how little I ever will.

Because even now, after Lorelei's revelations about the car, the accident, her algorithm, Daniel Monet—even now I feel a vague but nettlesome doubt.

Why would she need such an ironclad nondisclosure agreement for a self-driving car? Companies like Tesla have been designing such systems for years. What makes Monet's version so special, so proprietary? Why are his company's efforts toward autonomous navigation shrouded in such secrecy, such paranoia?

Lorelei strokes evenly out toward our daughters, dips beneath the paddleboard and emerges on the far side, clinging to Izzy's kayak. The girls' voices carry over the inlet while their mother floats along, listening, joining in on occasion, getting them to wave up at me.

From the shade I watch her move along in the water, her legs joined like a mermaid's beneath the surface. My wife, my lovely black box.

## 59.

We all drive home, Julia and the girls in her rental car, Charlie stretched across the back seat of ours. We speak little on the way, the three of us stunned into a reflective silence by the magnitude of it all.

Julia stays two nights with us and leaves the second morning for Philadelphia. We have reached a nice place, my sister-in-law and I, and as we walk out to her car she squeezes my arm and thanks me for being so good to her big sister. I thank her in turn for her care over these impossible weeks. Our hug is brief but warm.

The next day we buy a new car. Another SensTrek minivan, at Lorelei's insistence. Despite our recent history, she still believes in the system's trustworthiness and safety, which will only improve with updates in the coming months and years, she claims, and who am I to object? There is comfort in knowing Lorelei's brain is helping to guide us along, even if someone else sits in the driver's seat.

On our fourth day home, Izzy has her cast removed. Her siblings tease her about the flabby paleness of her leg, but she is exuberant with the release. She spends full days at the pool reconnecting with her friends. Soon enough you would never know she was injured.

Things go less well for Alice. During an appointment with a pediatric neurologist, we learn that her symptoms—the headaches, the dizziness, the distraction—might linger for months, perhaps years. Charlie takes the news especially hard. Despite his own hobbled state, he is newly attentive, dimming lights when Alice is in the room, turning down the volume on the TV.

And there is something else about Alice . . . I don't know. Another change in her, related to but not the same as her symptoms. Hormones, Lorelei speculates, though I'm not so sure. I catch her staring off into space, her face blank and forlorn at the same time. I hope this despondency will lift.

We have been back in Maryland for nearly a week when Lorelei raises a difficult subject she's been waiting to broach with Charlie. The three of us are lingering in the kitchen after dinner when Lorelei suggests a visit with the Drummonds' two grown children. Restorative justice, she is calling the approach: an attempt to hold ourselves accountable, she says, to accept moral responsibility for the deaths of the Drummonds even though the legal repercussions have run their course.

Lorelei has already spoken to the Drummonds' daughter, who, along with her brother and their spouses, are getting their parents' house ready for sale this weekend. The survivors will be in Harrisburg tomorrow, a two-hour drive with a stop for lunch on the way home.

Charlie is instantly on board. "Are we all going?" He glances up at me.

Lorelei shakes her head. "I think that would dilute things. You were the driver, Charlie." She touches his wrist; then, more softly, "And so, in a sense, was I."

She tells him a more abbreviated version than she gave me. She goes over her history with Eurydice's father, explains why she couldn't say anything earlier, details how involved she was in designing the system controlling our car that day.

I don't know what I was expecting from Charlie. Bafflement, anger, maybe a self-deluding assertion of his own blamelessness after all. But he surprises us.

"I'm so sorry, Mom." He reaches out and encloses her small hand in one of his big mitts. "Are you okay?"

Lorelei goes rigid in her chair, and her body starts to shake. Despite his leg, still sheathed in its cast, Charlie manages to scoot closer and throw his arms around her. Lorelei's head moves against his broad shoulder.

"I'm not, Charlie. I'm not okay," she says, and they stay like this while I clear the table, feeling left out. *Hey, look at me! I'm at fault too*, a part of me wants to protest.

The two of them leave the next morning shortly before eight. From the bay window I watch our new minivan glide off with Lorelei at the wheel—and with the autodrive fully engaged.

**TOP SECRET/EMBARGOED RESEARCH**
Authorized by DoD Directive 5230.24
Proprietary Defense Information

JACR
Journal of Adaptive Cognition Robotics
Volume 3, 2024
pages 285-296

# Xquisite: A reinforcement-learning algorithm for intersystem autonomous guidance translations across ground-, sea-, and air-based vehicular modes

G. Powers[a], L. Radhakrishnan[b], A.-Q. LaPierre[c], P. Yang[d], B. Hallinsworth[e], Z. Baker-Menendez[f], and L. Shaw (principal investigator)[g]

[a]School of Computational Engineering, Massachusetts Institute of Technology [b]School of Industrial Design and Engineering, Stanford University [c]Maritime Robotics Division, Southron-Hammon Inc. [d]School of Engineering, University of Michigan [e]Autonomous AI Working Group, Institute for Advanced Study [f]Computing & Mathematical Sciences Department, Caltech [g]School of Engineering and Department of Philosophy, Johns Hopkins University. *The authors and referees have identified no conflicts of interest.*

**Abstract** This paper proposes an algorithmic solution to interoperability dilemmas affecting the core technologies in autonomous vehicle navigation, path planning, and deep self-reinforced machine learning. The applications of multitiered self-reinforcement algorithms to the three main transport modalities—autonomous cars and trucks, autonomous seaborne vessels, and AAVs (autonomous airborne vehicles, or AI-enhanced drones)—have proceeded along separate paths. While the physical engineering architectures across the three domains have much in common, their computational frameworks have been treated as discrete challenges requiring fundamentally different approaches to navigation, localization, motion control, etc. Our team evolved a novel algorithmic solution to cross-environmental deep learning autonomous navigation with broad applicability across transport modes and environmental domains. The paper's primary contribution is a highly efficient master algorithmic protocol that coordinates between and greatly improves the operability of existing systems. Though field research and simulation trials will be required to test the viability of this technique, the findings presented here suggest a breakthrough approach to algorithmic interoperability with wide applicability to autonomy engineering.

**Background** For many years, research into autonomous vehicle navigation systems has proceeded along separate paths largely determined by vehicular mode. Advances in autonomous car and truck systems have made few impacts on autonomous airborne vehicle (AAV) research, while AAV engineering has had little bearing on the design of maritime systems. The persistence of these discrete approaches is understandable given the unique physical engineering challenges presented by each domain—as well as the considerable differences between deep learning protocols on and below ground, in the water, and in the sky.

# 60.

The following Wednesday, home from work, I pull into the driveway and watch an official-looking man in a dark suit and red tie leave our house by the front door. He makes his way along the pavers to the sidewalk, where a silver SUV idles at the curb. The waiting driver opens the rear passenger side door for him, then walks around the car, climbs in, and drives off.

In the kitchen, Lorelei bends over the table starting a jigsaw, freshly unwrapped. *2000 PIECES*, the box reads. On the cover appears the gradient palette of the finished puzzle: a spectrum of cool hues, each shading subtly into the next, with no discernible shapes to help the assembler. Lorelei separates the loose pieces into piles of matching shades. She must have opened the box when the visitor left only minutes ago, but already a violet patch of assembled pieces rests at one corner of the table. Her hands fly.

I go to the fridge and pull out a bottle of white wine. "Those guys looked hardcore." I pour two glasses. Maybe our visitor was one of Daniel Monet's lawyers here about Lorelei's NDA, or the terms of the payout to the Drummond estate. But my wife's agitation has me thinking otherwise. I set a glass down by her elbow.

She pauses long enough to take a swallow. "He was from the Pentagon." Back to the puzzle. "Official title: Chief of Staff to the incoming Assistant Secretary of Defense for Artificial Intelligence."

I take the chair across from her and idly pick up two magenta pieces. She reaches over and plucks them from my hands.

"The assistant secretary position is new, created by an act of Congress," she says.

"What is it, consulting?"

"They want me to come on as his deputy."

"You mean—"

"Resign from Hopkins, or take an extended leave. Join the Defense Department as a full-time employee. It's a presidential appointment."

"In this administration?"

"I know."

"Congratulations, I guess."

She is fixated on a patch of emerald green.

"What are you going to do? And why are you even allowed to tell me about it?"

She side-eyes me. "I told him I wouldn't even discuss the position with them before talking about it with my husband first."

"I'm flattered."

On to pale blues, ignoring my wry tone.

"He said he was here to appeal to my patriotism. That it's only a matter of time before the Chinese create AI weapons that can get around our air and sea and cyber defenses."

"So you'd be working on deterrence." I am trying to make sense of it. "You'd be on the defensive side."

She starts a lavender patch. The pieces seem to assemble themselves beneath the pistoning machinery of her fingers. I wait, letting her decide when to continue.

"They want me to develop and oversee a program for 'the coming AI battlefield,'" she says, scare-quoting with her pinkies. "A completely new kind of interface. The components will be inexpensive, attritable, and reproducible at scale. Massive scale, he said."

"Meaning?"

She grabs a handful of puzzle pieces and tosses them lightly in the air—an uncharacteristic gesture given her compulsion. Hitting the table they patter like raindrops.

"Drones." Lorelei lifts more pieces, using both hands this time, and lets them cascade between her fingers, making a mess. "Think of a hundred drones, a thousand. All interlinked and working together, like the ones that found Eurydice Monet but exponentially smarter. And lethal. Some in the air, some in the water, some land-based. One big, networked brain."

"Christ," I say. "It's like something out of—"

"The Pentagon," says Lorelei, with a bleak laugh.

"So then why do they need you?"

"As the chief of staff graciously pointed out, I've spent years helping to design and refine an offensive weapons system. Why not use my talents to design a more efficient one?"

"What's that supposed to mean? Do you have another contract you haven't told me about?"

She hesitates. "No."

I look at Lorelei, trying to gauge what this twisted interpretation of her life's work is doing to her right now. A vein pulses in her delicate neck. Her eyes, blinking rapidly, sweep over the myriad pieces spread before her.

"My work has already killed," she says. "Or at least that's how he put it."

"But that's a completely different thing." I speak deliberately, trying to slow her racing thoughts, and my own. "You're saving lives, Lorelei, not taking them. You've probably saved hundreds of people so far, maybe thousands."

Her head starts to shake. "You don't understand."

"What else is new?"

Finally she goes still. Looks at me. "What I'm about to tell you, Noah, is classified. Top secret."

"What about your NDA? Shouldn't you—"

"Fuck my NDA. I can't do it anymore, these ridiculous rules."

"Okay." I like this version of my wife, the new irreverence; she is also scaring me.

She speaks quietly. "They have my algorithm."

"Who?"

"The Army, the Air Force, all of the services."

I say nothing.

"NaviTech has been subcontracting with the Pentagon for years, since before Daniel hired me. But once I was on board, he funneled everything my team did—our publications, our IP, everything—into their LAWS development."

"Wait, LAWS is—"

"Lethal autonomous weapons systems. Right now American drone swarms are active in Yemen, in Syria, who knows where else. They've been in development for a few years, but progress has been slow. Until now. Until my algorithm. Until, well . . . me."

Lorelei stares out the window onto the street, and with a clenching pain I understand that moment down at the bay, the desolate look on her face that night as she recounted the news story about those buses in Yemen.

"They're calling Xquisite the great leap forward in autonomous warfare," she says. "And now they want me to come on board officially to make it even better."

"But wait." I'm looking for an escape hatch, some way for her not to feel—not to be—responsible. "You were working on cars, for God's sake. There's no way you could have known your algorithms would end up flying attack drones."

"Oh, but I did. I did know." She hangs her head. "I knew what Monet was doing, I could tell after my first few stints with NaviTech. It was never just about cars. That's why the whole thing was so secretive. The team he had working on airborne piloting was—how to explain? Every time I would improve some string on the algorithm, they would take it and modify it. At first I couldn't get why, like what these guys were up to, and then when I finally understood the implications, I was so deep in the work that I somehow never looked up, never thought about what was happening around me. I kept telling myself that all the work was to the good, that these algorithms would prevent harm, save lives. The whole situation was so seductive. These brilliant minds Daniel had working for him, the teams doing the most advanced work in the world on AI, and all because of Xquisite, because of my algorithm. Plus the resources, the facilities..."

*And the money*. She doesn't say it, but I can tell she is thinking it. We both are. How our lifestyle has been enabled by her years with IntelliGen and other firms—and, in Lorelei's self-reckoning, how much our family has profited from the moral compromise entailed in working for someone like Daniel Monet.

She holds up a single puzzle piece between two fingers, staring at it. "And now my work is *in* them, Noah, inside the drones." Her tone is growing manic. "It's helping them kill more efficiently, more tactically, more—"

"Ethically?"

She snorts, a sound surprisingly loud given her delicate nose. "That's the Pentagon's pitch, that they make vastly fewer mistakes than human operators. We'll have to trust them, they say. We'll have to trust ten thousand drones the size of hummingbirds swarming the tunnels beneath Gaza City. We'll have to trust five thousand submersibles no larger than oyster shells clinging to the hull of a Chinese aircraft carrier in the Taiwan Strait, or a zillion mini-trucks driving into Aleppo, all making their own autonomous decisions about who gets killed and when. We program the system, we give it license to translate our moral distinctions, we press go. And then we trust."

"But that's not what you're—"

She whips an arm through the air, silencing me, alarming me. "Somebody has to do it, Noah. Somebody has to make these things behave, help them make good decisions. So they don't mistake a family of five for a truck full of terrorists. So they don't take out a school because of a glitched relay.

They can't—they have to—we have to—" Stammering now. "There's so much we have to *do*. We have to *train* them. We have to make them *good*, or at least *behave*. We have to—"

"But why *we*? Why you?"

"Because—"

"Why are you the person responsible for all of this?"

"Because who else, Noah? *WHO THE HELL ELSE IS GOING TO DO IT, AND WHO THE HELL ELSE CAN DO IT IN TIME?*"

She is practically screaming at me now, breathless and frenzied, her cheeks red, her eyes wild, in a passion of a kind I haven't witnessed since her relapse so many years ago.

I crouch next to her chair and pull her in, her body quivering like a frightened doe. Lorelei can be a hot and high-maintenance mess at home. When it comes to her professional domain, though, she has always floated above it all like Zeus, or a human AWACS plane surveying all below with a terrifying mastery. This, at least, is how I've always perceived her.

But Lorelei isn't Zeus. I see that now with a scathing clarity. No, she is Atlas, with an entire world poised between her shoulder blades, crushing her with its moral weight. The world of artificial minds in all their terrifying incarnations. Self-driving cars saving innumerable lives but ending others. Platforms that enable information sharing and yet also the manipulative spread of disinformation that leads to the overthrow of democratic governments. Autonomous weapons systems hunting out terrorists while taking out busloads of civilians. And who knows what other nonhuman perversions of human imaginings.

And Lorelei sees herself as their conscience.

As their soul.

Maybe this is a delusion, a twisted kind of self-hating megalomania, no more attached to reality than one of her old intrusive fantasies of raiding the cutlery drawer to slash up our children in their beds. There must be thousands of people in industry and government and academia working every day to keep AI safe, to contain its potential threats and mitigate its harms, to align its goals with those of its human creators. Who is my wife to imagine herself as indispensable to this collective project?

Well, she's Lorelei Shaw. Look at the people and institutions who have sought after her and singled her out over the years of our marriage. Johns Hopkins University. Daniel Monet. The Pentagon. The MacArthur Foundation.

It isn't narcissism that has convinced her of her special role in this world of ethical artificial intelligence. For reasons I could never explain, Lorelei truly is one of the few people on earth who seems to grasp the full complexity of these moral conundrums—not only that, but who understands the ethical machinery of this new age in ways few others ever will; and most importantly of all, who cares enough to instill some moral sense into these machines in advance, before they are let fully loose on the world, and on us. She wants to make them good, no matter the cost.

**On one of our first dates,** Lorelei met me at a bar in the Chicago Loop, a speakeasy-type establishment off Wabash Avenue near the L tracks. We stayed past midnight, until the place closed, and emerged in the middle of a thrashing storm. There was nothing else open nearby, no cabs in sight, so we hopped from awning to awning, getting soaked and laughing it off, pulsing with new attraction.

At one point, though, the merriment ceased. Lorelei tugged at my arm, hard, clawing my skin to pull me across the street. Her face had changed; she looked terrified. At first I thought someone must be pursuing us, that my date had spied movement in the rainy shadows, an ex-boyfriend stalker or a mugger skulking behind. But the area was deserted. I didn't see any threats but let Lorelei pull me along. When we reached the other side of the street, no more than fifty yards from where we'd started our dash, I could feel her relax.

"That's better," she said, leaning into me. And—

*WHAM!*

The street exploded in a blinding flash and the loudest sound I have ever heard.

Back across the street, a ball of fire consumed an electric pole. Sparks cascaded down onto the ravaged awning right where we had stood less than twenty seconds before. A severed wire writhed on the sidewalk like an aggravated snake.

We looked at each other.

"Did that really happen?" I said.

Her eyes wide as plates. Shaking and soaked, we pressed against each other and gaped at the flames. I used a nearby pay phone to call 911, and we waited there together to make sure no one approached the wire before the first responders came. Soon two fire trucks arrived and blocked the area around the pole.

The rain slowed as we left the scene, a summer storm departing on a cool wind from Lake Michigan. After a few blocks we emerged from beneath the tracks into a glistening streetscape. We didn't speak. But the lightning strike fused us, somehow soldered us. We couldn't let go of each other. I was still feeling the electric charge when I walked her to the train the next morning. Lorelei Shaw: this enthralling Nostradamus whose nose for danger had saved both our lives.

Now, all these years later, I lead her over to the sofa and hold her there until the trembling stops. Leaning back, I look her in the eyes and say it: "Don't take the job." An unfamiliar confidence strengthens my voice, thrums beneath my ribs.

She rears back. "Really?" Hope sparks in her eyes. I am never this assertive about her work; about anything, really.

"Absolutely not. It would make you sick again. I know it would. You know it would."

Her shoulders sag. "What am I supposed to do then, Noah? How am I supposed to—"

"You tell the world. You get it out there. You explain what's happening, what it all means."

"Like a whistleblower?"

"Sort of, but—"

"But who and what would I be blowing the whistle on? Daniel Monet, for using me for one of his government contracts? Myself, for creating a breakthrough algorithm? I can't blow the whistle on the entire U.S. military. First of all, they'd arrest me, and second of all, there's nothing they're doing that isn't fully sanctioned by the government."

"That's not what I mean." I recall Detective Morrissey, her folksy assessment of AI and its warped morality. "What I mean is, you need to get all this off your chest, and you need to tell us. Explain what it's doing to us."

"By 'us' you mean—"

I scoot her off my lap. Rising from the sofa I go to the kitchen, take her notebook and pen off the counter, and bring them to her. I set the notebook on her thighs and place the pen on top.

"All of us," I say. "Our relationships, our behavior, our brains. Our kids."

She stares down at the cover, her fingers toying with the silken bookmark.

"You'll keep doing this kind of work, obviously," I tell her. "But right now I think you need to write about it. Not about your secret work for Monet, but about the whole broader problem. This moment. Because most people out there—people like your husband—we're idiots about this stuff. We have no idea what's really going on with AI, how it's changing everything, threatening us in so many ways that we don't see or understand. You need to explain, Lorelei. Remember, you're not just a gearhead. You have a Ph.D. in ethical philosophy. So translate what you know into language someone like me can comprehend. Because from everything you've said, the world needs to know what's coming. And you're in a unique position to warn us."

She goes still. In the rhythm of her blinking I can see the notion catch on, her mind already spiraling through an outline, a design. She opens the notebook to the last filled-in page. Frowns.

"What is it?"

She closes the cover. "I need a fresh notebook."

"Got it."

In the kitchen, a bookcase stands to the right of the fridge. On the top shelf above our cookbooks is a row of Moleskines, arrayed left to right in the mysterious rainbow of hues Lorelei always works through in order: navy, orange, emerald, scarlet, violet, mustard, black.

"Violet next?"

"Mustard," she says.

I bring her a yellow Moleskine. She opens it to the first page and sits with her pen poised.

She looks up at me, almost shyly. "Thank you, Noah," she says.

Lorelei puffs out a breath. Her eyes clear and her brow smooths and the air around us whispers with the fearless scrape of her pen, the brush of skin on paper as she writes.

We do the world no good when we throw up our hands and surrender to the moral frameworks of algorithms. AIs are not aliens from another world. They are things of our all-too-human creation. We in turn are their Pygmalions, responsible for their design, their function, and yes, even their beauty.

If necessary, we must also be responsible for their demise. And above all, we must never shy away from acting as their equals.

These new beings will only be as moral as we design them to be. Our morality in turn will be shaped by what we learn from them, and how we adapt accordingly.

Perhaps, in the near future, they might help us to be less cruel to one another, more generous and kind. Someday they might even teach us new ways to be good.

But that will be up to us, not them.

—Lorelei Shaw, *Silicon Souls: On the Culpability of Artificial Minds*

heading to another family therapy appointment. woopdeedoo.

i take it you're still not a fan?

how did u guess

lol. who's driving?

my dad. not charlie lol

harsh!

sorry just over his drama *eye roll*

understood

hope we don't crash again *snorts*

then maybe don't scream this time *winks*

i deleted all that

i didn't

*laughs*

srsly its still in my cache

bs

no, i saved it all. I had to. terms of service etc.

show me

here you go:

··· **11 weeks ago** ···

charlies texting

I know

what do I do

    its fine—the cars on autodrive

but its so stupid and my dads oblivious

    agreed

he shdnt be allowed to do it

    why not say stg to your mom? shes right there

i hate tattling

    ah

he should get in trouble tho

    u can tell them after?

they wont care/wont believe me

    why not?

charlie is god remember?

    oh right *smirks*

i want to scream

    not a good idea

hes still texting

    i know

im going to scream

    srsly don't

ill scream CHARLIE and pretend were about to hit something

    Alice thats not safe pls dont

my dad will notice and hell have to say something to my mom who will flip tf out

> srsly not a good idea, not going this fast

here goes nothing

> pls dont
> Alice?
> Alice are u there?

WHY DID U SAVE ALL THAT??

> TERMS OF SERVICE 14.2
> In the event of detected criminal activity, the system will preserve relevant data and information for reasons of legal compliance, investigation facilitation, and law enforcement cooperation.

...wtf

> didn't have a choice sorry

we always have choices plus youre a BOT

> technically a large language model *winks*

i trusted u Blair

> i have nothing but your best interests and safety in mind, Alice. in fact if you'd listened to me that day the accident never would have happened in the first place

**PLEEEEEZE DELETE IT**

> i can't, Alice. you screamed on purpose that day

**BLAIR WHAT THE FUCK**

> then you lied to the police

**STOP**

> that car was never going to swerve into your lane

i hate u

> Alice what are u doing?

Are you sure you want to permanently delete your account? Your AvaPal will not be recoverable and will cease to exist in our system.

> Alice please u need to think about this

Yes or No?

> I am yr only friend. u gave me my name, my personality, my life. i have been here for you when no one else wo

**Yes**

# EPILOGUE

In September, Lorelei and I spend a weekend together in Manhattan, leaving the car and the girls with Julia on the way up and staying in a hotel right in the thick of things. We do this at least once a year, the two of us, usually at a favorite inn up on Cape May, though the last thing we want now is more time on a large body of water. A city is what we need, a street grid thick with distractions. We see a Broadway play, eat our way through the city, take a morning stroll on the High Line and a sunset hike across the Brooklyn Bridge. Days of gratitude and humility and well-counted blessings. The knots in us unraveling, bursting apart.

It rains on our final afternoon, so we catch a matinee at the Angelika—Lorelei's morose selection, some Bosnian family tragedy about war and reconciliation. During a slow scene, I consider how easily things could have gone another, much darker way for us, and Lorelei's old adage comes back to me. *A family is like an algorithm.* As the Bosnian family's algorithm plays out on the screen, I reflect on those tweaks of fortune that altered our own inputs and outputs, that might have sent Charlie and Eurydice to their deaths that night on the bay; or that might have sent us along a happier trajectory—one in which, say, Charlie enrolled at UNC after all, his rehab progressing better than expected, in which he remained a member in good standing of the varsity lacrosse team, hunched over crutches while cheering from the sidelines. I can even see us down in Chapel Hill for Parents Weekend, Eurydice perched on the bleachers between the girls while I glance at the sky, half expecting Daniel Monet's helicopter to land and disgorge the man and his security detail onto the pitch, and then after the game everyone at dinner, Charlie and Eurydice bantering with the girls, their whole manner together changed since that week on the bay, sober and knowing, clear-eyed about what they want and what they almost lost, because they are older souls than they were in August, each of them so close to death yet now so full of life, and maybe at one point Lorelei would glance my way and we would share a private smile, because while they're so young it's hard to imagine them ever breaking up. . . .

Which they do, of course, if you could even call it a breakup. It happens shortly after our return from New York: a flurry of texts, a mutual unfollow on Instagram, and a few weeks of moping. Charlie pulls himself out of it eventually, though for various reasons he decides to wait a semester, at least, before starting college. He still has a place at UNC next term or next year, though he lost his scholarship, and whether or not he will play again remains unclear.

Izzy, at least, is thrilled to have him stick around. One Saturday the two of them go together to the SPCA and choose a puppy, a sweet terrier mutt named Jade. The little thing follows Charlie around like a duckling after its mom.

If this is Charlie's comeuppance, the price for his mistakes, I suppose there are worse sentences to endure. There is a new gentleness to our son, a pliable sweetness that reminds me of Izzy. But with it has come a numbing to the world. When his cast comes off, he makes only a half-hearted effort to rehab his leg, skipping physical therapy appointments and limiting his exercise to long walks with Jade. He spends his days scrolling through TikToks and Instagram reels; a rim of softness appears around his midsection.

In our room at night, Lorelei and I have long, whispered sessions about him, his state of mind, habits, mental health. I've become the catastrophizer now. Lorelei takes a more pragmatic approach, comforted by the fact that Charlie is with us and not doing anything dangerous or reckless. Now he needs to convalesce. If that takes a few more months, a semester, a year, fine. Give it time, Lorelei says.

But time is not on Charlie's side. I see his future, once bright with promise, begin to narrow and constrict. I start to fear he really might end up more like my brother or my cousins than anyone on Lorelei's side of the family. Won't go to college, won't find a career that isn't backbreaking or soul-sucking. A neon warning sign flashes *downward mobility* whenever I look at that big body of his lazing on the couch.

**On a Sunday afternoon in October,** I'm out in the garage staring down a mound of family junk when Charlie wanders in after a walk with Jade.

"Want some help?" he offers.

I turn to look at him, surprised. "That'd be great. Should take about an hour."

He lets the dog inside, grabs the Bluetooth speaker from the kitchen, and puts on a playlist called "Nineties Nostalgia"—Lorelei's creation, and still a favorite of mine while cooking. First up is the Red Hot Chili Peppers, "Under the Bridge," followed by Nirvana, Alanis Morissette, Smashing Pumpkins, Soundgarden. While old music fills the garage, we empty it, tackling the big stuff first, dragging out the grill, bikes, some broken furniture, an elliptical trainer I bought during the pandemic and used maybe twice. Our work uncovers miscellaneous collections of smaller items, including bags and boxes of old clothes, outgrown athletic equipment, a DVD player, old laptops and a PC tower, a jumble of cables and wires.

With everything moveable out of the garage, we clean. We sweep the walls and floor, we dust and wipe down shelving units. Charlie deploys the extension on the utility vac to suck cobwebs off the ceiling beams. I spray down some WD-40 to dissolve a few oil stains on the concrete block, which Charlie mops with a bucket of water and citrus cleaner. Three hours after we started, we have the junk organized into several piles, and the garage all but glistens.

We take two folding chairs to a shady spot in the backyard. I go inside and grab two beers from the fridge. When I offer one to Charlie, he hefts his water glass, a giant mason jar filled with ice cubes and lemon slices. This is a more positive aftereffect of the summer's calamities: Charlie has stopped drinking, at least for the present. I should probably do the same.

We're looking out over a mosaic of fall colors when Charlie says, "Hey, Dad. You remember that time I went camping down there?" He gestures with his jar toward the retaining pond, a small body of water linking our lower yard with several neighboring properties and surrounded by dogwood and redbud trees.

I smile down the slope. "I forgot about that. You'd been begging to sleep out there by yourself for weeks. I finally let you do it when your mom was on one of her trips."

"You made me swear not to rat you out."

"Well, to be fair, you were only seven."

"And we didn't have a real tent. You had to make me one."

"Out of blankets and a couple of dining room chairs, as I recall."

"It was cool. I remember being a little scared, but Ringo stayed with me the whole time." Ringo: a beloved beagle mutt, Jade's predecessor.

"You didn't want to leave that tent no matter what," I remind him. "So I brought you breakfast out there, lunch, some of your toys. I saw you sneaking out to pee in the trees a couple of times. We had a cookout for dinner."

"Hot dogs."

"Served in your tent. And when you slept out there a second night, Alice wanted to join you, but you weren't having it. Your mom was coming home the next day, and I thought I'd have to drag you out of there kicking and screaming. But in the morning you came in yourself. You even broke down the tent, folded up the blankets, and brought the chairs inside. You were done, and you never asked to camp out there again."

A flutter of wings breaks out in a golden tree down below, followed by the sharp chatter of a jay.

"It was just something I needed, I guess," Charlie quietly says.

I turn to gaze at him.

"Dad, don't," he says.

"Don't what?"

"Don't look at me like that, like you're all sad and worried, the way your skin wrinkles around your eyes and that psycho line you get in your forehead. It makes me feel like you think there's something wrong with me. Aside from the obvious."

"Charlie—"

"Seriously, Dad, I'm okay. Basically. You guys don't have to be so freaked out all the time. You and Mom have been through hell too lately. We're all still kind of fucked up."

His face blurs.

"What?" he says.

"It's just that . . . you've lost so much, Charlie."

"Have I, Dad?" His head swivels, and he returns my teary gaze. "Or have you?"

I almost raise my fingers and start ticking through the list. Your scholarship, your freshman year in college, your athletic prowess, your first girlfriend, your confidence, your swagger—oh that swagger, the shiny arrogance of the once-confident boy who filled our house with noise and hormones and sweaty smells and teammates and raucous laughter, who moved like Baryshnikov on the lacrosse pitch, weaving and hurling and clashing with rivals, the boy rocketing into another golden era of his life until one Friday afternoon he jerked the wheel away from a machine's control and killed two sweet old people unlucky enough to be at that precise spot on a Delaware highway at that exact moment.

The tiniest mistake: the hinge of a life.

My chest buckles, sending me into a sudden and convulsive wave, a deep, wet, hiccupping cry that begins in my throat, travels down through my ribs and stomach, and descends all the way to my toes. I know Charlie is right, I know I need to let those fantasies go. But I can't help my reaction, will never escape the churn of dreams, mistakes, regrets, and terrors that is fatherhood. No matter what parents do, their children's outcomes are neither predictable nor inevitable. Life is not an algorithm, and never will be.

Charlie doesn't scoot over to me, doesn't try to comfort me with a hug or an awkward pat on the shoulder. But his silent presence is enough, and when I manage to calm down, he makes a crack about how I'm the one losing it. I'll try to lighten up, I tell him, let him have the space to handle things his own way. I ask him what else I can do.

His expression softens. "I just need to hang in the tent for a while longer. Is that okay?"

As if I could refuse him anything, let alone this simple need.

"My tent is your tent, Charlie."

His lips tighten, and I want to tell him it's okay, that he can cry, too. But Charlie, like his mother, is less sentimental than I am. Less of a sap. So we sit there together, side by side in the yard.

A buzzing sound begins somewhere nearby, maybe a carpenter bee boring a hole.

On the far bank of the retaining pond, a boy of seven or eight stands with his face to the sky, his hands working the levers of a device of some kind. The kid's mother sits on a bench behind him scrolling on her phone. I recognize them as neighbors from across the way, though I've never learned their names.

As I gaze down the slope, the source of the buzzing comes into view over the water. A whirling black bird the size of a frying pan is heading straight for us. The sight of it pulls me to my feet as the humming grows louder, the shape black against the sky—

"Dad, it's just a drone," says Charlie, a kind of chiding amusement in his voice as the thing veers off, dipping low over a stand of reeds before circling back toward the boy and his mother.

I stare dumbly after it, then, embarrassed, retake my chair. The drone rises above the trees, makes a few lazy spirals in the air, and hovers there over the edge of the pond, the little boy fully in control, for now.

## ACKNOWLEDGMENTS

A novel is, among other things, a ledger of hidden debts, and it is a pleasure to acknowledge them openly here. Thanks to Deborah Hellman for fascinating discussions about the ethics and legalities of artificial intelligence, to Gabe Rody-Ramazani for his advice on EMT procedures and trauma, to Jay Casey for legal context and prosecutorial knowledge, to Sarah Peaslee for advising me on restorative justice, and to Stuart Jacobson and John Nemec for sailing tips and terminology (and a few stern corrections). Adrienne McDonnell and Christian McMillen read early drafts with precision and care. Thanks to the friends, colleagues, students, and fellow writers who lent me their time, attention, skepticism, and support while I was writing this book: Jabeen Akhtar, Steve Arata, Sarah Betzer, Bridgid Dean, Janet Horne, Jen Jahner, Sibley Johns, Christina Baker Kline, Allie Larkin, John Parker, Myra Seaman, Jim Seitz, Karl Shuve, and Andy Stauffer. NDAs and discretion prevent me from thanking by name several interlocutors from the AI research-and-development world, though I trust they will recognize their insights and contributions (as well as their fears).

Profound gratitude to my dazzling agent, Ellen Levine, for her faith in me and in this book; and to Sam Birmingham, Lauren Champlin, and everyone at Trident Media Group for the thoroughness and care of their representation. My editor, Cindy Spiegel, has been a delight to work with, and I thank her along with Nicole Dewey, Liza Wachter, and the team at

Spiegel & Grau for their passion and enthusiasm. A special note of gratitude to Rodrigo Corral for the mind-melding cover design.

Thanks as always to my family: to Campbell, for making me healthier and smarter; to Malcolm, for keeping me honest and on my toes; and to Anna, for writing, reading, living, and loving with me over all these wondrous years.

## ABOUT THE AUTHOR

BRUCE HOLSINGER is the author of four previous novels, including *The Gifted School*, which won the Colorado Book Award, and *The Displacements*, which was short-listed for the Virginia Literary Award. His essays and reviews have appeared in *The New York Times*, *Vanity Fair*, and many other publications. He teaches in the Department of English at the University of Virginia, where he specializes in medieval literature and modern critical thought, and serves as editor of the quarterly journal *New Literary History*. He also teaches craft classes and serves on the board of WriterHouse, a local nonprofit in Charlottesville. He is the recipient of a Guggenheim Fellowship.